JUDY BEEZLEY

# New Beginnings

## The Next Generation
### (CONTINUING STORY OF AMANDA)

**New Beginnings**
Copyright © 2025 by Judy Beezley

ISBN: 979-8894791869 (sc)
ISBN: 979-8894791876 (e)

The Reading Glass Books
1-888-420-3050
www.readingglassbooks.com
fulfillment@readingglassbooks.com

# Contents

# Dedication

To my wonderful husband, Bob Beezley, who has spent hours reading and re-reading to be sure all the corrections were made.

Thank you for your love and your support. Thank you also for loving these characters as much as I do.

I love you more than words could ever say.

# Remembering Tim and Amanda

*David Adler, a lieutenant with the Edgartown Police Department, was a close friend and confidant of Amanda Bradley Donaldson and her husband, Tim. He had known Amanda since she was a small child. Her dad had been the Chief of Police and David's boss. David and his wife, Lucy, were watching over the Donaldson's three children, twin boys almost 5, and a 3-year-old girl, along with their daughter also almost 5, while the Donaldsons took a quick weekend getaway. One never expects to answer the phone and hear the words that would change their lives, forever.*

*Lt. David Adler was Tim and Amanda's emergency number. He received the call about 8pm asking if he was acquainted with Tim and Amanda Donaldson. He assured the caller that he was. He heard them say, "we are sorry to advise you…" and then he really didn't remember hearing anymore. Lucy told him later that he fell to his knees, weeping, saying repeatedly, "not Amanda, God, please not Amanda". Lucy had taken the phone from him, identified herself, and asked the caller to please repeat what they had said. They explained that there had been an automobile accident involving 2 cars and a pickup truck and that there were no survivors. Lucy somehow managed to ask where Mr. and Mrs. Donaldson were being held and who was in charge so that she and her husband could contact them and make the appropriate arrangements. She wrote down the information, hung up, and tried to help David gain control of himself. He had been her protector, her big brother, her fill-in dad, her friend for as long as he could remember. He loved them both dearly, but Amanda was a big part of his heart. Lucy knew this and understood it better than anyone else. "David," she said, we have got to get ahold of ourselves and find the strength to go talk with Tim's parents. I don't want the children to see or hear the anguish that is in our hearts now as they have plenty of time ahead of them to feel grief. As Lucy was talking with David she turned and found Daniel leaning up against the doorway. The tears were streaming down his little face, but he hadn't uttered a word. Lucy ran to embrace him, but he pulled back and told her to help Uncy David and the rest of the kids. Sometimes there is a child that just seems to be special beyond words and that certainly was Daniel.*

*David gained control of himself, and he and Lucy got the children together and headed for the B&B. David had absolutely no idea what or how he was going to tell them this news. They arrived and started to knock but Tom opened the door saying that he'd seen their headlights. "Come on in. How's everything with you?" David started to say something, and Lucy interrupted him saying, "Let's get the children into the kitchen and find them a snack while we talk." She shuffled all the little ones into the kitchen and found them cookies and got each of them a glass of milk. Lorraine had come into the kitchen while Lucy was getting the children settled and taking one look at her signaled that they should go to the den with the men. "You kids stay in here while we talk with your Grandpapa and Grandmama", Lucy said as she left the kitchen. The ladies walked into the den and Lorraine looked at Tom and started to sag. Afraid that she was going to faint, or worse, David poured her a straight whiskey and told her to sip it. David and Lucy explained the best they could what they had been told. There were no survivors from the terrible crash and presently the bodies were being held at the Suffolk County Morgue. David suggested that they call Father McMurray, their parish priest, and arrange for him to meet them at the morgue in the morning. "It is too late to do anything tonight, David said." Tom agreed that morning would be best. Lorraine finally started to focus on her surroundings and asked, "What will we do with the children while we are in Boston?" Lucy said she would stay with all the children and David would go with her and Tom to the city. David said that he agreed with Lucy. "The less stress on the children right now the better. Lucy told me that Daniel is already fully aware of what is going on. He is such a special child. He will most likely help all of us to understand this tragedy."*

David and Lucy got the children into their pajamas and tucked them all in. Daniel and David were snuggled together as if they would never let the other one lose. Their eyes were huge and full of unanswered questions. Debra was unusually quiet and cuddled with Lucy for a few minutes. Alicia wasn't happy and was feeling left out until Daniel pulled her in between him and David. Daniel finally asked Lucy if his mama and papa were in heaven. All the children's eyes got very big, and tears were streaming down Debra's face. Lucy answered Daniel truthfully saying, "Yes, they are. They will miss you all very much, but they will be watching over you from heaven. We are all feeling very sad right now, but we know that they are happy with the Lord. Can you all help one another by hugging each other and wiping each other's tears away? You know how much your mama and papa loved you so just hold tight to those memories. Uncle David and I will just be in the living room if you need us, but you try your best to say your prayers and ask God to help you to rest tonight. Tomorrow we will have more information, and I promise that I will not keep it from you. I love you all."

The following days were a blur for everyone. Lucy went in search of a copy of Tim and Amanda's will that read:

> If I precede Tim in death, I bequeath all my monetary, real property, personal properties to him to handle as he sees fit.

> If Tim and I should perish together than know it to all men that David and Lucy Adler, Godparents to our children, shall have full custody rights without contest, until said children reach adult age. Further, David and Lucy Adler, shall act as Executor and will manage all my finances, to include personal, business, trust accounts, real estate, personal property.

> Personal bequests are listed as an Addendum to my will.

To say that there were going to be monumental changes in their lives was laughable. They were now responsible for the upbringing of 4 children under the age of 4. There were so many decisions to be made concerning where to live, how to manage the businesses, and so much more.

## *Saying Goodbye*

They got home in time to fix lunch and eat with the kids. Everyone was jabbering away, and the group seemed happy and content. After lunch David asked, "Aunty, can I ask you something?" "Of course, David, what is it?" "When can we go back to our house?" Lucy thought for a moment before answering him. "What do you think about living here instead, she asked?" David was cuddled in her arms and big crocodile tears were streaming down his little face as he said, "Aunty, I love you, but I want to go home. I miss my boo-ti-ful room and my bed that Grandpa and Papa made me and all my stuff. I miss my mama's perfume. I want to sit in my papa's big chair in his office so we can talk. Daniel 'splained to me that my mama and papa were in heaven, but if we aren't at our house, they won't be able to find us if they come back." Lucy was crying softly while trying to comfort this precious boy. "David, I need to talk with Uncy David and asked for his advice. Can you try to be a happy boy here for just a little while longer?" "Sure, Aunty, I love you." Lucy hugged him and told him that she loved him too. And then she went in search of her husband.

"David, Lucy told him, we have a real problem. Several, but one that is on top of the list right now." "What's wrong, Lucy, David asked?" She reiterated the conversation that she had with David (we've got to find a nickname for that child) and asked what his thoughts were. "I don't know, he said. Amanda's house is a little larger than this one, but not by much. The girls would have to share that small room which could be a problem. Given the information that we received from Judge Henry earlier today there is a benefit in our selling this house, which has a mortgage, and living in Tim and Amanda's house which doesn't. We could save a lot of money toward retirement by doing that. I haven't mentioned it to you, but I've been considering giving my notice at the precinct and taking over Tim's investigation business. I've been with the force long enough that I'll draw a retirement from them if I leave. I had considered asking Patrolman James to join me. He and I work well together, and it could be a good move for a young married man with a baby on the way. We could retain the office space, and it would be there for you to work out of while managing both estates that you have been charged with. What do you think?" "Good grief, David," she said, I don't know what to think. These ideas are sound, but this would be a huge move for us." "I know, he said, but think about the fact that you'll be paid twenty thousand dollars a month for managing the estates. That is almost double what you and I were making together while working long, hard hours." Lucy thought about what he said and replied, "Let's think about this over the weekend and talk again the first of the week. Another problem on my list that needs immediate consideration is, do we take the children to the funeral? If we skip that part, we could take them to the cemetery later so they'd know that they can go and visit their parents. Your thoughts, please?" David looked at her and said, "If you're sending them to pre-school during the service and interment, I would like to go with them. Honey, I don't know. I think they are too young to attend a funeral, let alone their parent's service. I think they'd be terribly frightened, and it will do them no good in getting through their personal mourning time. Let's arrange for pre-school and later in the summer, after the headstones are in place, we will take them to the cemetery.

As expected, the Catholic church was filled and overflowing in respect for Tim and Amanda. The service was conducted by Fr. McMurray who filled the hearts of every person present. Saying goodbye at the cemetery had never been more difficult for family and close friends. David, Lucy, Tom and Lorraine stayed behind at the cemetery after all the others had left. David was very worried about Lorraine, but Tom assured him she would rally; it was just going to take time. After final goodbyes, David and Lucy took their leave. Partway home

David had to pull over and just succumbed to his grief. His sobs were heart wrenching and Lucy had no words that gave immediate comfort. He was just going to have to work through it. After gaining control he headed for the pre-school to pick up the children. The kids were glad to see them and to be heading home as they had been promised tacos for dinner. Daniel stayed behind until all the other children were safely ensconced in the car. Daniel pulled Lucy's face down close to his and asked, "Aunty, are my mama and papa buried? Will they be okay? I'm terribly worried about them." The big crocodile tears were streaming down his little face. Lucy said, "Daniel, my darling, yes, mama and papa are buried. They are together in heaven and with the Lord that they both loved so very much. They are counting on all of us to do the best we can to be happy and healthy, to love one another, and to help each other every day. I love you and you know that. Mama is going to help me every single day to take the best care of you and your brother and sister that I can. Do you believe me?" "Yes, Aunty, he said. I know you always tell me the truth. Thank you."

David and Lucy and kids arrived home safe and sound. The children went to play while David and Lucy went to change into some comfy clothing. While they were changing David asked Lucy if she'd given any more thought to his idea about taking over Tim's business? "I have, she said, but I'm still holding out to think more and talk again next week. I feel as if my head is going to explode with all that is being pushed inside of me right now. I really cannot think straight. I also feel that I would like to talk with Tom and Lorraine next week about the house, job, and all before we move forward on anything. We need to know where they are at with all of this." Lucy got her comfy clothes on and headed to the kitchen to start the taco train. The children were all anxious to help fill all the bowls with the various ingredients that go to build their delicious tacos! Lucy started getting all the things out of the refrigerator and the boys started filling little bowls. Alicia and Debra oversaw the paper plates, paper cups, napkins, and plastic utensils. They had the table set in no time. The boys lined the little bowls up on the island and waited anxiously for Lucy to cook the meat and refried beans. There was happy laughter and chatter from all the children, which was music to her ears. David came in and was all smiles as he helped each of the children up to the island so they could devour their tacos. Lucy and David asked each of the children what they wanted on theirs and heard cheerful responses, "Everything. We want everything please!" David poured milk for the little ones and wine for him and Lucy and sat down to enjoy this simple, but delicious, meal. They looked at each other over the heads of the four and their eyes met and spoke volumes.

David and Lucy arranged to talk with the Donaldsons. They invited them over for a casual dinner and to have time to play with their grandchildren. They arrived right on time and Lorraine came into the kitchen with a beautiful berry pie for dessert. The children were thrilled to see her and had lots of things to show her and tell her about. Lorraine noticed that Daniel seemed more withdrawn than normal and asked Lucy about it. Lucy told her that Daniel was the child that seemed to know what had happened and was carrying the burden for his siblings. "I've tried to help him through it, Lucy said, but he assures me he's fine. I'm not so sure. Do you think we should call a child psychologist?" "Perhaps, Lorraine said, you'll know when it is time and what to do. Your instincts are impeccable." The ladies went into the den to find the men chatting away with a drink in hand. The children were in the playroom, so David began the conversation regarding the wills and what they had found out. "Given all the information that Judge Henry offered, we find ourselves in the middle of Tim and Amanda's lives. Lucy has been charged with administering their will, as well as the distributions of funds for the Brice will that Amanda had overseen. The children have said they want to go home, meaning back to Tim and Amanda's house. We are at a crossroad on what and how to proceed." "David", Tom said, "Lorraine and I were aware of how the wills read. Tim and Amanda brought them to our attention because they didn't want to hurt our feelings about leaving the children in your charge rather than ours. Lord! What would we do with all those little kids! We felt that they made the best and the correct choices regarding the will and how they were to be handled. If you guys are willing to put your place on the market and move to

Tim and Amanda's house, I'll be happy to do whatever I can to make more room for all the little ones. As it is the girls would be cramped. Not a problem now but it will be as they get older. We talked about converting the master suite to the boy's room which would give each of the girls their own room upstairs. We could convert the office area into a master suite for you two. I am uncertain how you feel about being on a different floor than the children, but I think with monitors and such installed that it wouldn't be a big problem. If you'd prefer the B&B we certainly understand and can move back to Boston." "Absolutely not, said Lucy. You two aren't going anywhere. I think your ideas about the house make sense. Long as we have monitors and can hear/see them when they are upstairs, I'm fine with being on a different floor. I believe that the trust will allow us to make these changes and pay for them out of the trust fund." "Yes, Lorraine said, You're correct. That is not a problem. Have you given any thoughts to what you'll do with the office downtown?" "Yes, David said. We talked but I've made up my mind. I'm giving notice at the precinct and taking over Tim's business. I'm going to ask Patrolman James to join me in this adventure. Lucy will need office space to handle both trusts each month and I think this makes perfect sense. I feel so much better knowing that we are all in total agreement."

It didn't take much effort to get the children to start packing their rooms up. The twins were very anxious to return to the only home they'd ever known. Debra seemed indifferent about it, but she was so young that she really didn't grasp all that was happening. Alicia Marie didn't care long as she was with David. Tom, David and James got busy renovating the master suite that would now be the boys' room. Debra's room had been redone by Tim and Amanda, so they painted a soft yellow in what would be Alicia's room. She had a beautiful bedroom suite for her nursery that would fit perfectly in the boy's old room. They would tackle turning the office/den into a master suite next. Lucy was busy getting their house on the market and familiarizing herself with the trusts that needed to be dealt with each month. David had given his notice, as had James. Between the renovation, the move, and Tim's business, they were very busy guys.

The children were eager to help pack and did a fine job of it. They are all four very bright children and hungry to learn something new every day. Alicia was a continually active child and Lucy felt that dance and gymnastics would be very good for her. Debra was content to go through a stack of books and whatever you read to her she committed to memory. She would sit her parents or grandparents down and read the book to them, practically verbatim. Remarkable for a child her age. David and Lucy continued to keep a close eye on Daniel. He was an overly sensitive boy and took everything to heart. If one of the children, Lucy, or David, had a problem or were ill, he just fell apart. They wanted to be sure that he was working his way through the loss of his parents. One day Lucy asked him if he would like to go to the cemetery with her to put flowers on his parents' grave. He looked at her with Tim's face and those huge blue eyes and told her, "Yes, Aunty, please. I would love to." He raced out of the house and started picking a bouquet of flowers to take with him. Lucy asked David to watch the other children while she and Daniel went by themselves to the cemetery. He asked her questions as they drove, and she answered each as truthfully as she could. When they reached their destination, his eyes were huge and full of unshed tears. "Are you ok, Lucy asked?" "Yes, Aunty, just very scared is all." "Me too, she responded. Just hold my hand tight." They got out of the car, and he went back for his flowers. He looked so little. She took hold of his hand and together they walked to the gravesite of his parents. The stone had been installed, and it was beautiful. Daniel stood looking at the graves for the longest time and then he just fell on his knees and sobbed. He talked to his parents for what seemed like a very long time. He told them how much he missed them and that they all wished they'd just come home. He lay on his mother's grave and wept until there were no more tears. Lucy pulled him up and comforted him and told him to say goodbye. He turned to his parent's graves, told them he loved them, and that he would bring David next time." With that he took hold of Lucy's hand and walked to the car. When she got him into his booster seat, he took pulled her down eye-level with him, and said, "Aunty, it just hurts my heart so bad. I miss them so much." The tears just streamed down his little face, and she feared him being ill. She was also worried that perhaps she shouldn't have brought him. She comforted him best she could and asked, "Daniel, will you be alright? Aunty didn't want you to be sadder than you already were. I thought perhaps it would help you to start healing." He thought for a moment and told her, "I've decided to be a priest. I want to help people get through these awful times. I'm ok, Aunty, I just needed to cry it out, I guess. My papa would sing to me and rock me in his arms when I hurt over something. I just miss him so very badly, Aunty. Do you suppose that Grandpapa would rock me and sing for a little while?" "Absolutely, Lucy said. We are going there right this minute. Throw kisses to mama and papa and let's go to Granny's house."

When we arrived at Tom and Lorraine's home Daniel undid his buckles and slipped out of his booster before I could reach him. He was grinning and threw his arms around Lucy's neck and squeezed her so hard she thought she'd pop. Tom heard the car arrive and met us at the door. Daniel flew into his arms and told him where we'd been. He looked up at Tom with those huge blue eyes and Tim's face and Tom just melted. "Grandpapa, I was feeling very sad and hurt and I miss my papa so very much. Would you rock with me in the big chair and sing to me? I just know it will help the hurt to go away." Tom's eyes filled with tears as he took Daniel's hand, and they headed for the den. There's a big rocking chair that is perfect for two. You could hear Tom's beautiful tenor voice singing Oh Danny Boy to Daniel. I peeked in and saw that Daniel was mostly asleep in Tom's arms but that his face was awash with tears. I decided to leave Daniel with his grandparents and go check on the rest of the family. Lorraine hugged Lucy and told her to take her time; that Daniel was fine with them.

Lucy headed home to check on everyone else. David was concerned as she was a bit later than he had expected. "Everything ok, he asked?" She explained the situation about Daniel, adding, "He's decided to become a priest. He wants to help people when they are hurting like he is." David turned away for a moment and Lucy saw him wipe his eyes. "Lucy, that is the sweetest thing I've ever heard. What a special boy he is." "I know," she said. He and Tom are rocking, and Tom is singing to him. Daniel said his papa always sang t him when he was sad." "Well, said David, the other children didn't even notice he was gone. So much for the twin-thing. When are we going to pick up Daniel?" "Can you go before supper," Lucy asked?" He assured her that he'd go get him in about an hour or so.

# *Changes*

Now that the remodel was complete everyone seemed to be settling into their new lives. The children were busy with school, sports, after school activities, and so on. The entire family attended mass regularly and were involved in church functions.

The holidays were getting close and Lucy wanted to be sure that they were fun times full of wonderful memories. Lucy found all of Amanda and Tim's decorations in the attic. She brought all the boxes down and staged them in the sunporch. She found a gorgeous artificial tree and decided she would set that up on the sunporch and get a real tree for the living room. The beautiful bay window simply cried out for a tree to be centered there. Precious hung out with Lucy while she sorted through boxes. She noticed that the cat kept sniffing the boxes and ornaments and would kind of whine or cry while she was doing it. Lucy finally decided that Precious had picked up Amanda's beautiful scent and was missing her. Lucy stopped and went and fixed Precious a little snack to try and make her feel better. We all miss them terribly, she thought, so it was not so strange that the cat would share in that longing.

Precious napped while Lucy went back to work. She found a beautiful advent calendar that appeared to be homemade. It was missing some of the presents, but she decided to hang it on the door anyway. When Lucy was searching through the attic, she found what appeared to be a train made of wood. It wasn't terribly big, the cars being about 12" in length. She wondered if Tim had carved it as he was very gifted with that sort of thing. It looked to be old, so she really was unsure what its origin was. She thought about the boys, but then decided she would varnish the train and give it to Tom (Tim's dad) for Christmas. David came home a little later and she asked if he would consider taking the children to cut down a tree for the living room. He inquired as to why she didn't want to join in that experience, and she told him, "Because I get to go shopping and to lunch all by myself while you do that with the kids." He just smiled at her and gave her a squeeze and a kiss on her beautiful cheek. Lucy checked the time and told him to go get the kids from school while she tried to come up with something for dinner.

The next morning after the children and David had left for school, she started working on the artificial tree in the sunporch. She started to get more decorations and noticed that the advent calendar seemed to be hanging strangely. She went to straighten it and found that a brand new one, complete with all the presents, was hanging on top of the one she had originally placed there. She found this peculiar but figured Amanda had decided she needed one that was new and complete. She found a small box with six beautiful stuffed elves in it. Each one was slightly different from the other and wee all cheerful looking. She found several spots in the room to place the little elves. Amanda had a collection of bird houses that she hadn't ever gotten around to placing outdoors. Lucy decided she would make them part of the artificial tree decorations. The tree was gorgeous. The children would be so excited when they saw it.

Lucy set about varnishing the little train set for Tom. She had invited them to spend Christmas Eve at their house. The children would put on a program for their grandparents and each one would be able to open one gift before bedtime. The varnish was dry, and Lucy had tied a string to the engine, maneuvered all the cars around so she could hide it in the front closet. Her idea was to give the string to Tom and tell him to follow it. She was hoping it would be a real surprise.

She had asked David the evening before if he had hung up the new advent calendar. He looked at her as if she was crazy. "Why? Where would I get it and why would I do that, he asked?" "Well, she said, I hung up the one that was obviously homemade and used and next day there was a brand new one hanging over the top." David just looked at her and laughed. He knew good and well that Amanda had placed the new one on the door. Lucy thought about this for a moment and said, "Seriously, you think Amanda is rummaging around in the attic?" "Well, said David, technically it is her attic."

David got everyone up early, fed them hot oatmeal, and put them in warm clothing for their adventure. They all kissed Lucy goodbye and headed out to find the tree. Lucy had toast and coffee, finished getting ready and headed to town to shop. Lucy's shopping spree went well. She had a burger at the Black Dog for lunch. She had found most everything on her shopping list and was very content. She ran into Marty, an old friend of Amanda's. They visited for awhile and then went their separate ways. Marty, like everyone else, could not bear to talk about Amanda without breaking down. The loss was still so raw. Lucy finished lunch and headed to the department store in Edgartown where she hoped to find her gift for Lorraine. Amanda had added several pieces to Lorraine's beautiful pottery collection and Lucy wanted to try and find the one that she was still missing. There was a beautiful chafing dish that she knew Lorraine didn't have and was hopeful she could find it. The salesperson was very helpful and told her she could order it, and it would be at the store for pickup in about 5 days. Perfect! She still had David's gift to get but she decided to do that another day.

Lucy got home about 30-minutes before the family arrived. She had made a big pot of soup in the crock pot before she left that morning, so dinner was all taken care of. The kids loved to pop the canned biscuits to open it so they would have those to go with the soup. The children came in whooping and hollering with joy over the tree they had found. David got the tree in and he and Lucy managed to get it in the stand. It was gorgeous! Lucy told the children that they needed to wash up for supper and that after they ate, they would decorate the beautiful tree. The children were thrilled! Lucy had set out the decorations and had dried lemons and popped popcorn to string on the tree. She had some cranberry chains already made up so the living room would smell delightful. The soup and biscuits were enjoyed by all. Lucy and David cleaned up the kitchen and the children went to sort through baubles and ornaments. Daniel came into the kitchen with big tears running down his cheeks. Lucy ran to him asking what had happened to him? "Aunty, look what I found. My mama made these for me and my brudder when we were little." "Oh, Daniel darling, don't cry. Mama and Papa made lots of stuff for all of you children and you'll continue to find cherished goodies for years to come. Don't be sad. Be joyful that you've been blessed with such wonderful memories of your parents." Daniel dried his tears and thanked Lucy before heading back to the living room. Lucy turned to David who was just heartbroken for the boy. "David, we are all going to find memories of her and Tim for years to come. There is no escape from it. I can't even decorate that she doesn't hang up new ones, she laughed."

The tree was simply a thing of beauty. It glistened from the beautiful lights and all the decorations were perfect. The children had done a great job of hanging everything at their eye level, so the tree was a bit heavy on the bottom. It was time for baths, stories and good night kisses and hugs. "Off to bed you go, Lucy said." The children all squealed with delight and were asleep practically as their little heads hit the pillow. It had been a wonderful day spent with memories that would last their lifetimes. David and Lucy went in search of a glass of wine and some time to just sit and relax. David told her all about the trip and how thrilled the children had been at finding the perfect tree…for her. "For me? Really? That's so sweet, she said." David told her that she was loved far more than she could even imagine. "They all fully realize how hard you work for them, he said." Lucy told him she was just doing her job. "I don't think so, he said, and neither do they."

The next two weeks just seemed a blur as they readied themselves and the house for the holidays. Lorraine and Tom had invited them for a quiet Christmas Day dinner after mass. She had also invited

Judge Henry and his wife to join them. On Christmas Eve David fixed his famous pancakes for everyone. The children helped to set the island for breakfast. Debra and Alicia made placemats because they are both very particular about etiquette… The pancakes and eggs were delicious. David had fixed fat little breakfast sausages that were the perfect addition to this meal. Everyone ate with gusto and asked for seconds. The boys had set the table with paper plates and plastic silverware that certainly helped to hasten the cleanup. So much for etiquette. Lucy asked the children to find quiet games or projects to work on in their rooms or the sunporch while she finished putting the dinner together. They were happy to oblige. The girls went upstairs to work on their projects and the boys kept themselves busy doing something on the sunporch. Lucy had a beautiful beef tenderloin for dinner. She was roasting small red potatoes and fixing winter vegetables to go with the meal. Tom and Lorraine were bringing dessert. David oversaw appetizers and the bar. He had gone to the local deli and gotten an array of goodies for an appetizer and thought Prosecco might be delicious for this evening's festivities. He bought non-alcoholic champagne for the kids. The table was set beautifully, and the girls had made place cards for each person. Lucy had made the girls gorgeous holiday dresses for both Christmas Eve and Christmas Day and the boys had got new slacks and shirts and bow ties for both days. David helped the boys get ready and got himself dressed so he could ride herd on the group while Lucy showered and got ready. She had gone upstairs and helped the girls with their bath and hair washing. Alicia's hair was like her mother's. The Asian blood had shown up in both their beautiful head of thick, jet-black hair. Debra's chocolate brown curls were always a chore but when Lucy curled the hair around her hand it was lovely. Debra is such a beautiful child that no matter what she does with her hair it doesn't take away from her beauty. The girls had their new dresses on with their patent leather shoes and were delighted to go downstairs and show David and the boys. Lucy soaked in the tub for a few minutes and then showered off and got herself ready. She had chosen an emerald-green hostess gown that fitted her slim figure perfectly. She donned her favorite gold earrings, watch and tennis bracelet, dabbed some lip gloss on and was ready to face the crowd.

David and the boys all whistled as she came out of the bedroom. The girls jumped with joy at how beautiful she looked. The doorbell rang announcing the arrival of Tom and Lorraine.

Lorraine helped Lucy with the dinner, and everyone thoroughly enjoyed their meal. David and Tom loaded the dishwasher and came back out with coffee and amaretto. The children were all on the sunporch getting ready for their program. The parents and grandparents were seated in the living room patiently waiting. Alicia came out first and recited a lovely Christmas poem. Debra came out next and tap danced while singing Jingle Bells. David was next. He recited a good portion of the Night Before Christmas. Daniel came out last and stood very straight and tall and sang O Holy Night in a beautiful clear, rich voice. Tom wept out loud while the rest of the adults just looked at this special child in awe. The absolute image of his father. When they collected themselves, Lucy explained that these were all surprises that the children had put together themselves.

The children were each allowed to open one gift from their grandparents. They were simply thrilled with their gifts, hugged and kissed granny and grandpapa and went to the sunporch to play. Lucy asked Tom and Lorraine to stay put because she had something for each of them. They started to object but thought better of it when they caught Lucy's look. She brought Lorraine her gift and told her to open it first and then she'd get Tom's for him. Lorraine opened the box and was speechless as she unveiled the beautiful chafing dish. "It's perfect! It was the one piece that I was missing and searched for. I can't believe you were able to find it. Thank you so very much." Lucy was so happy that Lorraine was pleased with her gift. She handed the end of a piece of string to Tom and explained that he'd have to follow the string to find his gift. Tom did as he was directed and when he got to the closet he opened the door, and everyone heard his gasp. "My Lord above, he said, where in the world did you find this?" He gathered it up and came to sit back down. Lorraine gasped as well as she most certainly seemed to know its origin. Tom explained that his father had made the train for him when he was a boy. I cleaned it up and gave it to Tim when he was about 8 years old. I had no idea that he had kept it all these years. Where in the world did you find it, Lucy?" "Well, she said, it was in the attic. I cleaned it up and revarnished it for you. I wasn't sure if you had made it or if Tim had but thought it would be best back in your care." "Lucy, my girl, he said, you couldn't have given me a better gift. I will set this up at the B&B for everyone to see and someday when I'm gone the boys will have it. You now know where it came from so, you'll be able to tell them should they forget." The children came to hug and kiss the grandparents and got ready for bed. Santa doesn't wait for sleepyheads, so they'd best get to sleep now. Lorraine and Tom went to tuck them in and told them again how much they had loved their program. "We will see you all tomorrow, they said."

Christmas morning began about 4:30am when the girls landed in the middle of Lucy and David's bed shrieking that Santa had been there! The boys heard the commotion and came to join them. David tried to convince the children that it was too early, but they weren't listening. Lucy got her robe on and went to make coffee while David made oatmeal for the kids. "We aren't hungry, they said." "Oh, is that right, David asked? Well, Santa left oatmeal for me to make, and you are all going to eat it before you attack that poor tree." They scampered up to the island and waited impatiently for their bowl of oatmeal to appear. Lucy had made cinnamon buns, and they were slightly more interested in those. Everyone finished their breakfast and went to the living room to see what Santa had left for them. Each child had three things they had said they wanted in their letter to Santa. They received all three of those and were obviously thrilled with their presents. The children were anxious to give Aunty her gift before they went to play. The girls had picked out beautiful earrings for her and they were jumping with joy as she opened them. The boys had gotten a beautiful bottle of cologne for her. Daniel explained that they knew it wasn't what she always wore, but they hoped she might wear this sometimes because it was their mom's favorite. Lucy had tears running down her face as she thanked each of the four children for their thoughtful gifts. She assured the girls that the earrings were her very favorite and told the boys that she had always loved that scent and would enjoy wearing it if it came with lots of hugs and kisses. The girls then gave David his gift. They had found him a beautiful shirt that they thought he'd be handsome in. He told them it was his favorite color, and he knew it would be his favorite shirt. The boys were given the honor of giving David Tim's pocket watch. They watched with huge eyes filled with unshed tears as he opened the box. When he saw the pocket watch he started to cry, and the boys ran to hug him. "I'm not sad, he told them, just overwhelmed with this beautiful gift. Where did you boys get this?" They explained to him that Grandpapa had the pocket watch cleaned for their papa but he was in heaven so Grandpapa thought Uncy might be the perfect person to have it. David told the boys that he loved the watch and would cherish it all the days of his life. "Just as I cherish each of the four of you, he told them."

Christmas Mass was wonderful. The choir was outstanding, and the entire program was truly heartwarming. They arrived at Granny's house (guess it will always be granny's house) and it was truly decked out for the holidays. The decorations and lights were beautiful. Judge Henry and Mrs. Henry were already there and came to greet each of them. The car was laden with gifts and David and Tom went to unload it. Lucy wandered through the dining room and noticed that all of Lorraine's treasured pieces were on the table and buffet. Lorraine greeted everyone with a hug and Lucy told her it was spectacular. Lorraine just waved a hand like it was an everyday thing. Lucy asked what she could do to help, and Lorraine told her that the turkey breast was resting, the beef tenderloin was resting and now let's go have an adult libation and let the kids have their tree. The den was decorated to the hilt. Absolutely beautiful! There were three gifts for each of the children. They had each made separate Santa Claus letters especially for Granny. These kids are smart! She and Santa had filled each child's wish list. There was screeching and hollering and shouts of joy from all of them. David and Lucy had given judge and Mrs. Henry a gift certificate for 4 of their favorite restaurants. They gave Lorraine a beautiful cardigan in her favorite shade of blue. They gave

Tom a casual shirt in the style he loves. Lorraine and Tom gave Lucy a quilted jacket that suited her to a tee. David was presented with a set of books that he had been longing for.

Judge Henry asked if he might have just a few minutes of everyone's time and they all echoed, "of course". "My beautiful wife and I wanted to tell you personally how grateful we are for the pair of you. Lucy, you had a prestigious position in one of the best law firms in the State of Massachusetts. You selflessly walked away from that position to take on the responsibility of your friend's three minor children. Not even a relative, but rather a friend. You have far exceeded all our expectations as an administrator of very complex estates, mothered your friend's children as if they were your own while still parenting your child and being wife-extraordinaire to your husband. You are most definitely "Mother and Aunty of the Year". Lucy was crying so hard she had to leave the room. When she returned the Judge told her, "Lucy, it wasn't our intent to make you sad, but rather to bestow upon you the title you so deserve. David, I know that you share in our love of Amada. You were her lifelong friend, a sort of big brother, a protector, a stand-in father. When you and Lucy met Tim, you knew instinctively that he was *the one.* You and he became fast friends. When the time came to make hard decisions, you never faltered. You walked away from a brilliant career. You have done an outstanding job building Tim's P.I. business. You're an exemplary father and Uncy. We simply wanted to take the opportunity to tell you both how we felt. Tom and Lorraine graciously allowed me to use this platform. We love you. We salute you. We thank you. Lorraine just smiled through tears and announced that she needed her glass refilled and that Lucy needed to help her put dinner on the table.

The meal was above fabulous! Lorraine had obviously cooked for a week and everything was delicious. The conversation was easy and in abundance between all parties. Uncle Judge Henry loved the children, so it was fun to watch him interact with them.

The new year brought dance classes, gymnastics, baseball, basketball, football, hockey, and more. It seemed everyday was filled with activities, laughter, and kids growing so fast that it took your breath away. They were all growing like weeds. They were each so intelligent and so very physically active. Each one of them had a distinct personality and a great sense of humor. The twins were prone to practical jokes which sometimes got them in trouble.

# *They're Growing Up*

The years seemed to come and go and before anyone realized it, the twins and Alicia were almost 10 years old, and Debra had turned 8. Everyone was busy and seemed to be going in separate directions. David and James had so many clients that they had taken on another investigator and a full-time secretary. Lucy stayed busy with the two estates, the children's school and extracurricular activities, David and the house. Lorraine and Tom stayed busy with the B&B and their multitude of friends. Uncle Judge Henry passed away shortly before Debra's birthday. His beautiful wife followed him just two months later. So many changes. So many tears.

The children seemed to fly through the rest of their elementary school years and junior high school. Reports cards were exemplary by anyone's standards. David and Alicia were still tied at the hip. They were never out of line as far as Lucy and David could see, but they were obviously *together*. Daniel was the helper at CYO meetings (the Catholic Youth Organization) and relished every minute that he was there. He oversees prayers at home and I'm almost positive that the other children are using his side of the bedroom as a confessional. Debra oversaw every project at school, or so it seemed. I don't know where her energy comes from as she wears me out.

The twins and Alicia were entering their senior year in high school. Debra was a sophomore. Daniel had not changed his mind over the years. He was entering the priesthood as soon as he completed college. He would major in Theology and Business which he felt would help him going forward. David and Alicia couldn't wait to be finished with school so they could get married. They had been attached at the hip for their entire lives, so this seemed inevitable. Debra excelled at everything she touched. She would obtain her high school diploma and associate's degree by the end of her sophomore year when she was just short of 17 years old. She had applied to and been accepted at Harvard for the following fall semester. She was already counting the days until she could pack up and move to Boston. She would live with her granny and grandpapa in Boston and her life would be just as she had planned; perfect.

The boys were active in every sport all through junior and senior high school. David was an outstanding hockey player and basketball center. Daniel had an arm that probably could have gotten him a major league contract if he hadn't wanted to be a priest. Alicia loved the arts. She was in every play all through school and while usually quite shy, she was a star on stage. She was a fair ballerina, a great tap dancer, and quite the gymnast. Debra was on every debate team, class President, and all-around teacher's pet.

Granny Lorraine had not been feeling very chipper of late and was talking about shutting down the B&B and moving back to Boston. Grandpapa Tom kept trying to steer her in other directions as he loved being close to the kids and loved the guests that visited the inn. Lucy tried extremely hard to take any strenuous activities off Lorraine that she could, but it certainly wasn't easy. That was one stubborn woman. Just before Christmas holidays Lorraine suffered a massive stroke and died instantly. Tom was beside himself as were the rest of us. We helped Tom to have Lorraine's body taken to Boston to be buried in the family plot. There was a huge mass held for her as she had been a member of that parish for 60 years and had been an active member of Boston as a prestigious attorney.

Lucy and David worried about Tom as he seemed to age in front of their eyes. He finally announced that he was shutting down the inn and moving home. He would be there to ride herd on Debra when she moves to start college. We all chipped in to help pack and make the arrangements necessary for closing granny's house. Lucy made Tom promise that he would call or text her every other day so she would know he was alright. He swore that he would. She warned him that if he missed even one day that she would call on Fr. McMurray to go straight to the house to check on him.

The children were all very sad with the loss of granny and now their grandpapa was moving so far away. Debra had gotten into the habit of visiting with them both quite often. When Debra was born Lorraine had told Amanda that she and Debra were going to be the best of friends. And they had been. Debra was counting the days until she could move to Boston with grandpapa and start her life as she had dreamed it would be.

# *Debra*

Debra had received her high school diploma and had acquired an associate degree by the time she finished her sophomore year. Within the month she was packed, enrolled/accepted at Harvard, and ready to move. Tom agreed to be her guardian and housemate. She and Lucy had talked all this over many times before. Lucy knew that Debra was as stubborn as a mule but very, very capable. While she wasn't exactly happy about her youngest flying the coop so soon, she understood that this was what was going to occur so she might as well get used to it.

Daniel hung around for the summer following graduation and then entered the seminary to begin his journey into priesthood. He would attend Boston University of Theology to earn his bachelor's degree. He could continue at Boston U Seminary to earn his master's or Doctorate. When that was accomplished, he would be ordained and receive an assignment within the church. His plan was to ask Grandpapa if he too could live with him while attending school. Tom was going to have a very full house!

Debra and Daniel were all moved in and settled in Boston. They had worked out chores, carpooling, and where they would look for part-time jobs while attending school. They were both dead set on being independent. They had dividends that were put into their checking accounts every month, but they didn't want to use them unless they had to. School was paid for. Books and incidentals were paid for. Rent was free long as they kept up their part of the household chores. Finding and working at part-time jobs looks good on their resume and gives them spending money for foolishness like pizzas and beer!

Seriously, for movies, friend's birthdays and stuff like that. They both loved school. They would sit of an evening and tell their Grandpapa everything they had seen, heard, and learned that day. He would just shake his head and smile. They took him out to the restaurant of his choice every Friday evening for dinner. They made a trip to Edgartown before the bad weather set in so they could see everyone. There were discussions about trying to come home for Christmas, but everyone decided they would talk on the phone and visit when the snow and ice were gone.

All four children were finished with their first year of college life. David and Alicia talked with David and Lucy and explained that marriage now was in everyone's best interest. David and Lucy were savvy enough to understand that this was the best decision. They wanted a small ceremony, just an immediate family, at their home. Plans were laid and it was truly a beautiful ceremony. Fr. James officiated in their backyard where a beautiful trellis of flowers had been erected. Daniel stood up for David and Debra for Alicia. They had already talked with the parents about living in granny's house until they graduated and then reopening the house as an Inn. Everyone had agreed that this was a workable idea. Lucy and David thoroughly enjoyed having Tom, Daniel and Debra for the rest of the weekend. The house is just so empty when they are all off doing whatever it is that they do.

David and Alicia had laid out plans for redoing granny's house before opening as an Inn. School didn't come easy to either of them, but they made good grades and kept good their promise to their parents. Alicia couldn't see the sense of it because she couldn't imagine using the degree for anything. David felt that down the road his degree would be useful.

Both Daniel and Debra are overachievers. They can't help it as it just seemed to be born in them. Daniel earned his bachelor's degree in theology in 28 months rather than the normal 4-years. He was accepted to the Boston U Seminary program where he would study for his master's degree before being ordained. He was certain he could do this in less than 2 years. He had found a job tutoring other students and helped the children at St. Jo's. That job didn't pay, of course, except for making his heart feel good. Debra, having graduated from high school at 16 years old and with an associate degree already beat out Daniel's time by a full 2-1/2 months. She was not quite 19 years old and would begin her graduate work toward a master's degree in law in the fall. She saw no reason to go for a PhD as she wouldn't need it. She is counting on being ready to take on the world by no later than her 22nd birthday. She had taken a part time job at the campus library and worked in the neighborhood deli on Saturdays. She hated both jobs, but she stuck with them.

David and Lucy were busy with their home and with their jobs. David relished the work that he was doing with the private investigation firm. Funny, he was much more involved in it than he ever was with the police department. He and James have built a business to be proud of. They are partnered with the police department, the county sheriff's department, the state police, and the district attorney's office. Lucy works diligently to distribute the Brice estate and manage the family estate (as she now thinks of it). The children have barely touched their rightful inheritances. Debra had purchased a car as had David. Her David had bought Alicia a car when she graduated high school, and she was still driving it. Daniel either borrowed Debra's or rented one as he wasn't ready for the responsibility of being a car owner.

Another year came and went with little or no problems or changes. Debra told her aunt that she was concerned about Grandpapa as he seemed to be declining and was somewhat forgetful. He didn't want to go to dinner with them or anyone else for that matter. He spent more and more time sitting in the den asleep in his chair. Lucy told Debra that there wasn't much she could do other than be sure he was eating and to insist on quarterly visits to his doctor to have his health monitored. Other than that age was taking its toll. Debra and Lucy talked about the fact that she only had another year, maybe eighteen months, and she'd be finished with her law degree. She mentioned that Daniel spent more and more time volunteering at St. Jo's and that she really didn't see much of him. Lucy commented that he still called home weekly, but his conversations were rather rushed. Let's just stay in touch and see how it goes.

Debra and Daniel convinced Tom to go with them to Edgartown for the holiday season. They packed up everything and were on the road with the idea of spending Wednesday-Sunday morning with the family and then taking the last ferry back home on Sunday afternoon. The weather had been cooperative, and they weren't worried about a major snowfall. They arrived at the house which is where everyone was going to stay. Lucy felt it would be too difficult on Tom to stay at granny's house. Rather than having the holiday dinner at David and Alicia's they would all gather at Lucy and David's house (home). They laughed because Lucy set David and Daniel up in their old room, Debra and Alicia in Debra's nursery and gave Tom Alicia's old room. Tom was happy to see David and Lucy and joined in the conversation without any prompting. David and Alicia showed up shortly afterwards and so there was lots of talking and laughing all through the house. Lucy had a spectacular supper all ready for everyone to enjoy. She had cooked a huge beef pot roast with all the trimmings which was everyone's very favorite. Dinner was enjoyed by all and everyone joined in to clean up and do dishes. Tom had a nightcap with David and then announced that he was tired. They helped him up to his room and he seemed ok. Lucy and David vowed to watch over him while he was there.

A wonderful Christmas Eve service at the local church was enjoyed by the entire family. Fr. James invited Daniel to sing and to read the scripture. He was thrilled and we were all so immensely proud of him. His voice, second only to his father's and grandfather's, was beautiful. Ok, well maybe it is even better than that, but we won't tell him that. Christmas morning was a blur. There were so many gifts under the tree that it took forever to get through them. The boys helped clean up paper and get it taken out to the garbage and they packed the car up with everything that was going back to Boston with them. Daniel and David packed David's car with his and Alicia's gifts. It was hard to think that they were leaving tomorrow but there wasn't any choice. They needed to get back to their schoolwork and their jobs.

Everyone helped to pull all the holiday leftovers out of the fridge in expectation of what Lucy was going to create for dinner. One just never knew what it would become. There was leftover ham and turkey, lots of veggies, mashed potatoes and mashed yams. Lucy checked her recipe collection and somehow, she turned it in to the best Jambalaya with spud/yam grits to go with it. A holiday miracle! They all sat around the big dining room table and talked and snacked on pies and cookies and told old stories. Tom excused himself again and went upstairs to bed. Lucy frowned and told them to just be patient with him.

The next morning after breakfast all the kids went upstairs and stripped all the beds and remade beds for the parents. The girls cleaned the bathrooms while the boys vacuumed all the rooms and the hall. They brought down all the dirty laundry and piled it on top of the washer just like they always had. Truth be told, it had been so fun coming home, staying in their old rooms with their siblings. A joyous holiday season. Lucy was already crying by the time that coats were being put on and goodbyes were being said. They promised to come home during spring break and reminded the parents that the road went both directions. David and Alicia headed home, and Debra, Tom and Daniel headed back to Boston. David and Lucy stood on the porch, waving and crying, long after the cars were gone.

Debra asked Daniel on the way home if he had gone to the cemetery. "You always go, she said, but you hadn't said anything." "Yes, I went. I stopped by when I went to the church to visit Fr. James. I could never come home without stopping to visit with the parents. Besides, I needed to talk to my mom, he said." "You did? About what, she asked?" "Pixie, he said, there are some things that just aren't any of your business." She just threw him one of her looks that was supposed to stop him cold. The trip was uneventful, and they arrived home in record time. Tom went straight in, fixed himself a drink, and went to sit in the den. No conversation, no nothing. Both kids were really perplexed by this. Debra told Daniel that she would perhaps make a doctor's appointment for him and see if anything was new.

# Sometimes Growing Up Is Very Hard

School started back up and both Debra and Daniel were so busy they barely saw one another. Debra figured she would be finished by spring break. Daniel will be done with seminary in the summer.

Debra awoke with a start but had no idea why. She looked around her room and decided to get up and check on Grandpapa. She barely opened the door to his room but could see his form lying in bed. She asked if he was okay but received no answer. She was frightened so she went and woke up Daniel to come and help her. He was there immediately and went to his grandfather's side. Tom was gone, probably having a heart attack. Daniel performed last rites for his grandfather and he and Debra knelt next to the bed and prayed together. Debra was sobbing and Daniel was holding her trying to tell her it would be ok. Daniel stayed with his grandfather and Debra went to call Lucy and Fr. McMurray. Fr. McMurray told her he'd be there shortly and that she needed to call the mortuary to pick him up. Lucy told Debra that she and her uncle were on their way and would be there within 6 hours. Debra went back to tell Daniel what she was told to do, and he said he would phone the mortuary if she would please stay with grandpapa as he didn't want him to be alone. She shook her head that she would but hadn't moved from the doorway. Daniel asked her, "Debra, what are you afraid of? It's just grandpapa sleeping. He's no different than he's always been. Please don't be afraid." Debra looked at him with huge eyes full of unshed tears and told him to go, she'd be okay now. Fr. McMurray was there in minutes and the mortuary was not far behind. Fr. McMurray came upstairs and found Debra sitting quietly by the bed holding her grandpapa's hand. She looked so little and so forlorn but had proved that she could be brave. She moved to allow the father to spend time with and pray with his old friend. Debra and Daniel were downstairs to allow the mortuary to enter. It wasn't long before they had left the house. It seemed so cold and so lonely suddenly.

Lucy and David, as promised, were there with David and Alicia in less than 5 hours. Everyone comforted each other. Lucy knew that Debra had been through a terrible ordeal. Daniel, on the other hand, seemed to be exactly where he was always meant to be. He got coffee for everyone and then asked that the family come together in prayer for their beloved grandfather's journey home. Lucy asked if Fr. McMurray had any idea about a service and Daniel told her that the mortuary would be ready to release the body within 3 days so possibly a Saturday afternoon mass.

The family and a horde of friends and business associates gathered to bid Tom a safe journey home to the Lord. Fr. McMurray asked Daniel if he would like to read scripture and if he had a favorite song that he would like to sing for his grandfather. He assured the father that he did and yes, he would love to read the scripture as well. "Actually", he said, "my uncle, my brother and my sister would also like to read some of grandpapa's favorite scriptures as well. Would that be alright?" "Absolutely, said the old priest." It was a hard day for everyone. Saying a final farewell at the cemetery was awfully hard on everyone as this was the last family member from Tim's family. Lorraine's sister was gone as was Tom's brother. David, Daniel, David, and Debra all read scripture that they knew had been Tom's favorites. Daniel explained to the congregation that when his parents passed away that his grandpapa had rocked him and sang to him this beautiful Irish classic. He of course sang "Oh, Danny Boy". David suggested that they all go back to the house and order dinner in. Debra said that she would order from their favorite Italian restaurant.

Dinner arrived and they all gathered around the table to eat supper. There had been many tears over the past couple of days but now was a time of joy in remembering all the wonderful times that they had been spent with their grandparents. They all told stories, and they laughed until they cried anew. Daniel was noticeably quiet, but David even more so. He had seemed to be the boy that was closest to his grandfather.

The parents inquired about how the kids were doing with their studies and if they were still on target for being done with their schooling. Daniel announced that he was about halfway done with seminary. He felt that about 18 months would do it. At that time, he would apply to be ordained and would obtain his placement with the church. He was spending a lot of time tutoring and helping at All Saints Parish. He was really hoping that he might be able to live at the seminary there while he finished up. Debra told the family that she had another 6-8 months to achieve her master's degree. She would see about setting up her bar exam after getting that pretty piece of paper. The family was concerned about her living alone if Daniel was going to move to the seminary. "Let's cross that road when we come to it, she said, as right now I don't see it as a problem." They all just stared at her.

The house was quiet with just Daniel and Debra living in it. There were glimpses of their grandparents everywhere. You couldn't go into the kitchen so that you didn't smell the wonderful pies and goodies that they would bake. You couldn't walk into the dining room so that you ignore the beautiful buffet full of all their grandma's treasures. It was going to be difficult to work through this, but they knew they could do it. They were Donaldsons after all and they were made of strong stuff.

# *Daniel*

Daniel was exhausted. Between school, tutoring and volunteering he seemed to be meeting himself coming and going. His nerves were shot, and he couldn't put his finger on the "why?". He finally decided to make a quick trip home. He needed to talk to his parents, and he needed hugs from Aunty and Uncy. Also, it would be good to see David and Alicia as well. He didn't even bother to invite Debra or to tell her he was going for that matter. He really felt he needed to make this journey alone for a change. He left the house early and was at the ferry dock in time for the first crossing. He drove straight to the cemetery, got out of the car, and laid down on his mother's grave and wept. He laid there for a long while before finally sitting between his parents and tried to explain what he was going through. He was so tired and so distraught from school, but mostly from his tutoring job. The children were so special, but so desperately in need of help and guidance. He tried the best he could, but he couldn't reach them all. He told them he had spoken with Fr. McMurray, but he had pretty much told him it was what it was and there was not much he could do except to pray for them. "The children are all so special, he told them, and nobody seems to care. Most of the children I'm tutoring are in foster care and not very well taken care of. It is breaking my heart." He sat there, praying, and waited for a sign. He noticed there was a young woman and two small children walking toward him. He stood up and smiled and bid her good day. She asked if he knew the cemetery very well and he answered that he did. "I'm looking for the children's section, she told him." He assured her that he knew right where that was and would be happy to show her the way. While walking along he introduced himself to her and the children and she told him that she was Mary, and that the little boy was Jeb, and the little girl was Carly. "These are my sister and brother, she told him. Our other sibling is buried here, or so we were told." "I'm so sorry, he said. Has your loved one been gone for long?" She explained to him that she received word that her younger brother had been the victim of a hit and run. That he was pronounced dead at the scene. Some wonderful people paid to have him buried here and have spent the past two years trying to locate me and my family. Our parents are long gone. We haven't heard from either of them for about four years now. I'm in charge of our family now." Daniel told her how deeply sorry he was for her loss and all her heartache. He also asked where she and the children were from, and did they have adequate accommodation here in Edgartown? "We live in Plymouth. My younger brother was staying with our cousin, or so I was told. I haven't been able to locate that cousin for more than a year, and no we don't have accommodation yet, but I'm sure we can find something suitable." Daniel told her that he was studying to join the priesthood and that he was well acquainted with the Catholic church here locally. My brother and sister-in-law, he said, have a huge house that is presently undergoing renovation, but I know they would be happy to put you up for the night. Shall I call them?" She looked alarmed for a moment but then told him that if it wasn't a lot of trouble that she would be grateful. He told her that he was going to go say goodbyes to his parents and would call his brother and wait by the car for her and the little ones. She thanked him again and watched him walk away. She and the children knelt by their brother's grave and prayed and cried. She told him how sorry she was that she hadn't been there for him and hoped he would forgive her. They spent a few more minutes and then went in search of Daniel.

She found Daniel near his parents' graves. She and the children waited by the car that was parked close to the gravesite. Daniel helped them into the car and told them that his brother and sister-in-law were looking forward to their arrival. "You're certain we won't be a bother, she asked?" "Not at all," he said. I noticed that you just have a small bag, so I assumed you weren't planning on spending much time here?" She told him that they lived in the back of a grocery store in Plymouth. "The folks that own it, she told him, have been wonderful to me and my siblings since our parents left. I cleaned the store and helped stock in exchange for the rent on the small apartment. The children attend the local school, and they love it. Jeb is in 4th grade and Carly is in the 2nd grade. I had to drop out to take care of everyone. I would have graduated last year if I hadn't had to quit."

On the drive to Granny's house Daniel attempted to explain the family and what he was doing in Edgartown. He told her about Uncy and Aunty and how they had been like family his entire life. "My twin brother, David, married Uncy and Aunty's daughter, Alicia, who was born the same day we were. Our younger sister, Debra, is in law school in Boston. Our parents were killed in a car crash when my brother and I were 5 and my sister just 3 years old. They arrived at Granny's and David and Alicia came to greet their guest. Alicia had a snack ready for everyone and the children were thrilled to munch the sandwiches, cookies, and milk that she had prepared. Mary and Daniel joined David and Alicia at the dining room table where they could get acquainted. Alicia inquired whether Mary was happy in Plymouth or was considering relocating. Mary explained that she had no funds to relocate with. "Well, said Alicia, it just so happens that I need help keeping this huge house in order. Would you be interested in working for us and living here?" Mary started to cry, and Alicia went to hug her. "Are you serious, she asked? Really, work here and live here?" "Yes, said Alicia, I'm profoundly serious. This house is way too much for me to manage on my own and we are trying to get the renovation done and open as an Inn." Mary looked at her with huge brown eyes, and said, "We would love to live here. I need to return to Plymouth, though, and get what little bit of stuff we have and thank Mr. and Mrs. O'Shea for their years of kindness to us." Well, said Daniel, I must return to Boston tomorrow or the next day and Plymouth is sort of close. How about we go get your stuff and then you can hang out with Debra and me in Boston until the following weekend when we can bring you back. Will that work?" "Yes, of course. Will your sister be okay with us coming there, she asked?" "She will, he said, but it wouldn't really matter. I'm the big brother and she's the little pixie sister. I'm going to excuse myself and go to the parent's house before they find out I'm here and haven't come to see them yet. Mary, relax and enjoy getting acquainted with these lovely folks. I'll talk to you all tomorrow." He hugged David and Alicia and headed on his way.

Daniel arrived at the house and not a moment too soon. Obviously, like always, mom and dad had alerted Aunty and Uncy that I was in town as they were on the porch waiting for me! "How do you guys do that, he asked?" Lucy told him that her heart always alerts her when her babies come home. Uncy helped get Daniel's bags into the house where there was food galore waiting for him. They headed into the kitchen to hang out at the island and catch each other up on what was going on. Daniel explained, best he could, about Mary and the kids. "It is so strange, he told them, but since we were here last, I've had a cloud hanging over my head. I had no idea why, but I knew I had to come home and talk to my parents. While I was doing that, Mary appeared from nowhere really. It was as if I was supposed to be there at that very moment to help her and the children." Lucy inquired why this young woman had come to the cemetery to begin with. Daniel explained about her brother being the victim of a hit and run. Lucy shook her head and looked at David. She asked Daniel, "Do you know the name of the boy that was killed?" "Yes, Daniel responded. It was Patrick. Patrick Donohue. At least that is what the head stone said. Why?" "Because Lucy said. Your uncle received notice from the local police department that a young boy had been struck down and died and nobody knew where he came from or where he was staying. He had a wallet with a little money and identification on him. Your uncle and I paid for his burial." "Oh, my Lord, said Daniel. This is just too strange. Talk about divine intervention. I believe that this is a perfect example." Daniel went on to explain that Mary and the children were at David and Alicia's house. Alicia has hired her to help clean and keep the house and she and the children will live there. I'm going to take her back to Plymouth to collect her belongings and then on to Boston until we can get her back here.

Aunty and Uncy and I had a wonderful evening together talking, eating, drinking, and just reminiscing. I always enjoyed my time with them. We talked about the children that I was tutoring and the work I was doing at All Saints Parish. I told them how genuinely profiling the work was and how happy it made my heart. "They are so grateful for any time spent with them. They respond in such a positive way even though so many have nothing to be positive about. Recently I met a boy that is just 11 years old. He is fostered by a family that obviously were looking for cheap labor and a monthly paycheck. His clothing is threadbare as is his dinner plate. The father is quick tempered and happily takes it out on the boy." Aunty was just aghast at people being so cruel. Uncy, of course, had seen all the ugliness while in police work. "I explained that I had best go and call Debra and let her know what is going on. Knowing her quiet demeanor I'm sure she'll be understanding." I went out on the porch and dialed her number. She picked up on the first ring demanding to know where I was. "I'm sorry, I told her, I simply forgot that you were in charge of everyone's lives." "That's not funny, Daniel, and it isn't fair. I've been worried sick." "Really, I asked? Did you call the parents or our sibling to ask if they'd seen me or talked with me?" "No, why would I?" "Well, I told her, because you would have found me. I'm home visiting family." "Really? And it never occurred to you to either ask if I wanted to go with you or to tell me you were going?" "Nope, I said, neither of those things entered my mind.' I heard the click letting me know she had hung up on me. I'll give her 5 minutes to cool down and then ring her again. I looked around the neighborhood and decided that it hadn't changed in all my years on earth. Everything was the same as always. The land that the Brice house had set on was cleared and made a lovely park area in the neighborhood. My mother had overseen those decisions and Aunty had completed her wishes. There were benches throughout the park, each with a plaque memorializing the people of the neighborhood that had passed on. My parents' bench was in the very center. Mrs. Brice's bench was just off to the left of theirs. Aunty had decided against a bench for Lois or Leonard. Nobody wanted to remember them anyway.

My phone was ringing, and I noticed that it was Debra calling back. She is apparently over being angry. I answered and she was softly crying telling me she was sorry for her outburst. I assured her that it was fine as I was well acquainted with her outburst. She asked why I had not invited her to go along. I reminded her that I had something to discuss with the parents and it seemed the right time. "Yes, she said, I recall you saying that something was on your mind." "Well, he said, as it turns out I was exactly where I was supposed to be when I arrived at the cemetery." I told her about Mary and the children and that Aunty and Uncy had been responsible for burying the young boy. "Oh, my goodness, she said, that's just terrible. Will the young woman be alright? Where does she live?" I told her that she lived in Plymouth and then went on to tell her that Alicia and David had hired her to work for them. "They what! She said. Why on earth would they get involved with this total stranger?" "Well, he said, for starters because they are really nice people. And apparently Alicia needed help around that huge house." "Oh, she said. I suppose so. How is she going to get to Plymouth and back? Does she have a car?" "No, I told her. They traveled by bus. I'm taking her and the kids to Plymouth to fetch their belongings and then I'm bringing them to Boston to spend the week with you." "What? What are you talking about Daniel? I don't need houseguest here right now or anytime soon for that matter.' "Well, I told her, they can just stay in my half of the house until the weekend so I can return them to Edgartown. Will that meet with your approval? "Whatever, she said. Do whatever. I need to hang up. Safe travels." With that I heard the final click and then the dial tone. Such a sweet, understanding girl she is…

I went in the house to see what everybody was doing. Aunty had made coffee and cut a beautiful berry pie that was screaming for ice cream. "I've got a movie all set up for us, she said." "Wonderful, I have dibs on the big chair." We watched a wonderful family-style movie and ate our wonderful dessert. Uncy fell asleep about halfway into the movie but Aunty and I enjoyed the entire thing. "I'm thinking I'll fetch Mary and the children tomorrow and head to Plymouth and then onto Boston. I'll return them the following weekend, probably on Thursday afternoon or Friday morning. Would you be up to having lunch with me on Saturday? I want to get an early start back and will probably forego mass Sunday morning. I can always attend the evening service in Boston." "That sounds good, Daniel. And, yes, lunch on Saturday sounds grand. Just you and me?" "Yes, I said. Just us." It was getting late, but Aunty inquired about Debra's mood when he called her. "Not good. She is a tad self-centered and more than a tad spoiled. She thinks everyone and everything should revolve around her. She'll just have to try and grow up as she progresses into these very grown-up decisions she is making." Aunty just smiled. "Yes, Daniel, she is all those things, but she is also a girl with an enormous heart that adores you. She is probably worried that this person will take away some of her time with you." "I suppose that might be true. Unfortunately, though, not all of us have the luxury of only thinking of ourselves." With that he bid Lucy goodnight and headed up to his old room for a good night's sleep.

Daniel was up bright and early and downstairs for breakfast. He had already packed his bag and it was by the front door. Uncy greeted him as he walked in the kitchen. They visited for a while and then Lucy joined them to put the finishing touches on their delicious breakfast of sausage gravy and hot homemade biscuits. Daniel ate until he groaned. "I'll never be able to stay awake all the way to Plymouth, he said. I'm just stuffed." They helped him get ready to leave and told him they'd see him next week. They stood on the porch waving long after his car was gone.

# Getting To Know Mary

David greeted him when he arrived at the inn. Mary and the children were already to travel. He noted that she looked so happy and relieved since dropping her off there yesterday. This was going to be a wonderful move for her and the children. Alicia hugged each of them and told them to hurry home. Mary had big unshed tears in her eyes as they pulled out. She and Daniel chatted to the ferry landing. He took the children on a quick walk around the area as it was very scenic. They enjoyed their walk and were ready for the rest of the trip. The ferry crossing went smoothly, and Mary directed Daniel after he turned onto the highway headed for Plymouth. "Have you always lived here, he asked?" "No, I don't think so. I know we lived somewhere else before moving to Plymouth but I don't know where. My brother took off, angry, when our parents left, and I just hunkered down and made the best out of what we had." The O'Sheas have been wonderful to us. I know they'll be happy for our good fortune. They arrived at the grocery store and Mary told him she would go in and tell the O'Sheas what was going on. "Do you want me to come in and introduce myself, he asked?" "Not yet, she said. I'll let you know when." She was inside the grocer for quite a while before a short, balding man came out and knocked on the car door. I got out of the car and went around to meet him. I introduced myself and he seemed pleased with what he saw. "I'm concerned for the girl and the children, but she says you're good people. May I inquire as to where you come from? I gave him a quick summary of my pedigree and gave him all the phone numbers and addresses for the entire family. "You can call anytime, and you are always welcome to visit if you want." "Mary says you're entering the priesthood, is that correct, he asked?" "Yes, I'm almost finished with my studies at seminary and will then be ordained and receive a position with a church." "Did Mary tell you that she's had no formal church upbringing? Her parents were, are, trash. They don't deserve any of these fine children. God rest of the soul of their newly departed brother." "Yes, she did tell me that and it's fine. If she and the children have any interest in church, they will be welcomed into any faith that they would choose. May I go and help her get her belongings?" "Sir, she can carry them out in a garbage bag. They don't have anything. My wife and I have tried our best to help them. She's a hard worker and a proud young woman. This new job will be wonderful for her. I can see that on her face already." Mary came down the stairs and told the children to go and thank and hug Mrs. O'Shea. They scampered away to do as they were told. Mary hugged and kissed Mr. O'Shea's cheek which was damp with tears. She thanked him over and over for his love and his kindness. "I will write, she said. Please write me back." He promised to do so.

The children came back outside, and we got everyone into the car. Mr. O'Shea stood and waved until the car was long gone. I asked Mary if she was okay, but she assured me she was more than okay. "I'm so excited about my job and our room is simply gorgeous. They gave me a room and the children a room next door. Miss Alicia told me that the children could only share a room for another year or so and then they'd have separate spaces. A year or so! Can you fathom that she's thinking of keeping me for that long?" I just smiled and told her I figured she'd be there forever or until she meets a nice young man. She stared at me so strangely before saying, "I don't see much chance of that happening. I'm not pretty and I'm not very smart. I can barely read and I'm not good with my numbers at all." "Well Mary, I told her, my brother is a scholar and he will most likely take you under his big, sweet wing and teach you anything you want to learn. Also, I know they are already considering asking you if you'd like to continue your studies and get your diploma. Don't be afraid to let them help you. They want to or they wouldn't offer." "Alright, she said. Thank you for sharing that with me." "Oh, and by the way, I said, you are very pretty. They have mirrors at the house, so you need to look closely and learn to appreciate your God-given beauty, both in and out." She just smiled.

We were about an hour from the house and I stopped for gasoline and called Debra. She said that she had ordered in and there was plenty to eat for everyone. "I've made up two rooms, so they are ready as well." Then she hung up. That's my Debra. We wound our way through the traffic and pulled up in front of the house. Mary gasped at the beauty of the exterior of the home. "It's a palace, she said." "Well, not quite but it is genuinely nice, I told her. Come on. Grab your stuff and the kids." Debra had the door open and was busy greeting everyone as they entered the house. She told Mary where hers and the children's rooms were located and to get them settled in and then come down for dinner. Mary ushered the children upstairs and I came in behind them. I raised an eyebrow at baby sister who just stuck her nose up in the air and turned and walked off. This was going to be a long evening. I took my bag upstairs and came back out about the same time as Mary and the children were ready to go downstairs. We all walked down together and went to the kitchen where Debra had the island all set up for the 5 of us. She had ordered spaghetti and meatballs and sausages, green salad, garlic bread, and a tiramisu for dessert. The children were just thrilled and delighted in everything put before them. Mary was shy and rather quiet but answered whenever Debra asked her anything. When everyone was finished with their meal Mary jumped up and started clearing the island. Debra told her to relax but Mary said she'd get everything cleaned up. "Shall I make you coffee, she asked?" Debra thanked her but told her no, she didn't drink coffee of an evening. Debra had gotten out some of the toys and games that she and her brothers had when they were small. She took the children into the den and showed them the games. They were thrilled and genuinely appreciative. Debra told them if they needed anything to just come and ask. "We will have our dessert a little later and then you two can get baths and get ready for bed. You've had a long, busy day." Debra went back into the kitchen and found that Mary had everything washed, dried and just needed direction on where to put things away. Debra showed her where things went and told her to relax that she was a guest, not a servant.

Daniel was sitting at the island waiting patiently for his sister to decide to forgive him and talk to him. She sat down across from him and poured them another glass of wine. Mary asked if it was ok for her to go see how the children were doing. "Mary, you're a guest in our home. You can do whatever you want without asking. If you're hungry, find something to eat. If the children need something, get it for them. Please, just relax and be comfortable." Mary thanked her and went in search of the children. Debra glared at Daniel but finally told him that she thought that Mary and the children were lovely. "Alicia called me, and we had a long visit about them and her plans for them. I believe that she will be as much of a blessing to them as they are to her." Daniel told her that he absolutely agreed. "I believe that I was supposed to be at the cemetery when she and the children arrived." "Yes, I believe that too, Debra said. I'm not questioning that at all. I just feel that you were unnecessarily rude to me to not even bother to tell me you were leaving. Please, take a moment and imagine me doing that to you." "Point taken, he said, and I apologize. You are correct. I would have been upset and worried. Please forgive me?" "Ok, she said. This time. I would suggest, though, that you not repeat this in the future." With that she got up and went into the den to find Mary and the children.

Debra was up early the next morning but found that Mary and the children were already bathed, dressed, and waiting patiently for the rest of the household to wake up. "Good morning, Mary, Debra said, have you and the children had your breakfast already?" "I fed the wee ones, Mary said, but I held breakfast so the three of us could eat together. I hope that was alright?" "Absolutely, replied Debra. Just let me go holler for Daniel." "Oh, Mary said, he's out for a run. He should return shortly." She poured Debra a cup of coffee and started getting the breakfast laid out. Debra asked her if she and the children had warm clothes as it gets nippy in Edgartown. "Well, Mary said, I'm fine but the wee ones could use winter coats. I'll get those for them after my first pay. Mrs. Donaldson has already explained what my hours are and what my pay will be. I'll have no trouble buying coats with that kind of money." "Well, said Debra, how about you and I go do a little shopping this afternoon. We can get the things you and the children will need and worry about the money part later. You can consider it a gift." Daniel walked into the kitchen just as they were finishing their conversation. Mary jumped up and put breakfast on the table for them. She was obviously an accomplished cook and the meal looked and smelled wonderful. After they finished up Mary cleaned up the kitchen and Debra went to get ready for their shopping trip. Daniel was checking emails when Mary asked him if he thought it was alright for his sister to be gifting things to them. "What? Mary, of course it is okay. We are very happy to help you and the kiddos and are so appreciative that you'll be able to help David and Alicia. They are really looking forward to your being there." Debra walked in as they finished their conversation and asked if Mary was ready to go. She was so they gathered the children together and took off for the mall. The children and Mary sat in the car and didn't utter a word unless they were spoken to. Finally, Debra couldn't stand it any longer and told Mary that she was going to turn the radio on so they could all sing. Mary looked rather taken back but shook her head in agreement. The children were singing at the top of their voices and both Mary and Debra were singing along and laughing. They reached the mall, parked and headed into the local children's store. Debra found coats, gloves, hats, shoes, and several outfits for the kids to try on. Mary was gasping at all the items Debra had selected for the wee ones. "It's too much, she said. I won't be able to repay you for all these things." Debra told her that she wasn't repaying anyone for anything. "This is my treat, she said. Let's just enjoy our day. I never get to go shopping!" The children came back out with their new items on and Mary and Debra exclaimed over how adorable they looked. She paid for the purchases and grabbed backpacks while she was at it. "Let's go get you some new duds," she said. Are you planning on wearing dresses or slacks and tops?" "I don't know, Mary said. I have two dresses and a nice pair of black slacks and a white blouse and a pink blouse." Debra looked at her and said, "Well, I think you'll do well in slacks and tops. I'm assuming that part of your duties will be the cleaning and that means a lot of bending over and reaching up, so slacks are a better choice. Do you tend to be warm or cold all the time?" Mary thought for a moment and told her that she was mostly comfortable in short sleeved blouses and a cardigan if needed." They headed to the lady's wear store and found 5 outfits for Mary to work in and two new dresses for Sunday Mass. Debra told her they needed to go to the shoe store. You need good comfortable shoes for working during the day and are you accustomed to wearing heels with your dresses? "I have never had a pair, Mary said, so I'll be fine with my work shoes." "Uh, said Debra, I don't think so. We will start out with nice low heels that will look attractive with your new dresses. I noticed you have a decent winter coat so that will do fine for church. They found Mary a pair of good athletic shoes for work that had good support and would be comfortable for her. Debra found a beautiful pair of black low heel pumps and a matching handbag. "We just have one more stop to make and then we can go find something to eat. I'm starving!" There was a hair salon that welcomed walk-ins. "Let's get your hair trimmed, Mary, and then you'll be all set to go." "Trimmed, Mary asked. What does that mean. I've never been to a barber shop before. I've always cut my own hair when it looked tangled." "Well, Debra told her, you're going to love this." They went in and as luck would have it there was availability right now. Debra told the lady that she wanted Mary's hair washed, conditioned, and trimmed. "Leave plenty of length for her to pull it up, or into a ponytail, while still looking good with it down." Debra and the children visited while Mary was being treated to this new experience. It wasn't long before Mary walked back out. She was simply beaming and looked gorgeous! "Your hair is beautiful, Debra told her, simply gorgeous!" They went to the local restaurant to grab burgers and shakes before heading home.

Daniel was at the house to greet them and unload the car. He told Mary how beautiful she looked, and she was radiant over the praise. "It's just more than I could ever have imagined, she told him." Debra asked Daniel if he could get away earlier than the weekend to return Mary and the children to Edgartown. "I have students to tutor tomorrow, but I could leave early Wednesday morning. Are you going with us, he asked?" "Yes, I need to get away from the house and the books and the ghosts that continue to haunt me." Daniel didn't say anything but was concerned that this was how she was feeling. "Ok, he said, let's head out early Wednesday morning and then we can return on the first ferry after Mass on Sunday." "Perfect, she said."

Debra spoke with Alicia and let her in on what she had purchased and how she had handled it. Alicia was very much in agreement. "I'm thinking, Alicia said, that her duties will be split between cleaning, helping with the garden, some cooking, seeing to their laundry needs and watching the children. I believe that with that schedule she will begin to settle in to being more independent and less afraid. I don't perceive her as feeling like a victim, but I do know that she has barely scraped by even before her parents up and left them. I really think there is a chance that she has been physically abused in the past. She's fine with me, but she won't even look at David when he speaks with her. How is she with Daniel?" "Well, Debra said, now that you mention it, she is better with me. However, she has talked with Daniel and even confided in him so that may be because he's almost a priest. Let's just keep a close eye on the situation. We are leaving early Wednesday morning to head home, so you'll need to be ready for them that afternoon. Are they registered for school yet?" "No, Mary will need to do that when she gets here. Hopefully she phoned the school to have their records transferred as I suggested to her." "Yes, I know she did that because I heard her speaking with them. Another thing you'll need to do, Alicia, is to get them set up with a Pediatrician and Dentist. They'll need at least an annual checkup. I'm positive the children have had their vaccinations, or they couldn't have attended school in Plymouth." "Yes, Alicia said. I'll get appointments set up. I'm also going to suggest to Mary that she attend classes at the local community college to get her G.E.D." "That's a wonderful idea, said Debra. She needs to do that so that eventually she and the children can live independently. We'll see you Wednesday afternoon. Love and hugs to you both."

Mary was busy putting the children's and her new items away when Debra found her. "We are going to leave here early Wednesday morning to head for Edgartown. Alicia and David are so looking forward to your return. Can you think of anything else that you and the children will need to get started?" "No, Miss Debra, you've been more than generous with all of us and we are so very grateful." Debra told her that she was going to need to get the children enrolled at the local school as soon as they got there. "Also, she told her, Alicia is going to make both doctor and dentist appointments for the children to get annual checkup and establish themselves locally. Should she set up an appointment for you, also?" Mary's eyes got very wide as she assured Debra, she didn't need to see either a doctor or dentist. "I attended the free clinic and had my teeth looked over and cleaned. They told me that they looked good and just to be sure to brush regularly and to floss also." "How about a doctor. Were you seeing anyone at the free clinic for regular checkups?" "Yes, and I'm fine. No problems at all." Mary seemed to be busy putting stuff away again, so Debra took that to mean the conversation was over.

## *Secrets*

Wednesday morning arrived before they knew it and they were on the road at 5:30am to make the 7am crossing. Daniel had spoken with Lucy late last night and she said everyone was coming to the house for dinner on Wednesday evening. Daniel knew better than to argue with her. The crossing went well and the trip to Edgartown was without incidence. Daniel told Mary that if she and the children wanted to visit her brother's grave while he was there that he'd be happy to take her. "Thank you, she told him, but I've already said my goodbyes to him." Daniel chose not to mention it again. They arrived at the Inn and both Alicia and David were at the door to greet them and welcome them home. David went with Daniel to help him unload the car. David took advantage of the time alone to ask if anything was going on. "What do you mean, Daniel asked?" David told him that he and Alicia had noticed that Mary was comfortable with Alicia but not with him and they were concerned that she might have been abused in some way. "Well, Daniel said, I can't say for a certainty. She talks at me, but not always with me. I know she was angry at her brother that died, but I'm unsure what went on there. Perhaps in time she will be more comfortable and come forward with any concerns she might have. In the meantime, let Alicia be the one that deals with her." "Yes, I agree. I'll keep my eyes open though., David said." They got everything unloaded and upstairs. Daniel asked Mary if she was up to getting the children registered this afternoon and she said she was. He took her to the school and asked if she wanted him to accompany her? "No, I'm fine, Mr. Daniel, thank you. I'll not be long." She went into the office with the paperwork that she had in hand. She was back in about

30 minutes and said that the children could begin classes as early as Monday. "There is a bus that will pick them both up at 8am and the bus stop is practically in front of the Inn. They will both attend all day and so they'll get home about 3:30 in the afternoon. They can either bring their lunch in a sack or eat in the cafeteria. I explained my position and told them I was just starting a new job so they said the children could receive food coupons for the next month. I'll be able to pay for their hot lunches after that." "Mary, I would have been happy to pay for their lunches until you are on your feet, Daniel said." "No, Mary said, your family has done more than enough for the likes of us. We will be fine. Thank you." They started on the drive back to the Inn and Mary asked if she might ask Daniel something privately. He assured her that she could ask him anything. "Your sister bought me dresses and specifically said that they were for Sunday Mass. I'm Catholic, born and raised, baptized and all, but I choose not to attend church if that is okay with all of you?" "Mary, might I ask why? Is something wrong? Do you need help with working something out? I'm here to help you however you might need me, he told her." "I can't speak of it now, she told him. Please, I just don't want to attend church. Can we just send the children with Mr. and Mrs. Donaldson for now?" He thought about it for a while but finally told her that of course, whatever she decided would be fine with all of them. Something was not right but he was not sure what it was.

They arrived back and the Inn and Mary told the children about starting school on Monday. They were thrilled.

Jeb was so excited about riding the bus and Carly was excited that she would get to wear her beautiful new clothes to school. Debra reminded everyone that they needed to get freshened up, dressed up, and ready to go to Aunty and Uncy's house for dinner. The children scampered away to decide what to wear. Mary excused herself and went to help them. The three of them came back downstairs about 20 minutes later looking beautiful. Jeb had on new jeans and a cowboy shirt that he had chosen. His beautiful curly red locks were brushed and as mannerly as they could be. Carly put on a beautiful dress and her new patent leather shoes. Her face was glistening from her good scrubbing and her beautiful long auburn hair was pulled into a soft ponytail. Mary had chosen one of her new pairs of slacks, a white lacy blouse and a coral-colored sweater. She was also wearing her new pumps. She had pulled her thick auburn hair back with two of the combs that Debra had loaned her. She looked gorgeous. Well, said Daniel, it would appear we are ready to make our appearance at the parent's house. With that they all piled into two cars for the ride over to Lucy and David's house.

Lucy and David greeted them all at the front door. There were hugs and kisses all around and Daniel noted that the children were right in the middle to receive theirs. Mary hung back a bit but accepted the hug from Lucy and thanked her for inviting them. "Nonsense, you are family. We always get together at least once when these rapscallions come home for a visit." Mary noticed that Lucy had a tight hold onto Daniel and could tell that he was certainly a favored son. They all settled in the living room area and David asked for everyone's order for drinks. The children wanted 7-up if that was ok and he assured them that it was. "Mary, what will you have?" "I don't know, she said. I don't drink coffee, tea, or spirits. Water, I guess or 7-up would be fine. May I help you get it?" "Nope, he said, you can go sit down and be a lady of leisure while I get your beverages." Everyone was visiting and Lucy excused herself to go put the final touches on dinner. Mary wandered into the kitchen to ask if she could help. Lucy patted the island and said, "Sit down for a moment dear, and let's get acquainted." Mary sat down at the island and Lucy joined her. "You've had quite a change in your life, Mary. You must feel as if you are in a bit of a tailspin. Are you comfortable with all the changes? Are you okay?" "I'm fine, Mary told her. It's a bit overwhelming but I feel that I've really received a blessing from your entire family. I feel like I'll be able to start making a decent living for myself and the wee ones." "Yes, I believe you will. You're going to be a huge help to my daughter who has felt a bit overwhelmed with the size of the Inn. She and David are very excited about getting that much closer to opening the Inn the way they want. I wanted you to know that I was deeply sorry about your brother. I don't know if Daniel told you or not, but my husband and I were the ones that took care of getting him buried." Mary told her that Daniel had confided that to her and that she was incredibly grateful for the gesture. "He was a troubled lad, she said. He always had been. Then when our parents left us, he became even more belligerent toward me and the wee ones. I wasn't sorry when he finally decided to leave us. I'm just sorry that he had to die." "Well, Lucy told her, there isn't anything we can do about that now. I just wanted you to know that should you need a shoulder mine is always here for you. Now, let's get dinner on the table."

Lucy had prepared Spaghetti, Meatballs and Italian Sausages for the dinner knowing that it would probably be something the little kids would enjoy. There was garlic toast and salad to go with it. Jeb gulped down a glass of ice-cold milk and asked if he could please have more. David went and got him a fresh glass. Mary explained that milk wasn't always on their menu. Everyone ate with gusto, complimenting the chef on the wonderful dinner. Lucy announced that she needed the children to help her with the dessert. Their eyes got huge as they excused themselves from the table and went to help her. They came back toting bowls of fresh strawberries, a beautiful sponge cake cut into squares and whipped cream. Lucy went back and got the vanilla ice cream for those that preferred it to whipped cream. The children were just busting with joy as she had them help dip up dessert for everyone. Jeb oversaw cake and Carly oversaw the berries. Lucy came behind them asking if the person wanted whipped cream or ice cream. When Jeb fixed his own bowl with a piece of the cake and Carly put berries on it he asked if he could have both whipped cream and ice cream. Lucy assured him that would be fine. Carly said she wanted the same. Mary just smiled at the pair of them as they devoured their delicious dessert. Alicia, Debra and Mary cleared the table and told Lucy to go relax while they got the kitchen cleaned up. Lucy said that she had games for the children on the computer so she would entertain them while the girls did the woman's work. They heard her giggling as she went in search of the children. Lucy got the children set up in the office with the computer and they played some fun games that they hadn't ever seen before. She watched them closely to see how they reacted to some different things in the game. There wasn't any violence but there were some surprise popups. Carly jumped back when the first one appeared and seemed truly alarmed. Lucy asked if she was okay and she said she was sorry, but she didn't like that game. Lucy found another that didn't have scary popups. Something had happened to this family and Lucy wasn't going to rest until she found out what it was. Mary came in to check on everyone and told Lucy that her kitchen was restored to its previous glory. Lucy asked the children if they wanted to stay and play games, but they decided to go back to the living room with Mary. Alicia announced that it was getting late and that they should head home. Daniel and Debra were staying at the parent's house, so they were already home. Lucy and David helped the children out to the car as they were already drifting off. Probably from too much food. Daniel and Debra bid Mary goodbye and told her they'd see her for sure before they headed back to Boston. Debra told her, "If you need anything just let me know." Mary assured her she was fine.

Daniel and Debra went back into the house and David had already poured everyone a coffee and a liqueur to go with it. They decided the kitchen island was the best place to chat. Lucy opened the conversation by saying, "Something isn't right. Something or someone has frightened those children, and Mary is hiding something." Debra agreed and finally, Daniel shook his head in agreement. David announced that he was going to do some nosing around and see what he could find. "I may make a trip to Plymouth to visit with the O'Shea's unless one of you has an objection to that." Neither one objected. In fact, they both thought it was a good idea. We finished our coffee and cordial and everyone headed to bed.

Daniel was up early for his run and Debra staggered downstairs about an hour later in search of coffee. Lucy told Debra that Daniel was running, and David had left early for Plymouth. "He and I talked," she said, "and we both felt that we need to know what is going on before we go any further with this. Those people are ensconced in our family's home, and we need to know that David and Alicia are safe." "I totally agree, Debra said, something is not right, and I just can't put my finger on it. What are we doing today? Would you like to go out for lunch or go shopping or for a drive?" Lucy thought for a moment and told Debra that she would love to go to Oak Bluff and take the ferry to Cape Cod. I haven't been there for years, she said. Can we?" "Absolutely," said Debra. Get ready while I run to put on traveling clothes. I need a toast to hold me over though." Lucy fixed her some toast and jam and started getting everything ready. "There is a brew pub there that serves buttermilk chicken with grilled peach and bourbon sauce that I recall was out of this world delicious." "I know the place, said Debra, and that sounds perfect. When will Uncy be back do you think?" "I'm going to text him right now and see if he's round tripping it or if he's staying over. He might well go to the Boston house for the night." She texted David and he called her right back. She told him that she and Debra were headed for Cape Cod and if he was gone to stay over, they were going to make a night of it. David laughed and said, "Make a reservation. I'll stay at the Boston house and come home tomorrow. Have fun and I love you." Lucy hollered upstairs to Debra to pack an overnight case that they were staying in Cape Cod for the night." Debra was dressed and packed and back downstairs in less than 15 minutes. "Let's go, she said. I am really excited about this get away." They were loading the car when Daniel came home and asked where they were going." "We are running away from home for the night," Lucy told him. "We'll see you tomorrow. We love you." He just laughed and told them to have a great time.

Debra drove and while they were headed to the ferry Lucy got them a room for the night. "I booked us at the mansion. We each have a full-sized bed to stretch out in. All we must worry about is where to have dinner." They laughed and chatted all the way to the ferry dock and most of the ferry ride. When they arrived at Cape Cod, they found they were starving so they headed straight to the pub for their lunch. The mansion was about 12 miles from the downtown area, so they decided to go check in and then return to the downtown corridor to walk and shop. Their room was magnificent. Everything you have ever wanted in a luxury hotel room was in this one. They signed up for massages at 10pm figuring they would be back, tired from their drive and sightseeing and that a massage was the perfect way to end their evening. The masseuse would come to your room, so it was very private and just what they were needing. They hadn't brought any fancy clothes so they opted to eat dinner in town rather than at the hotel which they knew would require after 5 attire. "We could buy a new outfit if you'd rather eat here, Lucy said." "Nope, I don't feel like dressing up just to eat, Debra replied. Let's just go with our original plan. There is a ton of stuff to see in town so if you're ready let's head back and start our excursion." They drove back to the downtown area, parked and did all the museums that were on their sightseeing map. They stopped and had lattes and a pastry about 3pm or so and then started looking through the tourist booklet on where they wanted to have dinner. Cape Cod wasn't busy at all mid-week, so they were sure they'd have no difficulty getting seated at any of the restaurants for dinner. They finally decided on a seafood restaurant that bragged about having the best lobster in Massachusetts. That was right up their alley. They continued their sightseeing and stopped in a couple of different boutiques where they each found beautiful blouses and Lucy found a dress that she couldn't say no to. Debra found a beautiful tote bag that was calling her name. They put their purchases in the car and decided it was the perfect time to go in search of adult beverages and lobster. They settled into the bar area for their drinks and an appetizer. They told the hostess that they would like a table in about an hour or so. They relaxed with their drinks and had a seafood platter for an appetizer which they both thoroughly enjoyed. The hostess came to tell them their table was ready, and they followed her to a lovely table by the window where the gorgeous views of Cape Cod were to be enjoyed. They both ordered the Lobster Louie and a bottle of ice-cold Crisp Pinot Gris to go with it. They ate until they thought they were going to die. They passed on dessert and decided to order coffee, a cordial and share a dessert via room service at the hotel before getting ready for their massages.

Debra and Lucy had an early breakfast at their hotel and then headed to the ferry landing. They had shared such a wonderful time together; one that they would always cherish. Lucy was anxious to hear what David had found out. She thought about calling him but figured they'd probably all get home about the same time. Debra was chatting away about school and her future, and Lucy listened as attentively as she could. She had a bad feeling and just couldn't put her finger on what it was. The line at the ferry was long but luckily, they managed to board the ferry. If traffic and weather were cooperating, they should be home between 2-3pm. She jumped when her cell buzzed. It was David and she silently thanked the Lord for his incoming message. He told her that he was at the ferry landing and should be home by 2pm or so. She texted back that they were on the same wavelength, and she'd see him at home. Debra glanced at Aunty and asked, "Are you ok?" "Yes, Lucy told her, I get very jumpy whenever any of you are traveling to and from Boston." "I know you do, Debra responded, we all do." She reached out her hand and grabbed Lucy's and gave it a squeeze. The rest of the ride home was a happy one.

Debra and Lucy parked in front of the house just moments before David arrived. They were unloading the car and he jumped into help them. Daniel wasn't home so they figured he was probably either at the church or at the Inn. They got all the packages into the house and David announced that an early happy hour was in order. First, he called Daniel to see where he was. He didn't answer but in moments texted back that he was almost to the house. They all gathered around the island anxious to hear what David had found out. David told them that his first stop was at the O'Shea's grocer in Plymouth. "Really wonderful people, he said. They truly care about these children. Apparently, they tried desperately to locate the parents but didn't have the financial means to carry it very far. Mr. O'Shea told me that he had suspected abuse in the household for quite some time. He had personally called the police several times for the loud fights and Mary's father's excessive drinking. He suggested that I check with the local law enforcement which was my next stop." Everyone had exchanged worried glances while David reiterated his findings. After a couple of minutes, he continued. "My next stop, he said, was the local PD. I knew one of the captains from my time on the force. He wasn't in but they called him, and he agreed to meet me in about an hour. I left my card and told the desk sergeant that I would be back within the hour. My next stop was the free clinic. The doctor on duty was up to his neck with patients but agreed to meet me at 5pm. I got me a bite to eat and then went back to the PD. Capt. McCormick was waiting for me in the foyer. We caught up on careers and family and then went to his office to talk privately. I explained the situation to him and asked if he had any information that he might be able to share. He stepped out of his office and then returned with a rather large file. "The senior Patrick Donohue was a scoundrel, said the Capt. He was an excessive drinker, as was his wife. They beat the children and I'm pretty sure he abused the girls although I don't have proof of that. He was in and out of jail for mostly domestic issues. They took off together, leaving those poor children on their own. The O'Shea family agreed to keep an eye on them. We probably should have taken action to remove the children from the home and put them in foster care, but frankly, Mary did a fine job of taking care of them, so we let it be." David told him that he had an appointment with the doctor at the free clinic at 5pm. "Good, said the Capt., he'll be able to fill in some blanks. If you have difficulty extracting information from him, call me and I will come and help."

David told the group that he was thinking that driving from Plymouth to Boston after a 5pm meeting was looking less and less favorable, so he found a motel for the night. "I got myself settled in and then went for my meeting with the doctor. He was really a nice genuine fellow and was willing to share whatever he could without giving up confidential information. "Mary is over 18 years of age, he told me, so her records are private as of her 18th birthday. Prior to that date, her being a minor child, I'm not held to the same laws. That said, I will tell you that Mary had been molested by both her father and her brother, Patrick Jr., since she was no more than 13 years old. Her mother would stand watch to be sure they couldn't be heard by any neighbors. When the parents took off her life with Patrick Jr.

became more and more unbearable for her. The police knew about this situation and chose to ignore it. I stepped in, probably shouldn't have, but I did. I told him flat out that I had enough information to put him away for a long time and that his best bet would be to leave the area and not return. I never dreamed that the move would cost him his life." I knew that I couldn't push him to divulge anything more, David said, and I understand that, I guess." All three of the people sitting around the island were softly weeping. None of them could fathom what this young woman had gone through. What to do now?

David finished his drink and told them that he stopped by and shared a beer with the Capt. He admitted that he and the doctor had both turned their heads and not done anything to put the children into foster care. "It just seemed better to leave them all together, he told me." "What I cannot understand, David said, was how far did this abuse go? That is the part that the doctor would not divulge." Lucy spoke up and said that she understood the doctor's position. "He was so negligent in not acting on what he saw, she said, that he just didn't want to go any further with it. The fact that Mary didn't contact the police was probably one reason why he didn't pursue it. Daniel asked, "What do we do now? Do we confront her with what we know? Would that resolve anything? None of this is her fault. She is simply the victim here." David agreed and said, "We all have skeletons that we don't want stirred up, so I think it is best to just keep this amongst ourselves and be there if she wants to confide in any of us." Lucy looked at him and couldn't resist asking, "Skeletons? Would you care to share?" He just glared at her from across the table.

Daniel's heart was heavy with worry over Mary, but of course, that is his nature. Lucy talked with him and tried to convince him that there was really nothing to do only to show her love and support. He agreed. "I know you're right, Aunty. It is just such a horrible thing for a young girl to go through alone. I'm going over to the church. Do you need anything on my way back?" "No, I'm good, she said, but thanks for asking. Any special request for dinner? You two are due to leave tomorrow you know." "Yes, I know. I'm not necessarily looking forward to returning but I must. Could we have steaks and baked potatoes tonight?" "Absolutely, my darling. Anything for you." He hugged Aunty and headed out the door.

Debra was over at the Inn visiting with Alicia. She felt that Alicia needed to be armed with this information to help and support Mary going forward. They visited in the garden where they wouldn't be overheard. Alicia was noticeably upset but told Debra that she had suspected as much. "She smiles, kind of, at the children, she said, but otherwise not at all. I've never heard her laugh or even giggle. I don't know how to help her other than to continue to support her in getting ahead and becoming financially independent. David will stay away from her while still being cordial and helpful. As I become better acquainted with her, I'll be able to determine her strong points and maybe that will help her to look to the future." Debra absolutely concurred. Debra visited for a few minutes with David and then went to say her goodbyes to Mary and the children. She gave Mary a hug and while she didn't exactly return it, she didn't pull away from her. She hugged and kissed the children, and they hung on her thanking her again for all their wonderful stuff. "You must write or call me and tell me how you're enjoying school, Debra told them." They agreed to do just that. Mary thanked her again and then just walked away.

Daniel talked with Fr James about the situation. The old priest echoed what David and Lucy had said. Leave it be and see where it goes. Daniel told him that his heart was heavy, and he really felt that they should just head for home first thing in the morning. "I can attend Mass tomorrow evening, he told him." Fr James said he understood and God's speed as they travel home. Daniel decided to stop by the Inn and tell everyone goodbye before heading home. Mary was sweeping the front walkway when he drove up and she waved and went in the side door without talking with him. He visited for awhile with David and Alicia and then went to bid the children goodbye. They were all hugs and laughter. Mary was in the kitchen busy doing something. He went in to tell her goodbye and she thanked him for his thoughtfulness and turned to walk away. "Mary, have I offended you in some way, he asked?" "No, of course not. You're nothing but a gentleman. I'm sorry if I seemed abrupt, she said." "It's fine, really, he said. I'm just hoping that we can always be friends. I bought you a present, but it was with selfish reasons. He handed her the cell phone that he had purchased for her that was in a bright, girly case. "Oh my, she said. It's beautiful!" "Well, I put my number, Debra's number, Aunty and Uncy's numbers, Fr. James' number, and of course, Alicia and David's numbers. I'm hoping that you will text or call and keep in touch, so I'll know how you and the children are doing." "Yes, of course. I will ask Miss Alicia to help me learn how to use it and I will certainly keep in touch with you and Miss Debra." "Great, he said. Take care of yourself." He started to turn and walk out but not before she caught him and gave him a hug and a smile. "Thank you so much, Mr. Daniel. I really appreciate all that you've done for me and the wee ones." With that she fled the room. Daniel felt renewed. She doesn't hate me!

# *Time To Return To Boston*

Daniel returned to the house and told Debra he wanted to leave first thing in the morning and that they could attend Mass tomorrow evening after their return to Boston. She told him that was fine, and she'd be ready to go. He found Lucy in the kitchen putting dinner together. She pointed to the salad fixings and he got started with that. They've always had a wonderful relationship and worked well together in the kitchen. Lucy had steaks ready to grill and the potatoes were already baked. David came out of the bedroom a few minutes later and said he would get cocktails ready and then go grill the meat. Debra came downstairs just in time for happy hour to begin. They visited about everything and nothing and shared a wonderful meal and evening together watching a movie they all wanted to see. Lucy was sad thinking about them leaving but understood that they had a life and needed to return to it.

Daniel returned from his morning run and he and Debra opted for cereal and toast and coffee so they could get on the road. There were hugs and kisses and perhaps a few tears like always. The ferry crossing and ride back to Boston was without incidence. They unpacked the car and Daniel asked if Debra wanted to go to Mass with him. She decided to forgo it for now and said she'd go to the mid-week service instead. Daniel headed out the door and Debra set out to unpack and do laundry, so she'd be ready for classes in the morning.

Daniel and Debra's routines rolled along without any problems and before they knew it, Daniel had finished his seminary and been ordained. He was officially a priest. He had achieved his goals thus far and been assigned to the parish he was anxious to work with. Debra had about a month left to have her degree. She was happy with her decisions and was looking forward to starting her journey.

Debra was curled up in the big chair staring at her diploma she had earned from Harvard University. With her law degree in hand, she applied to take the bar exam in Massachusetts. She received notice of the date for taking the exam and let her friends and family know that she would be MIA for the next 60-75 days while she studied like crazy. She was 22 years old and had accomplished everything she expected of herself up to this time. As soon as she has the bar out of the way she will release the letter to the Massachusetts Prosecuting Attorney's office where she hopes to be a part of. It has been her dream for as long as she can remember. She had read everything her Grandmother Rebecca (Amanda's mother) wrote while she was the Assistant District Attorney. She felt that she was armed with everything needed to make her dreams come true.

She was really missing visiting with Daniel. She had not heard from him in more than a week which was unusual for him. He had been assigned to All Saints Parish in Boston's suburbs and was happy doing what priests do. Personally, I felt like it was a waste of an incredibly handsome man that was one of the sweetest men I've ever met. Daniel was, if possible, more handsome than our father was. It had been nice to be able to get together with him while I was in law school.

My brothers and Uncle David and Aunty Lucy had all been disappointed to learn that I wanted to build my career in the greater Boston area rather than Edgartown. They argued that I was terribly young to be living on my own in such a huge city. Maybe, but I saw it all as an opportunity waiting to happen. At this time, I felt like all my energy should be directed to passing the bar.

My cell was ringing, and I couldn't find it anywhere! I finally found that it had slipped under the cushion on the couch. I dug it out just as the caller hung up. I checked my recent calls and found that it was Daniel calling. I returned the call and he answered immediately in his always chipper way. "How's it going baby sister?" He asked. "I'm fine, I said, thanks for checking…finally." "Hey, it hasn't been that long since we talked last. What's going on?" "Well, I told him, I was about to send the entire family a note asking that you not expect to hear from me for the next 60-75 days while I study for the bar exam." "Are you really worried? He asked. You always pass everything with flying colors, and I expect this to go to the same way." "Well, I hope you're right. Anyway, why were you calling? Anything important?" "No, he said, I just wondered if you were free for dinner tonight?" "As a matter of fact, I am, and I know just the place you can take me. There's a new Italian place about one-half mile from your church that I've been wanting to try." "I know the place, he said. How about you meet me there at about 7pm?" "That's perfect. See you there." She was glad that he had called. It would be a pleasant evening playing catch up with him. He always has great stories about his parishioners and he's a wonderful storyteller. Truth is I just miss him terribly. David is so involved in his life and Alicia that he doesn't even know anyone else exists. I don't mean that he doesn't care about us because he does, but he's a very isolated human being. A very strange group are we.

I went upstairs to soak in a tub before getting dressed for my dinner date with Daniel. As is my custom I fill a glass with ice cold white wine and soak in my bubbles for at least 30 minutes. It literally washes away the worries of the day and refreshes the body, mind, and spirit. Hmmm, I believe my mother did this very same thing. I finished up my bath, towel dried my mop of hair and did my makeup. I looked in the mirror trying to decide what to do with this mass of chocolate curls that I had been blessed with. I finally pulled it back in a loose ponytail and secured it with a huge barrette. I had already laid out my dark blue dress and navy shoes to wear. I found a beautiful multicolored scarf that would set off the dress as well as my almond-shaped green eyes. When I look at photographs of my grandmother Rebecca, I fully realize that I'm the incarnation of her. I'm barely 5'2" tall and am a petite size 3. My mother, while slim like a runner, was right at 5'9" and my dad at 6'3". Obviously, I hadn't taken after either of them!

I gave the valet my car and went in search of Daniel. Bottega di Capri was less than half- mile from All Saints Parish so he might already be inside. I walked into the foyer and there he was. He still takes my breath away. There is simply something wonderful about the way he looks and the aura that he emits. He rewarded me with his big, beautiful smile as he walked toward me. "Hello Pixie, he said. You look divine." "Thanks Daniel. You're not half bad yourself." He got the hostess' attention and she showed us to our table. He had already ordered for both of us. Obviously, this is a hereditary thing passed down from our father. He had chosen a beautiful bottle of Chianti and bread with garlic infused olive oil to munch on. The waiter poured our Chianti and left us to visit. "How's life at the church, I asked?" "Good, he said. I've had a couple of young families that I've been counseling, and it has proved very rewarding. I believe there was always a hint of a teacher lurking inside of me." "Yes, I would agree with that, I said. Not to change the subject but have you spoken with David recently?" "No, I've left messages but so far no response. He and Alicia are truly a strange pair. The only good thing is that they are happy with each other so that's at least comforting." I told him that I had talked with Aunty about it, but she felt the same as we did. She told me that she and Uncy have always been concerned by their relationship, but that it seemed to work for them. Aunty actually hinted at the fact that she felt they were both a bit selfish." That made both Daniel and I laugh out loud! We talked about my studying for and taking the bar exam. Daniel asked, "are you actually concerned about passing it? You've never been worried about tests before." "Well, I'm not actually worried but rather more concerned. If I don't pass it there is a considerable waiting period and I really need to get on with my life." Daniel laughed, and squeezed my hand. Pixie, I don't think you have a thing to worry about. Are you really planning on applying at the District Attorney's office here?" "Yes. I want to be a prosecutor and I don't think there is enough happening in Edgartown to offer me the challenges that I want. And, I have the Boston house that I can live in here. If I were in Edgartown I would either need to live with Aunty and Uncy or with David and Alicia. Neither of those options are very appealing to me. I love them all, but I don't want to live with any of them!" "Ok, he said, that is a good argument for staying here. I rather like having you close at hand anyway. Our salads arrived and we both ate hungrily. I asked him when we finished salads what he had ordered for an entrée?" "Well, I know how much you love lamb so I had called ahead and asked if they would prepare Osso Bucco with lamb shanks. They were happy to oblige." "Oh, Daniel. My mouth is watering at the thought of it. The aromas alone are enough to send me into a frenzy. Thank you so much for thinking of such a lovely treat." "You are most welcome, Pixie. Anything for my favorite little sister." The entrée arrived and I think everyone in the restaurant tried to figure out what that wonderful aroma was. We devoured our plates! I swear I would have licked the plate if I'd been home alone. We passed on dessert as we were stuffed and getting sleepy. Daniel walked me to my car, hugged and kissed me, and told me to study hard and let him know when it was over. I promised that I would. On the drive home I couldn't help but think how lucky I was to have this wonderful man for a brother. My parents would have been over the moon at how this son had turned out.

I set up my study area with a small microwave, coffee maker, and a small refrigerator. I figured this way I wouldn't need to be running back and forth to the kitchen and could concentrate on studying for the exam. During the next 5-1/2 weeks I only left my study area to bathe, sleep, and tend to other necessities. I'm ready! I'm sure of it! My exam is scheduled for next Wednesday at 9am and I plan on being their star pupil. I discovered that I was starved to death for something that hadn't been cooked in a microwave. My ideal kitchen is a large, well-illuminated area, preferably with an island that seats 4-6 people, professional chef appliances, a well-stocked freezer and pantry as well as someone who is adept at cooking, which isn't me. I found my stack of take-out menus and decided on Thai food. I called in my order and poured a glass of white wine to accompany my dinner. It wasn't more than 20 minutes until the doorbell rang and a wonderful young man delivered my dinner. I had already set up a place in front of the television so I could eat while catching up on my list of recorded favorites. By 10pm I was full, sleepy and needed a good night's rest.

I decided to forego my bubble bath and instead found my pajamas and was asleep by the time my head hit the pillow.

Wednesday was going to arrive before I knew it. I had some grocery shopping to do (I like to have plenty of juice, wine, yogurt, coffee, and pastries) to choose from. I also had a couple of birthday gifts to search for. I showered, pulled my mop of hair up into a large scrunchy, threw on jeans and a tee and grabbed my coat on the way out the door. There's a great mall not too far from the house and they have a couple of nice specialty shops. I had two girlfriends that were celebrating birthdays in the next couple of weeks. I found a beautiful water-colored scarf and pin for one of them and a lovely compact with her birthstone on it for the other. I grabbed cards, wrapping paper and ribbons before leaving the store. I found a beautiful pair of boots as I was walking to the parking lot so I went inside to try them on. They were kid leather, light tan, and fit like a glove. I shouldn't, but I did. Hey, what are monthly dividend checks for if not for splurging occasionally. A quick stop at the grocery store and then home.

I spent the rest of my free time answering emails, making some phone calls to friends, and finally was able to reach David and Alicia. They made excuses that they were just terribly busy. We caught up on what everyone was doing and how the inn was coming along. Alicia said they would look forward to hearing how my exam goes. "Well, I said, if I pass, I am hoping to come home for a couple of weeks to visit with Aunty and Uncy and you guys. Would you have room for me, or should I ask Aunty?" Alicia thought for a moment, and then finally said that she thought they would have an available room for me. We visited awhile longer and then hung up. I sat at the island, drinking my wine, and thinking again what very strange people they are. I called Aunty and Uncy to see how they were doing. Aunty brought me up to date on the townspeople and what was happening. She and Uncy were both feeling good; busy but that is how they like to be even though they're in their late 60s and early 70s. I sure hope that I have that same endurance.

# *Passing The Bar*

The time went quickly, and I found myself parking my car and walking toward the building to take the first part of the bar exam. I will be back again tomorrow to complete the test. There were to be 3 written exams to be taken over three 7-hour days. I was nervous but not scared. I knew my subject. I excelled at my subject. I would be a great lawyer! I finished day 1 in just under 6 hours and felt good about my answers. I had written a competent brief on contracts and torts (civil law) and I handed in my paper and left. The next day I completed my brief on criminal law in just under 6-1/2 hours, turned in my paper and left. The next day I took the entire 7 hours allotted to compile my court brief on crime. I was extremely excited about the next portion of the test which was oral.

I arrived home to the landline phone ringing which was strange. I answered and was greeted by someone trying to sell me a new roof. I ran upstairs to change clothes but got waylaid by my cell ringing. This time it was Daniel wanting to know how things had gone. "Ok, I think. Tomorrow is the big day that I've looked forward to. If that goes as planned, it'll be easy street going forward. What are you up to?" "I just finished a counseling session, he said, and wondered if you wanted to share a pizza and a pitcher of beer with me?" "Yes, give me about 30 minutes and I'll meet you there. Get a good table." I ran in the bathroom to run a brush though my mop of hair, freshen my makeup, and change into something a bit more casual. I threw on jeans and a hoody and decided I was good to go. Daniel was holding a table at our favorite pizza place. I noticed that he was already sipping his beer while waiting for me. I joined him at the table as he stood up to welcome me with one of his wonderful bear hugs. I swear every woman in the place was drooling and wanted to scratch my eyes out. They probably thought I was having an affair with this handsome priest! I just looked around and laughed while Daniel looked on with his always innocent look. The fact that we look absolutely nothing alike makes situations like this happen quite often. Daniel is 6'4-1/2" tall, has gorgeous coal black hair, bright blue eyes, and a dark ruddy complexion just like our father. I, on the other hand, barely hit 5'2" tall, am diminutive in stature, have a mass of chocolate brown curls, almond-shaped bright green eyes, and if I were any fairer, I'd be invisible. Just like my maternal grandmother.

Our pizza arrived and we strategically maneuvered our halves, guaranteeing that we would get our fair share. Their pizza is thick crust that melts in your mouth with sauce that emits garlic that stays with you for days, salami and pepperoni that is made in-house. There is just nothing else on earth that is as good as their pizza. Daniel and I visited non-stop while scarfing down our pizza and beer. He is extremely excited about the couple that he is counseling and feels that he's learning a great deal from them. "They are just the nicest people, Pixie," he said. They are so open and honest about their feelings and want very much to get through the difficulties that they are experiencing without it costing them their marriage." "Wow, I said, that is really something. I'm so glad you're able to help them, Daniel." "I know, he said, I feel so blessed to be able to work with them." "Well, I said, you are a wonderful priest, and they are very lucky to have you." Daniel just smiled that wonderful smile of his and squeezed my hand. We finished our dinner, and he walked me to my car. I don't usually do mushy things, but I just felt compelled to put my arms up around his neck and tell him how much I loved him. "I feel the same way, Pixie. You are my favorite sister." With that he was off to his church.

I soaked in a tub of bubbles for a while and then decided I would read until I got sleepy. Apparently, I got sleepy before turning off my light or putting my book down. It couldn't have been the beer I drank. I woke up about 3am and tried to figure out what was going on. I used the bathroom, got me a cold glass of water, and went back to bed. I awoke early feeling refreshed and ready to face my day. I grabbed a slice of toast and a cup of coffee and headed out the door. I was wearing my favorite *uniform.* I had chosen my dark navy suit and ivory lace blouse. I felt that it looked very professional. I found a good parking place and walked to the building in plenty of time to freshen my makeup and hair before going into the room where the exam was being administered. It covers material relating to seven legal practice areas. They are Civil Procedure, Constitutional Law, Contracts, Criminal Law and Procedure, Evidence, Real Property and Torts. There might be multiple choice questions injected at the administrator directions. The board of law examiners were looking very stern this morning. This day of testing is to determine the examinee's knowledge of the law, ability to perform under pressure, to correctly interpret the law, and generally to test their lawyering qualifications. I was tested for 3 full hours before we were granted a break. I felt that I had done a good job and that my answers had been clear, concise and on point. When I returned to the room one of the board examiners asked if I was related to Rebecca Bradley. I was surprised with the question but responded saying she was my maternal grandmother. Further she asked if I was related to James Bradley. Again, I responded with an affirmative and that I believed he was my 2x great grandfather. The board examiner then asked if I had any other ancestors that had been attorneys. I told them that my mother had studied and passed the bar in Illinois but had been an estate lawyer who had reciprocity in Massachusetts. They didn't offer any reason why they were asking these questions. The testing continued and finally the administrator said that my testing was concluded. I was told that the results of my text would be sent to me in 6-8 weeks. I thanked each of the panel members and the administrator and walked out to my car. I must admit I felt a bit uneasy but decided that I wasn't going to let it get to me.

I called Aunty and asked how her next few days were looking, and would she like to have company? She was elated and told me, "Your room is ready for you". I told her that I wanted to spend a few days with her and Uncy and then I would go impose on my brother and sister-in-law for a couple of days. "When will you be here," she asked?" "I'm going to go pack, and I'll see you tomorrow." I called Daniel on my way home and told him that I had survived. I also mentioned the strange questions by the one examiner. "Well, I wouldn't be concerned about that, Pixie. Mom, Granny, Grandmother Rebecca, and Great Grandfather James all had fine reputations. Furthermore, Grandmother Rebecca passed the bar exam in the State of Massachusetts with the highest score, both written and oral, ever recorded in the state." "She did? I didn't know that." "Yup, you come from smart people." "Ok, I said, well I wanted you to know that I'm headed to Edgartown in the morning. I'm going to spend 3 or 4 days with the parents and hopefully 2 days with our brother. Would you like to accompany me?" "Hmm, can I call you back in about an hour and let you know?" "Certainly. Try though cuz I don't want to go by myself." We hung up about the time that I pulled up in front of the house.

Daniel called back within 20 minutes of my getting home to say, "Yes, pick me up!" "Great, I said, how'd you swing the time off?" "Well, he said, it seems that Fr. James would like a Sunday off, so I am going to conduct the services on Sunday in his stead." "Super, I said, be on the sidewalk waiting for me at 7am tomorrow morning. Pack for 5 nights; 3 with the parents and 2 with the sibling." "You got it, he said, see you then." I hung up feeling absolutely elated. I phoned Aunty and told her to expect her favorite son too. She was thrilled! I then called Alicia to let her know that Daniel would be joining me for 2 nights at the inn. She simply said she would see us when we got there and that our room would be ready. Such a warm welcome. I fixed a sandwich and a cup of soup, ate, drank a glass of wine, and headed upstairs to pack. I needed to wrap the birthday gifts with me as they were for Edgartown friends. After that I decided to watch a little TV before turning in. It would be early morning for me and that was certainly a trait I had not inherited from my parents. I could sleep until noon every day…happily.

My alarm screamed at 5:15am! I took my shower, did my hair and makeup, got dressed in comfy travel clothes and lugged the suitcases downstairs. It was pouring rain, so I put my rain slicker on, grabbed a Paddington Bear hat, and headed out to pack the car. My next-door neighbor, Mr. Johnson, was leaving for work so he came and helped me load the car. Such a sweet man. I locked up and headed to Daniel's place. He was sheltered under a tree when I pulled up. He loaded his suitcase in the car and offered to drive. I happily changed places with him. He inherited our father's natural driving expertise. We chatted all the way to the ferry landing. The rain had subsided somewhat when we got there so we made our way to the café and grabbed coffee and pastries to munch on during the crossing. The ferry arrived about 10 minutes later; we loaded on and were homeward bound shortly thereafter. We both seemed a bit emotional about being headed home. We were independent people and had lived away from family for several years now. Daniel asked if I minded him stopping at the cemetery on the way into town. "No, of course not, I said. It'll be good to stop and say, hey, to our parents." We arrived at the cemetery about 20 minutes later. Daniel drove to the exact spot as it was etched in his mind and his heart. We got out and walked together to mama and papa's graves. Both of us were crying as we were nearing the spot. Daniel knelt between them and sobbed. When he gained control of himself, he prayed a beautiful prayer. He told our parents what we had been doing, marked the successes of both of us, and told them we were headed home but we wanted to stop and visit you guys first. I've always tended to stand back when we visit. My heart always feels like it will burst. Daniel spent a few more moments with them as I walked back toward the car. He got in, squeezed my hand, and we headed home.

Aunty and Uncy were sitting on the porch when we arrived. I swear our parents must have called them and told them we were close. They ran out to hug and kiss us. They both looked wonderful; older but wonderful. Uncy's beautiful black hair has turned white but otherwise he looks the same. Aunty hasn't aged a day in the more than 20 years I have known her. She is truly a beautiful woman. They helped us with our luggage, and we walked into the house. Both of us caught our breaths as we entered. We always do. Even though the furnishings are different it is still *our home*. Fluffy old Precious had been replaced with an equally ornery kitten whose name is Jack. Jack is a beautiful fluffy gray and white kitten who is about 3 months old. When you reach out to pet him, he automatically slaps your hand away and hisses. Aunty assures us he will mellow with age. We are not so sure. We took our luggage up to our rooms, freshened up and went back down to the kitchen. Aunty had coffee, iced tea, water, and sandwiches laid out on the island. Daniel and I both discovered we were starving. Aunty has always made homemade bread that is rich with butter and delicious. She had sliced turkey and pepper jack cheese with a delicious sauce. Daniel went in search of the potato chips to go with his sandwich.

We all visited non-stop for the next hour. Uncy asked me how I felt the bar exam had gone. "Well, I feel like I did as well as I could. I was confident in my written briefs, and I feel that the oral exam was somewhat exemplary. You know. Typically, me." We all laughed at my rather humble comment. "There was a strange thing that happened though after the lunch break. One of the examiners asked me if I was related to Rebecca Bradley and James Bradley. Then they inquired if I had any other relatives who were attorneys. I of course told them my mother was. When you fill out the application you list your parents, their parents, and so on so I guess that is how they tied things together. I'm uncertain how any of that would pertain to my application." "Well, said Uncy, "given your family's records in practicing the law I would think all of that information would be favorable toward you." "Yes, that is what Daniel said, too. Certainly, Grandmother Rebecca's credentials were remarkable." "Not to change the subject, said Daniel, but I need to borrow someone's car so I can run over to the church." "Here's the keys to the truck," said Uncy. Use it while you're here." "Thanks, Uncy. You're a peach. I want to speak with Fr. James and find out what is going on. I spoke with Fr. McMurry last evening and he thinks that Fr. James is unwell. I just want to see if other than the Sunday Mass if there is anything else that I can do to help him. I'll only be about an hour. Does anyone need anything while I'm out?" Nobody needed anything that they could think of but would text him if that changed. Daniel took his leave and Uncy poured us another cup of coffee. I had the impression that he had something on his mind. "Debra, how are you fairing in that huge house in Boston? Are you truly set on trying to find work there?" "I'm fine, and yes. If I wasn't living in the house, where would I live, I asked?" "Well, he said, we were thinking of getting you a condo closer to the area you'll be working in. It would be a bit more modern, a little less work for the housekeeper, and so on." "Oh, I said, well that does seem like an attractive offer. I haven't touched the money that was left to me by my parents. I did my schooling on a full ride scholarship and worked to pay for books and such. I have always hoped that when I used the money it would be for something profoundly important. Would a condo be purchased through the trust?" "Yes, Aunty said. We would sell the Boston house and that would flow back to the trust and the new purchase would be housed in the trust. Depending on the new appraisal of the house we might be able to avoid capital gains if we use the money for a new purchase within the year." "Well, I guess this is all depending on whether I pass the bar, and whether the Boston D.A. wants me. If these things fall into place, I know the exact building that I'd like to consider. It is literally within walking distance of the D.A.'s offices. I'm really kind of excited at the thought of this. I'd be closer to Daniel's parish and wouldn't feel so all alone in a huge rambling house that squeaks and creaks at night." "Well, Uncy said, we'll keep that on the table for now. You certainly know that we'd like nothing better than you to move home and work locally, but we understand your dreams and respect them. On another note, have you spoken to your other brother lately?" "Yes, I, well no, I spoke with Alicia to let her know that we wanted to spend two nights with them. Why? Is something wrong?" "We don't know. Alicia hasn't said anything and knowing how they are we haven't approached either one of them with questions. We just feel that something is going on with him." "Well, the best person to nose into that is Daniel. I'll put him to work on finding out what's what with his adorable twin. I wonder if Mary has anything to do with it. Now, I'm going to throw on some comfy clothes and help Aunty with whatever she needs help with." Aunty laughed out loud before coming around to give me a hug and tell me how much she loves me. "Why don't you unpack, she said, and then when you come back downstairs it'll be wine time, and we can visit while we drink." "Oh, that sounds perfect, Aunty. I'll hurry."

# *Difficult Choices*

Daniel arrived at the parish and went in search of Fr. James. He found him in his office doing some paperwork work. He jumped up to come around and hugged me. He seemed so frail or so I thought. "How are you, Father?" "I'm doing better now that you're here Daniel, or should I say Fr. Daniel?" "No, Daniel is simply fine. Tell me how things are going and what's new around here." "Well, we have lost a few and gained a few which is always the way. There isn't much in the way of news around town or not that I've heard anyway. How about you? Are you enjoying your new position?" I told him that I was and brought him up to speed on what I was working on. "I understand, sir, that I'm going to relieve you on Sunday so you can have a little R&R." "Yes, that would be wonderful, Daniel. I have some personal things to tend to and it will ease my mind to know that you're taking care of Sunday Mass." "I'm happy to help, Father, I just hope that you are feeling ok? You know you can count on me for whatever you need." "I know, said Fr. James, you're a wonderful man, a wonderful priest, and an incredibly special friend to this old man. Now come, let me acquaint you with where things are so you'll be at home come Sunday. Do you know what your sermon will be?" "Yes, I do. I plan on speaking around Mark 11:22." "A wonderful scripture, he said, I'm so happy you thought of it. Everyone can use a little inspiration in that little word *faith*." Fr. James showed him where the robes were, the candles, the items for the altar and so on. He reminded him that the choir convened about 30 minutes prior to mass. Most of them will ask you to hear their confessions in that noticeably short amount of time. Anyway, it's always good to have everything you need out of the way before they arrive as you won't have any additional time after that. Also, before you leave, I'll give you a list of prayer requests for people that are in care centers or hospitalized. Can you think of anything else? Oh, and Daniel, if I need help for a couple or few more Sundays do you suppose your supervisor would allow it? Should I phone him personally, do you think?" "I do think you should call him, I said, and yes, I'm happy to help. Father, are you alright? Is there anything I should know?" "No, my son, it will be okay. I'm certain it will be. I'll call Fr. McMurry and see if I need to go any higher up the ladder than that to be granted this favor." Daniel got the list, bid the good father farewell and assured him he'd be back early Sunday morning.

Daniel got to his car, made himself comfortable and phoned Fr. McMurry. He told the father what he had discussed and shared his concerns with him. "I'm happy to help but I feel that he is not being forthcoming about the help he needs. Also, I don't want to traipse back and forth between Boston and Edgartown if that is what is needed, I'd rather just stay here until he's back on the job." Fr. McMurry agreed with Daniel on all points. "Let me speak with him and see how that conversation goes and then, if I may, I'll phone you afterwards and catch you up." "That would be wonderful. Thank you, Father, for your time and your help. May the Lord bless and keep you safe." He hung up and headed home with a heavy heart.

Daniel arrived at the house and went in through the back door. Aunty and Debra were in the living room and Uncy was in the kitchen. David took one look at Daniel, poured him a glass of white wine, and pointed to a chair. "What's wrong, Daniel?" Daniel told him about his visit with the elderly priest and of his concerns. "There isn't much you can do, Daniel. At least not until you hear from Fr. McMurry." "I know. You're correct. I just feel terrible about it." "I know, but that is because of your great big heart." Daniel just smiled at him and then after thinking for a moment, got up and went around to the other side of the island so he could give his uncle a hug. "I love you, Uncy. So very much." "I know you do, Daniel. I love you as well. Your parents were very precious to me; your mother especially as you well know. But over the years I've come to love each of their children as if they were my own." David's eyes were full of tears but neither man said another word. They drank their wine and then went to find the girls.

The girls were busy looking at patterns and material that Lucy had tucked away. Lucy is a very accomplished seamstress and over the years had made some beautiful summer dresses for both Debra and Alicia. Debra had picked out three patterns and material for each and Lucy had promised to have them done for the summer months. David asked, "What's for dinner, Lucy? Should we have a cocktail hour before we eat?" Lucy looked at him and I swore he backed away. "I believe we're just about finished here, David. I'll go get to my wifely chores here in just a few minutes." "Lucy, you know I was just being cute and that you're not angry with me. Right?" "No, she said, I'm not angry at all. While you two gentlemen are standing around doing nothing why don't one of you make cocktails and the other pull the cold poached prawns and sauce out of the refrigerator and set on the island?" "Yes dear. I'm on it." The girls just looked at each other and burst out laughing. The boys, not so much. They got the island set with the goodies and David mixed up Old Fashions for everyone. The girls went in the kitchen to join them. Lucy put her arms around David's back and hugged him as she went by. He just smiled at the kids. "I asked David and Alisha if they wanted to join us, said Lucy, but they were busy. Too bad, it would have been nice having everyone together." "I think that perhaps while we are staying over there that we can plan a night with everyone together." "That's a great idea, Pixie, Daniel said." David asked Lucy what they were having for dinner as we were very hungry. Lucy walked over to the oven, opened the oven door, and displayed a beautiful New England dinner that was all ready for them. "Oh, that's what you were doing this morning, he said." She just shook her head at him and announced that she wanted another drink. Daniel smiled and went to make it for her. He and Debra set the dining room table as her New Englund dinner looked fabulous. There was also a salad in the refrigerator chilling. Daniel found a wine that would be perfect with it. Lucy and David got the platter out of the oven to set on the trivets on the table. She warmed up rolls and had fresh creamy butter and raspberry jam to go with it. Everyone ate and talked and ate some more. Debra announced that she was stuffed, and Daniel looked guilty as he went for his third helping.

The next couple of days were spent visiting the parents and helping with anything that needed to be done around the house. Daniel and Uncy found lots of little things to work on, and Aunty and I did some gardening, and I watched while she cut out the patterns and sewed. It was truly a blessed time to spend with two people that we loved with all our hearts. I could still see Uncy in the early days as he tried so hard to get past life without our mother. She had truly been a big part of his heart.

I called Alicia to see if we could perhaps all have dinner at the inn on Saturday night. She hesitated for a few minutes before saying, "Yes, of course. That will be fine. Mary can do the shopping and help me get things ready." I told Aunty and Uncy to plan on being at the inn Saturday around 4pm for cocktails and dinner with the entire family. "It will be nice, I said, to be able to visit with everyone. I'm sure we're all planning on early mass Sunday morning to support Daniel in his efforts to fill in for Fr. James." "Yes, Aunty said, we plan to be there. I don't know about David and Alicia. They don't attend very often." "I want to try to get to the bottom of this, I said. I need to speak with Daniel."

Later in the afternoon I was able to steal Daniel away for a few minutes. "What's going on, he asked?" "I need you to call your brother and invite him for lunch or a beer or something and find out what is going on with the two of them. Aunty says they don't attend mass; they don't return phone calls, they haven't been to their house in months. Something is wrong and we need to get to the bottom of it." "Ok, he said. I'll call him but I don't guarantee he will open to me either. I'll let you know."

Daniel phoned David later in the morning. Alicia answered his call and said he was busy. Daniel told her that he really didn't care if he was busy or not, to put him on the phone. Something in his tone must have gotten through to her because David came to the phone. They chatted for a few minutes and finally David agreed to meet him for a quick bit of lunch. Daniel hung up the phone feeling very strange. His brother sounded like a total stranger to him which is weird between identical twins.

Daniel went upstairs to shower and change into clean clothes for his lunch with David. He came back downstairs looking every inch the priest. He wiggled his eyebrow at everyone, hugged us and headed out the door. Daniel got to the restaurant a few minutes early, parked the car, and decided to wait at the entrance door. David showed up a few minutes later. David walked up to Daniel and started to offer his hand. Daniel engulfed David in a big hug and finally he hugged back. They went into the restaurant and found a table in a quiet corner. They ordered and then Daniel looked at David and without hesitation asked, "What is going on?" David said that nothing was going on. What did he mean? "Well, for starters you've never shook hands with me in our lives. We have loved each other from the second we were born and have always been very demonstrative to one another." "Well, said David, things change." "No, brother," Daniel said, they don't. People change but things don't. I really feel that I need you to talk to me. If there is a problem I want to help. If you're sick, I need to know. I need to know what's wrong, David." After a few minutes David looked at Daniel and tears welled up in his eyes. "I don't know where to start, Daniel." "The beginning. Start there and we'll work forward, Daniel said." David told him that everyone had always teased him and Alicia about their relationship. "From the time we first met, he said, it was as if we were predestined to be together. I loved her and she loved me." We've also heard the quiet comments about us being selfish with our relationship. "That is about as far from reality as it can be, he said. From the time we were children we've always dreamed of having a big family and sharing that family with all of you. This year Alicia has miscarried twice. We haven't told anyone because we didn't want everyone to worry. We have worked closely with our doctor to try and get pregnant and then have held our breath hoping that we could get through the pregnancy. We figured if we could get through the first trimester that it would be okay to share the news. So far, we've not gotten that far. The doctors don't know why this is happening. They've assured us that there is no medical reason why we can't carry the child to full term. Alicia is the strongest one in our relationship. She carries all these hurts inside but can cry and rid herself of some of her grief. I, on the other hand, am not built that way. Seeing her hurt, losing our child not once but twice, has just ripped my guts out. I can't think, I can't sleep, I just hurt." By this time both boys were shedding tears. Daniel got up and went to sit next to David and hug him. He really didn't care what anyone else in the restaurant might think about this. He only knew that his brother was hurting and needed his comfort. David seemed to be better, and Daniel moved to the other side of the booth. The waitress had been very thoughtful of what she had seen and waited until that moment to set their lunches down in front of them. Daniel thanked her and said they would need coffee and the check. She quickly provided both. When she departed Daniel said, "David, you need to go to mass. You need to cry. You need to scream at the heavens and tell them you are hurt. This isn't something that you tuck away inside you because it will grow to such a huge size that you'll not recognize yourself." "I know what you're saying is true, David said. It has just seemed such an impossible task." "Well, lucky for you, Daniel said, I'll be officiating at this Sunday's mass, and you will be attending to support me." David smiled at his brother and told him how much he loved him. "Of course, I will be there. I will always be there for you, David said." They ate their lunch and just visited about everyday stuff. When they were finished David thanked him and told him he looked forward to seeing everyone on Saturday. "Should I tell everyone when we're together, David asked?" "I think that would be a good idea, Daniel said. See you Saturday."

When Daniel arrived at the house everyone was sitting in the living room with anxious looks on their faces. Daniel sat down on the ottoman and picked up Jack who had been weaving in and out of his legs. Daniel looked at each of the three faces and finally said, "David will tell you on Saturday." Lucy couldn't contain herself any longer and blurted out, "Are they okay? Is someone sick?" "They will talk to us all on Saturday, he said. It is not my place to speak for them." Uncy announced that cocktails were early today and went to fix drinks for everyone. He came back with glasses and a huge pitcher of margaritas. Luckily, he remembered chips and salsa to go with it. "I understand, David said, why you can't divulge this conversation to any of us. What I find difficult to understand is why our daughter and son-in-law couldn't tell us what was wrong or going on from the get-go." "I know, Daniel said. I feel the same. It is never fair to keep things from immediate family. People need to share the truth with each other so that they gain the love and support that they deserve." We all puttered around the house for the rest of the evening and Daniel and I packed to be ready to go to the inn early afternoon. We figured we'd get settled in before the parent's arrival.

Saturday morning Aunty had pancakes, bacon, sausage, and eggs for our "going-away" breakfast. She was already missing us. We ate like it was our last meal and then helped clean up the kitchen. She and I took a last look at the dresses to be sure that no further alterations would be needed. Daniel helped Uncy move a heavy chest to the storage unit. I tried on the three dresses and Aunty marked the hems. "I think I can have these done for you before you leave on Monday, she said." "Oh, that would be super, Aunty! Thank you so much." "I guess you kids better get ready to go. Let's go have a lunch together first though, she said." "Yes, Aunty, that sounds perfect." We grabbed Daniel and Uncy out of the back yard to come and have lunch with us. Aunty had apparently gotten up very early this morning because she had homemade fish and chips and clam chowder for our lunch! "Man, that looks delicious, Aunty, Daniel said." "Yes, it does, I said, my favorite!" We all ate with gusto and laughed and visited throughout the meal. We helped clean up the kitchen and then went to get our bags and load the car. Aunty was trying her best to hold back her tears as we started to leave. "We'll see you in a couple of hours, I said." "I know that, she responded, but it's just never the same. We do so very much love having you all home. You make our lives complete. You always have." With that she was hugging us and headed back to the house. Uncy just smiled, hugged and kissed us both and said he'd see us shortly.

Daniel and I stopped at the grocers and bought goodies for cocktail hour and wine and liquor also. We knew they'd have it covered but this way we could replenish their larder. "I sent them a check for both of us for two nights, I said. I don't want them turning away paying guests to entertain family." "I agree, said Daniel. I'll give you back my half when we get home." "That's hardly necessary Daniel. It's all out of the same pot. You can continue to buy me dinners weekly." "Done, he said." We arrived at the inn and were warmly greeted by both Daniel and Alicia. Mary and the children came out to greet us, also. Mary phones Daniel every couple of weeks letting him know how things are with her and the kids. She is a Godsend to Alicia, and they all seem content together. They helped us with our luggage and got us signed in. Alicia had a fit that I'd sent her a check, but she understood and appreciated it. The inn was fully occupied, so we were lucky that she got us in at all. We got our luggage put away and came back downstairs to see if we could assist with the dinner preparation. Alicia and David had things pretty much under control, but they gave us each task to keep us busy, and out of their way. Originally our great grandparent's home was a single-family dwelling. When our granny and gramps moved here from Boston, they turned it in to a bed and breakfast. The original office/library was converted into a master suite as it had a bathroom attached to it. There is also a lovely sitting room that is part of that area and that is where David planned on the family gathering tonight after dinner, so we'd be out of the way of the guest. They had recently converted part of the coach house into an apartment for Mary and the children and that seemed to be working well. I checked my watch and determined that I needed to go shower and change for the evening's festivities. I checked with Alicia to be sure that was okay with her. She told me to hurry and that I could man the place while she did the same thing. I ran upstairs to my room, showered, did my makeup, pulled my hair into a rather large curly ponytail, pulled on a gray dress and matching heels, my mother's gold earrings, and headed downstairs. I went in the kitchen to help Daniel while David and

Alicia went to change clothes. Daniel is just like our father when it comes to the kitchen. He's a marvelous chef, knows everything about food and loves working with it. Me? No, I don't think so. That's why we have take-out/delivery. I am, however, an accomplished bartender.

I set up the bar at about the same time as the parents arrived. I fixed everyone a drink in the kitchen while we were waiting on Daniel and Alicia who showed up about 5 minutes later. Everyone hugged and talked non-stop for a few minutes and then Alicia said to the dining room and she would serve dinner shortly. We inquired about the other guests and were told that the entire group were meeting up with friends in town and would be gone until at least 10pm. We took our drinks and got out of her hair. Daniel and David stayed behind to help serve. The parents and I sipped our drinks while we waited on the boys to deliver our salads. They showed up with beautiful bowls of crisp leafy lettuce, orange and grapefruit segments, and avocado. Absolutely delicious. David went into get the entrée which was served family style. He had made spaghetti, with meatballs, and big plump sausages that looked divine. Daniel ran in to get the garlic bread. Everyone ate hungrily and kept telling David how delicious everything was. "You certainly inherited both your parent's ability to cook, said Uncy." David thanked him for his kind words. After dinner David asked if everyone could retire to their sitting room with coffee and an after-dinner liqueur. We all followed them in, got our coffee and liqueur of choice and found a seat. Alicia was tucked in tightly next to David while he addressed the room. "I don't have to ask whether my brother said anything regarding our lunch conversation, because I already know the answer to that. So, here goes. This last year has been hell on earth for my wife and I. We have tried since we married to start a family and have had no luck. We finally consulted with a specialist who has been guiding us for the past eighteen months. Because of how fragile this situation is we decided that if we were fortunate enough to conceive that we would say nothing until the first trimester had passed so that we were sure everything would be okay going forward. We became pregnant 8 months ago and were thrilled, but terrified. The doctor told us to just be careful and see how things moved along.

Alicia miscarried five weeks later. We were distraught and mourned the passing of our child that was never to be. Then 4 months later we conceived again. This time we didn't even make it for three weeks. My wife is such a strong, capable woman. She has done her crying and moved forward. I, on the other hand, have forsaken my God and my church, and even my family. I have withdrawn to such a point that I didn't even realize how bad it was until Daniel and I talked today. I'm sorry. I'm sorry that we didn't include you. I'm sorry that we've been unavailable to all of you. I pray you can forgive me for being so selfish. Aunty couldn't stand it another minute. She was sobbing so hard that you could hear her all over the inn. She raced over to her children and hugged and kissed them both telling them how much she loved them; how sorry she was for their lost babies. Uncy waited until Lucy had moved back and then went to hug his kids. He just stood there with tears running down his face. After the parents went to sit down, I was able to go and hug both David and Alicia. When everyone was somewhat calmed down Daniel addressed the family. "We are all aware of how difficult and personal something of this nature can be. I know we all support David and Alicia in their grief and will pray that, be it God's will, a child will soon be conceived and carried to full term, or should that continue to be a problem, that they will adopt the child that is waiting for them to find him or her. I would like all of us to pray together now, as a family, with the confidence that our Lord and Savior will hear our cry and heal our hearts. We all tearfully joined Daniel in that prayer. Daniel and I decided to go for a walk around the grounds giving Aunty and Uncy time with their kids and all this news. We grabbed mugs of hot coffee to take with us and wandered out to the garden where there are benches. "Daniel, I said, I must tell you that tonight is the very first time that I've witnessed you in your role as priest. You really are quite remarkable. You never wavered during the heartbreak that was going on around you. You stayed steady and targeted on exactly what needed to be done. I am enormously proud of you and just a little bit in awe of you." "Aw shucks," he said. Thank you, Pixie. It means a great deal to me. I have felt that the family was not altogether supportive of my decision to be a priest. I can't recall a time in my life when I didn't feel the call of the Lord. It is such a comfort to me to be His servant." "I'm glad, Daniel. I'm very proud of you and I love you very much." They felt that the family had been given enough time to discuss things, and they went back in. Daniel gave huge hugs to every family member, bidding them goodnight. "I have a sermon to review for tomorrow morning. I'm hoping to see all your faces in the crowd." We all bid him goodnight, assuring him that we would be there to cheer him on. I wasn't far behind him in saying goodnight to everyone. I was tired and felt a bit worn out by all the news of the evening.

The inn was quiet when I awoke. I remembered that the other guests were late getting home from their party so tried to be considerate of them sleeping in. I showered, did my hair and makeup, chose my navy dress and shoes, my mother's ring and bracelet and her gold hoop earrings. I grabbed my shawl to use as a coat as it was a beautiful morning. I went downstairs to the kitchen and found David and Alicia all at the bar with breakfast. Alicia jumped up and filled my plate and grabbed a cup of coffee for me. "Daniel left about 5:30am this morning, David said. I know he wasn't nervous at all, but I think he's a bit of an overachiever when it comes to things like this." He was laughing at his own joke. We are all very aware that our brother is a bit of an overachiever in work ethics, school grades, you name it. I ate my omelet and toast as if I'd not eaten for days. At this rate I'm going to be a blimp! I checked the time and asked what time they wanted to leave and were we taking one car or two? "I would think we could all ride together. I told the folks," David said, "that we'd pick them up too. We'll go to early mass, go have pastries and lattes and go back to the 11am mass. How does that sound?" "Perfect! I'm so excited to see him in action!" David texted the parents and told them we were on our way. Aunty and Uncy were waiting on the curb when we drove up. Uncy jumped in front with David and the three of us ladies huddled together in the backseat. Everyone chatted away on our way to the church. Daniel was at the front door, greeting everyone as they arrived. He looked so handsome, so much like our dad and gramps. A truly beautiful human being. His beautiful smile broadened as he spotted all of us. We were all rewarded with warm hugs and assurances that he'd talk with us later. We found a pew toward the front that would hold all of us and settled in. The choir sang softly as people were ushered in and then Daniel walked up to the center of the altar. He greeted everyone and asked the Lord's blessing at the gathering and today's message. Then he did what only Daniel, our dad and our gramps could do, he sang The Lord's Prayer in the beautiful rich baritone voice that he inherited. I doubt there was a dry eye in the church. His message from St. Mark was on faith and what it truly means. It was a beautiful sermon and at the close of it he sang again. This time he sang an old Irish hymn called "Change Our Hearts". It was beautiful. Following the call to come forward to receive holy communion he wished us all God's blessings and bid us good day. The choir again sang softly in the background. He made it, somehow, to the front door to say goodbye to everyone. We heard parishioners after parishioners praising his message and his beautiful songs. Daniel seemed pleased but somehow rather solemn as he received these compliments. When it was our turn, we too thanked him for his beautiful message and song and told him we would be back for the 11am mass. His eyes were full of unshed tears as he hugged us and said he'd see us later. None of us quite knew what to make of it. David was genuinely concerned and started to go back to talk to him, but Uncy stopped him. "David, Uncy said, whatever is going on, he'll share it later if he can. Let's give him the space he needs to do his job." "You're right of course, David said. Thanks for stopping me." We found a lovely little café where we could share pastries and fancy coffee drinks. Aunty was upset. She has such a huge heart and always seems to take on all our pain. When it was time, we headed back to the church.

Again, Daniel was at the front door to greet us all. He looked somehow older than he had an hour before. I squeezed his hand and mouthed that I loved him, and he did the same. We went in and again found a pew close to the front. The choir had been humming a quiet tune in the background. We didn't see him, but we heard Daniel sing Ava Maria. It is a song that takes me to my knees every time I hear it. Our father would sing this song, and I would just sob. Daniel's voice broke twice during the song, and I knew instinctively that he was crying. What in the world is going on? After the song was finished Daniel walked to the center of the altar, greeted everyone, and asked the Lord's blessings on each of us. He stood there with tears streaming down his face as he delivered the news that Fr. James had passed away earlier this morning. The congregation all gasped at the news. Daniel tried to explain that he received word from the hospital that Fr. James had come in for some tests to be done, had been ill, and was in critical condition. He knew this at the earlier mass but didn't want to say anything without more information. He asked for the forgiveness of the parishioners for his selfishness in not sharing the information that he had. "I will call each person after mass today and express my sorrow in not having shared this news with them. At this time, I have no idea what the church's plans are or how things will be handled going forward. I'm sure there will be a priest assigned to your parish quickly so none of you will be without counsel. Rather than delivering my sermon that I had planned I would like each of you to share memories or stories about Fr. James and what he meant to you." It didn't take much nudging as one of the choir members started and many, many more followed. Uncy was able to share the story of our parent's practice wedding. Everyone was laughing at the memory as most had attended the ceremony. Daniel quoted the scripture and spoke very personally to each of us on the importance of always telling each other how much they mean to us and how much we love them. As you probably all remember," he said, "our parents left us when we were very young. I can remember the crushing heartbreak that I felt and still do, to this day. However, I also know that my wonderful, loving God sent the Holy Spirit to dwell within me and comfort me every minute of my life going forward. I am so grateful for my faith and for His abiding love. Go forward today knowing that Fr. James is with the Lord and will always remain in our hearts. As I, or another representative of the church, learn anything further you will be notified. May the Lord bless and keep each of you safe as you leave today." He again met every single person at the door on their way out. Each of them thanked him for his encouraging words and assured him that he had nothing to be forgiven for, that he had done everything just right. He told us that he wanted to stay to call the early parishioners and give them the news personally and that he would be home when he could. We assured him that we understood.

We all went home with rather heavy hearts. Aunty and Uncy came back to the inn with us as we all determined that we needed to be together. Aunty and Alicia went about fixing lunch for all the guests and for us. We ate in the kitchen at the island leaving the dining room for them. Alicia and David started the preparations for dinner as there were 12, other than the family, that were there for dinner. David and Uncy fixed a beautiful beef stew, Aunty made homemade bread, and Alicia made 4 pies. I watched while I sipped on my wine. I went upstairs to pack for our return to Boston tomorrow. I guess we're returning to Boston tomorrow. I'll have to wait and see what Daniel has to say. I didn't have a lot longer to wait as he showed up about 45 minutes later. We all congregated in the kitchen to hear his news. We were about an hour or so before the guests' dinner needed to be served so we had time. Daniel told us that he had spoken to each of the parishioners that had attended the early mass, and they were all of the same mind as the 11am parishioners had been, that he had nothing definite to report and had chosen to say nothing at that point. "Further, he said, Bishop Cornell had called him wishing to speak with him directly rather than through his mentor, Fr. McMurry. It seems that Fr. James had spoken freely with Fr. McMurry expressing to him that he had been ill for some time now and that he was having a biopsy taken to confirm the doctor's suspicions. He indicated that the doctors were upset because he had not seen to this when he first noticed he had problems. Anyway, long story short, he did wait too long and as you all know, he died. Fr. McMurry spoke with Bishop Cornell who in turn called me directly. They would like me to consider taking over St. Liz' here locally." "Oh, my goodness Daniel, that's wonderful!" That was pretty much the cheer that went up throughout the kitchen. Daniel looked at me and said, "Well, Pixie, what say you?" I said nothing. I simply turned and ran out of the kitchen into the backyard. I was sobbing when Daniel found me out by the swings. "Tell me, he said." "I can't. It doesn't make any sense to me at all. You're my brother. I'm thrilled for your success. It's what you've worked so hard for. I feel so selfish. I don't want you to be here. I want you to be in Boston with me where you belong." And then, more tears. "Pixie, listen to me, he said. I understand exactly what you're saying because I feel the same way. I can't fathom being back here without you. We're buddies. We have always been buddies." "What are we going to do, I asked?" "I don't know just now. I was told to take my time thinking on this and that a substitute pastor would be assigned to St. Liz until I determine what I want to do. I figure we take two weeks to work through this." "That sounds fine, Daniel. I'm sorry that I'm such a big crybaby. I have no idea where I get that from." "Oh, me either, he said. Me either." With that he hugged me, and we walked back to the house.

## *So Many Decisions To Be Made*

We had a wonderful dinner with the family, said our goodbyes for now, and managed to get everything together for an early getaway tomorrow morning. We wanted to leave good and early so decided to just escape, have breakfast at the landing and go from there. No such luck. These people get up early in this town! The parents were already in the kitchen and breakfast was waiting for us. Hello, it was 5:30am! We laughed, set down our luggage, enjoyed the wonderful breakfast and then everyone walked us to the car. There were cheerful, tearful hugs and kisses all around and they waved us into the sunset. We had promised to text them as soon as we arrived home. Also, that we were to let them know as soon as I had my exam score and Daniel's decision. Yes, yes, yes. It was an uneventful trip home to Boston. The weather was perfect, the traffic minimal, and we were able to chat all the way. Daniel had both favorable and not favorable thoughts on returning to Edgartown. He really liked Boston. He loved the restaurants and the ethnic choices he could make. He had made lots of friends and had parishioners that he loved and cared about. He loved working closely with Fr. McMurry as he always shared wonderful stories about his dad and his grandparents. It truly felt like home and Pixie was close at hand. On the other hand, this was a tremendous opportunity for a young, unseasoned parish priest. "Pixie, is there any chance in this huge world that when you pass the bar that you'd consider moving back to Edgartown?" "I knew you were going to ask that sooner or later, I said. I don't know, Daniel. I don't dislike Edgartown but rather I love Boston. Aunty and Uncy were just asking me about finding a condo close to where I'd be working so they could sell the big house. It would all fund through the trusts. There is a condo close to the D.A.'s offices that I've had my eye on for some time now. It's a huge question!" "I know, he said. I just thought I'd ask." We had driven for a while when I turned off the radio and said, "You know what, Daniel? Yes, I would consider it. I can't not live close to you. I want to be close to David and Alicia especially if they finally conceive so I can help with the baby. And, I want to be close to the parents as they aren't getting any younger. I noticed Uncy was slowing down considerably. So, yes, if that is what we need to do then I'm ready to do it. I just need that paper declaring me a full-fledged lawyer." "Ok, he said, I think we may have a plan laid out." We drove on in pretty much silence as both of us had our heads full of thoughts. Daniel dropped himself off at the church where he lived in the back of the building. He had asked if I wanted dinner, but I decided I just wanted to go home. I drove on to the house, unloaded the car and went in to warm the place up and get myself settled. I retrieved the mail out of the box on the porch, went in and poured myself a glass of wine and settled down in the den to sort through things. Most any mail that comes to the house is either an advertisement or personal mail as any bills go straight to Aunty to handle them through the trust. I got to thinking about the fact that she must be in her mid-60s and still working hard to handle things that were tied to my mother's business. I know that part of one of the trusts that she handled for the family that lived across the street was supposed to expire 23 years after inception which would mean it was either already complete, or very close to it. She's probably still up to her neck in distributing funds plus handling all the family trusts as well.

I went into the kitchen to sort through the takeout/delivery menus so I could decide on my dinner. There is a wonderful Italian bistro right around the corner from the house, so I decided maybe I'd just walk over there and have supper. Our street is very well illuminated, and all the families have lived here forever. I went and grabbed my coat and headed over there before changing my mind. The bistro is just so cute. It's very homey and full of wonderful smells. The owner greeted me and showed me to a nice table in a corner where I would be comfortable on my own. I ordered a glass of red wine and he brought it along with some bread and olive oil. I couldn't get pass the lasagna, so I ordered it before I changed my mind. I was finishing up my glass of wine when one of my neighbors walked in. I called out to him and he was all smiles as he came over to the table. He's in his 70s and just the sweetest man ever. I invited him to join me if he didn't have another date. He thought that was hilarious. Said he hadn't had a date for 40 years. They delivered another glass of wine and some additional bread. I asked them to hold my order so we could visit for a few minutes while he decided on his supper. We talked about the neighborhood and what I'd been up to. He thought it wonderful that I had taken the bar exam and just knew that I would pass with flying colors. "Your father, mother, grandfather, grandmother, and both great aunts were all brilliant! Brilliant! I just know you'll get the highest grade ever." I told him I certainly hoped he was right. He chose Chicken Milanese for his entrée and yes, we had another glass of that delicious red wine. I asked if he had walked over and he told me he had. "But I always call for a cab to take me home, so I don't fall over after all that wine." Perfect. A taxi it would be. Our dinner arrived and it was delicious. We shared a piece of tiramisu and had a cup of espresso to go with it. I insisted on paying the bill so he said he would pay for cab. He walked me to my door, kissed my hand and bid me goodnight. It was a wonderful evening.

# *A Job For Debra*

I decided next morning that I couldn't sit around like a lump waiting for the results of my bar exam. I looked through the paper to see if anyone needed a temporary paralegal or something like that to keep me busy and out of trouble. It so happened that the District Attorney's office was looking for a temporary, part time administrative assistant. I have no idea what that means but I was convinced that I was more than qualified. I called them and secured an appointment that very afternoon. I was so excited that I ran upstairs to sort through my closet to find the perfect outfit for the interview. I have a lovely black dress, long sleeved, high neck that shows off my mother's pearls and matching earrings perfectly. I found my black comfy heels, pulled out my steel color cashmere coat and felt that I had the perfect ensemble. I went back downstairs to fix myself some breakfast and a cup of coffee. After eating I cleaned up the kitchen, read the newspaper, and answered some emails. I went upstairs to soak in a bubble bath before getting ready to leave. I had already decided that I was going to swing by the condo that I was interested in and see if they have one set up for viewing. I toweled my mass of curls as dry as I could and then pulled the sides up high and held it in place with a gold comb. My hair is probably halfway down my back, but it is so curly that it appears shoulder length. After getting my makeup done and getting dressed, I stepped back to review the finished product. I decided that I looked rather good and was sure my prospective employer would agree. I locked up and headed downtown. The condo is about 2-1/2 blocks from the D.A.'s office so I found a parking spot partway between the two. There is a sales office on the bottom floor of the building, so I went in to see if they had model to look at. The lady that waited on me was lovely and highly informative. She took me up to the mezzanine floor to view the model. It was an open loft-style with 2 bedrooms, 2-1/2 baths, a chef's kitchen with a huge island, which of course is wasted on yours truly, a den/office and a balcony with a kitchen setup and pizza oven. Fabulous! It would be so fun to furnish. I inquired as to how many units were available and was told there were two units with no pending offers. The sales price was $3.5m. That should make my Aunty happy. She provided me with a pamphlet that held the information regarding the builder, the amenities and such. I thanked her and walked back to the car to drop the literature inside. I checked the time and found that I had just enough time to grab a quick bite of lunch. There is a deli about two doors from the D.A.'s office. I went up to the counter and ordered one-half corned beef on rye with mustard and a diet soda. I found a small table and devoured my lunch. I used their restroom to brush my teeth and touchup my hair and makeup. Time to go.

I walked quickly to the building and stopped to identify myself. I was shown to a small room off the lobby area and asked to fill out the forms on the desk and have identification ready to copy. I did as I was directed, and the young lady showed up to gather up the papers and take my ID for copying. She returned my identification in just a few moments and told me that someone would be with me shortly. I didn't have to wait long as an older lady showed up within minutes. She identified herself as the Human Right's Manager and sat down across from me. We visited about my interests, education, and background. She reviewed the forms that I had filled out and I saw her eyebrows shoot up at something she was reading. She laid the paper down and asked, "Are you by chance the granddaughter of Rebecca Bradley?" "Yes, I am. She passed away before I was born so I never knew her personally. My paternal grandmother, also deceased, was Lorraine Donaldson." She smiled and said, "Yes, I knew them both and that would make you the daughter of Amanda Bradley Donaldson." "Correct, I said." "My dear, she said, you come from darned good stock!" "I know. I'm very proud to be the offspring of all of them. My father and grandfathers on both sides of the tree were equally as impressive career-wise." "Why are you applying for this position, she asked?" "Well, I'm waiting on the results of my bar exam which, as you know, could drag on for a couple of months. When I saw that you had a part time, temp position I thought it would be a great way to get my foot in the door. When I receive my credentials showing that I've passed the Massachusetts bar I'm hopeful that I can secure a position with this office. It has been my life's dream to eventually be the Suffolk County District Attorney. I love the law and I want to work in the heart of it." "Wow, she said. when you dream, you don't miss a beat. Given the contents of your resume and application and what we need for the next 3-5 weeks I would like to offer you the position." "Thank you! I'm very happy to accept the offer. When do I start?" "You just did. I'll walk you over to the payroll department and they'll get you banking information as pay is direct deposited every two weeks. Welcome aboard, Debra." We shook hands and she walked me to payroll where I gave them Aunty's information for deposits to be made to the trust account. The payroll person didn't say anything, but her look was one of, "why are you working?" I was told that I'd be paid an hourly wage of $25.50 per hour which amount represents two times the minimum hourly wage. I was asked to sign a confidentiality paper as I would be handling confidential files. She walked me to the elevator and up to the 3rd floor where she showed me the area where I would be working. She introduced me to the person that I would take my direction from and left. Lindsey, my supervisor was lovely. She showed me where the locker was to put my coat and handbag, where the lunchroom and restroom was and then helped set up my desk with the tools necessary to perform the task at hand. I was given about a 25" tall stack of folders that were active cases. They needed to be read, notes transcribed in the most readable manner possible. Lindsey told me to work my way through the first folder, to jot down all questions, and to let her know when I had accomplished that. "At that time, she said, I will assist you in transcribing the information in a manner that is acceptable to this office." "Thank you. I will let you know when I'm ready." It was 1:15pm.

I went after a cup of coffee which was ok to take to my desk. I started reviewing the first folder on the top of the stack. I jotted down my notes as I went through the file. I numbered the handwritten notes according to the dates written. I transcribed those into full sentences, showing the author, the date recorded, the contents and any other pertinent data. If the writer referred to a specific case for comparison, I pulled that information and added it to the transcribed data with the appropriate references. I looked at my watch and was a bit discouraged by the fact that it was 2:30pm and I had only just finished. I went to Lindsey's office and told her I was ready for her. She raised her eyebrow but followed me to my desk. She sat down in the extra chair, reviewed the file and my notes and transcribed data and told me that I had completed the tasks and that nothing else was needed from that file. "Your notes are on point, your transcription is accurate, and I applaud you for the way you completed the task. You are authorized to work 6 hours per day, 5 days per week. You can select the hours that work best for you and if weekends are better than weekdays, we're fine with that too. The stack of files is your job. When you finish the last file in the stack the position will officially be over. Let me know if you have any questions. I'm here to assist you with any needs you may have." With that she got up and went back to her office. I decided that I would research the next file, get as far as I could and be off the clock by 7:15pm to complete my 6-hour shift. The research went well, and I had worked through two complete files before the end of my day. I had begun on the next file, but it would have to wait until tomorrow. On my way down the elevator and the walk to the car I decided that Tuesday through Saturday from 8am-2pm would work perfectly for me. I would eat a hearty breakfast and then stop at the deli for a sandwich or salad after the end of my day. I was feeling darned good by the time I got to my car.

I had my cell phone turned off when I went for my interview and continued to leave it off for the rest of the day. When I turned it on, I saw that there were messages from Daniel. Apparently, his next step was the police if I didn't call him back soon. I decided to wait until I got home to call him. The traffic had pretty much died down, so the ride home was easy. I parked and headed up the stairs. Sitting on the stoop was Daniel. "Where have you been, he said. Are you ok? How come you're all dressed up? What's going on?" "Hi Daniel. I'm fine thanks, how are you?" With that I brushed past him and went through the door. I threw my coat and purse on the chair in the foyer and headed for the kitchen. I needed wine. Lots of wine. I poured my glass, glared at Daniel and poured one for him too. "I understand, I said, your being curious or even upset that I hadn't responded to your phone calls. However, you should have considered that I must be busy. I was planning on calling you as soon as I got home." "Ok, he said, sorry. Where have you been all day?" "At work." "Work? What do you mean you've been at work?" Well, I woke up, looked around, had nothing to do until I hear from the board of examiners, so I looked through the paper and found where they needed a part time, temp position that I was perfect for. I looked wonderful, gave them my best smile, and got the job." "Where, he asked?" "The D.A.'s office of course. Where else would I want to work?" "Are you kidding me, Pixie! That's fabulous! Congratulations. This calls for a celebration. Where are you taking me? And, before I forget, where were you last night? I called and texted and never heard back." "Oh, that. I had a dinner date. We went to the little bistro around the corner. I'm going to go change clothes." "Debra!" "I'll be down in a minute. Help yourself to the wine and take-out menus." Daniel just laughed, poured another glass of wine, and decided on Chinese delivery. He made the call and they told him it would be about 30 minutes which was perfect. Date? Right.

Debra came back downstairs in sweats and a tee shirt. She filled her glass and asked what they were having, and he told her Chinese. "Sounds wonderful. Let's go set things up in the den to eat. We can watch some TV later." They set up trays in front of the comfy sofa and browsed through the channels to see what was coming on. They finally decided on a movie that was starting in about 40 minutes. It would be over in time for her to get a good night's sleep before work tomorrow. Dinner arrived and they enjoyed every morsel. Daniel cleaned up while she got the movie ready. When he came back in he asked, "Really, you had a date last night? I didn't know you were seeing anyone." "Well, truth be told, I decided to dine alone but Harold from two doors down showed up and we joined forces and had a wonderful time guzzling wine and eating rich food. He paid for our taxi home. It was a lot of fun and I hope to get together with him often." Daniel smiled that beautiful smile of his and told her that was wonderful. "Hey, before we start the movie, I have something I want to tell you. I spoke with Fr. McMurry and Bishop Cornell both. We talked at length about how this would impact my path as a priest and possibly advancement someday. They are both thinking very positively about my taking the position. I asked about living arrangements as I don't recall seeing where Fr. James lived. It seems that there is a small cottage on the back of the property and that would be mine to live in. I could commit to 2-years and at the end of that time either ask for a transfer or make my plea to stay on in a permanent position at St. Liz. They want the decision in 48-hours and then they want the move to be immediate. What do you think?" "I think you need to do whatever is going to make you happy, Daniel. If moving back to Edgartown and having your own parish is the answer than you certainly have my support and my love." "Will you come with me, he asked?" "Eventually, but not immediately. I need to see this temp job through and leave my mark in that office. Again, I was quizzed on our grandmothers and mother. Apparently, they all had wings when it came to the law. I want the people of Boston to know I'm alive. When my certificate arrives saying I'm a full-fledged attorney at law I will be better armed to take the next step." "Ok, he said. I respect that and it makes sense. If you go back home, where will you live? With the parents?" "No, absolutely not. I'll want my own place close to my work so I can walk whenever possible. The winters are so long that the thought of being able to walk in the spring/summer season is very appealing to me. Also, I'm concerned about the workload on Aunty. I need to delve into that matter more closely when I'm there the next time. When are you leaving?" "I'm thinking next Monday. I need to get things cleared up and cleaned up here. I need to get a car as I'm kind of stranded at the moment. I understand that the cottage is furnished but most of it belonged to Fr. James. I'm thinking I'll want to redecorate a bit. I'm sorry you won't be there to handle that but perhaps Alicia will help me?" "Yeah, or most any woman on Martha's Vineyard… Ouch. That hurt Daniel." We watched our movie and snacked on the popcorn that we microwaved. About halfway through it I was dozing, and Daniel noticed. "Hey, let's continue this another night. You're tired and you have work tomorrow." "Thanks Daniel. Hey, take my car. It is new and you like driving it. I can taxi or Uber until I decide on another set of wheels." "Are you sure?" "Absolutely. The registration is in the glovebox with the insurance information. Change the name on the insurance and ask Aunty to change the title from me to you. Just don't drag your feet or forget because both parts of that statement are important and necessary." "Will do, he said. I love you, Pixie. I'll be talking to you." I locked the door behind him, turned off lights as I went and headed to bed.

I was up early next morning and ready to face the day. I fixed myself some toast and jam and a cup of coffee. I called for an Uber to pick me up at 7am just in case there was bad traffic. The driver texted me with his name and the code number assuring me that he was who he was supposed to be. I locked up and walked down to the car. He told me the destination address that was dispatched to him and I confirmed that was correct. "Sir, would it be possible to order a steady 7am pickup Tuesday-Saturday and a pickup at the destination you just gave me at 2:15pm on those same 5 days?" "Of course, he said. I will enter it in the log when we get to the destination, give you a printout and our dispatcher will have the information. It will probably be me that picks you up each day and I'm unsure of the driver at 2:15pm. You will be texted a code for that driver." "Perfect. Thanks so much." He dropped me off at 7:45am so I still had 15 minutes before I could report to work. I walked quickly to the corner deli and got me a coffee to take back with me. I caught the elevator just as I walked in and was at my desk at 8am sharp. Lindsey greeted me as she walked by. For the next several days I plowed through one folder after another. Daniel and I had dinner together before he left for Edgartown and I really was happy for him, even if I had difficulty showing it. Less than 3 weeks into my temp job I had all of the folders completed. I took the last of the pile into Lindsey's office and told her I had completed my task. She smiled at me and said, "Wow. You really don't mess around, do you?" "I don't, I said. I come from hard working people who believe in giving your best to whatever task is laid before you. I wanted to tell you thank you for your help through this and that I have enjoyed my time here." We shook hands, I got my coat, briefcase, purse and headed for the elevator. I checked my watch for the time, called Uber and told them to cancel my evening pickup. I hailed a cab and headed home.

I got my clothes changed and went out to collect the mail. My neighbor hailed me while I was on the porch and asked if I had plans for dinner. "I don't. Are you buying, I asked?" "I am, he said. About an hour?" "Perfect. I'll meet you on the sidewalk so we can stroll over to the bistro." I went in and tried to decide what to wear that would be comfortable but okay to go out to dinner in. I grabbed a glass of wine, went upstairs and stared at my closet. Jeans? Slacks? Oh, that's a pretty little dress. I grabbed that to put on. It was perfect. I went in and freshened up, tied my hair up in a loose ponytail, donned the dress and flat shoes and headed back downstairs. I still had about 20 minutes so I went in to check email while I waited. Well, well. What have we here. An email with certification from the Board of Examiners for the State of Massachusetts. I'm official! Also, they had sent along my scores for the exam. Congratulations to Miss Debra Lorraine Donaldson for having scored the highest marks ever recorded in the State. Sorry Grandma Rebecca! I win!

## *Father Daniel Goes Home*

Daniel arrived safely in Edgartown and after stopping first at the cemetery to say hello to his parents he went to Aunty and Uncy's house. I had decided that the best course of action was to perhaps stay at the house until the cottage was habitable. Bishop Cornell had told me that Fr. James had lived there for more than 20 years while pastoring the church and that he felt it probably needed a good cleaning if not a full-fledged renovation. I thought I would ask Uncy to accompany me and help me make some decisions before moving in. As always, they were waiting on the front porch. How do they do that? Do my parents contact them or what? I laughed to myself at that thought. They came to help with luggage and to bestow hugs and kisses on their favorite son. They got everything into the foyer and Jack attached himself to my leg. I reached down to disconnect the kitten and petted him before putting him back on his ottoman. Aunty was simply thrilled that I was there and announced that there was food and drink in the kitchen. I took my luggage upstairs and then came back to check out the goodies in the kitchen. Aunty had made scones and cream cheese pastries and the aroma was drifting through the entire house. My stomach was rumbling as I picked up the pastry first. Delicious. How does she do that? Everything that comes out of her kitchen tastes like love. We chatted about my decisions to take this assignment and what my next steps were. I asked Uncy if he might go with me to the cottage later in the day? He said he was ready whenever I was. "Aunty, I'm supposed to remind you to change the title on the car from Debra to me. She told me to change the insurance, but I haven't a clue what it is or how to get a hold of them. I'm sorry to be so dumb, but this is new to me." "It fine, Daniel, she said. I'll take care of both parts. Will Debra be moving home, or do you know?" "She told me that her plans were to move home *eventually*. That is all I know." "That's fine, Daniel. Thank you."

Uncy and I got to the cottage and I let us in with the key that I'd been given. I could feel the presence of Fr. James everywhere. I felt a bit like an intruder. Uncy started looking around and then came back and said, "Daniel, let's hire a contractor to first, demo this entire cottage and then renovate so that it is habitable for this century. I doubt you could even use a computer here." "Ok, I said, but Uncy I've only been given $300 for this project." "Well, give it to the church fund. We'll take care of this ourselves. You aren't living like this, Daniel." With that Uncy was out the door. I guess we've made a decision. I just laughed to myself as I locked up. Uncy said, "Let's go visit the fellow that I want to do the work now if that is ok with you." "You bet, which way, I asked?" "Right downtown about 3 doors from your mother's office, he said." "Uncy, I've been meaning to ask you, do you miss working?" "Not really, he said. I still help James if he needs it, but I've been trying to help Lucy as much as possible. She has quite a heavy load." "I'm sure of that. So is Debra. That was one of the reasons she felt she should move home, I said." "That would be grand, Daniel. Your aunty could use the help." We arrived downtown, found the office we were looking for and a parking spot right in front. We went in and Uncy talked with the contractor about doing the job. "We can go look at the site tomorrow morning and start the following day if that works for you? We would like someone to be on-site and also to give us an idea what all you want done." Uncy told him that we'd both be there at 7am tomorrow morning to meet him. We left and Uncy seemed downright pleased with our progress. "Let's go shopping, he said." "Ok, what are we shopping for, I asked?" "Furniture, bedding, bathroom, kitchen, everything. We're perfectly capable of doing this ourselves. We don't need women to get us what we need." I was laughing at how cocky he was being. "Ok, let's go to the furniture shop and then one of the big box department stores. Oh, wait, we don't have any of those!" "We have a furniture store, smart boy, and we have department stores. They're simply locally owned establishments, said Uncy."

We got to the furniture store and Uncy said we would look around and decide what we needed and liked. "We can pick out, pay for and tell them to hold until we call them. All amazingly easy." We found a queen size bed set, a chest of drawers and a dresser that I liked. We found a sofa and two comfy chairs for the living room along with coffee tables and end tables. Uncy said we should hang the TV on the wall above a nice credenza that could double as storage. We found a small dining room set with 4 chairs that would be perfect for the area. Uncy told the manager that they needed to replace the range, refrigerator, dishwasher, washer, and dryer also. The manager showed us a catalog and we selected those items. Uncy told the manager that our contractor would coordinate with him on the appliances and that the other items should be held until one of us call for delivery. "Ok, Uncy said, let's go see about the other stuff." There is a nice department store in town that carries linens. We found 3 sets of sheets, a couple of blankets, a quilt, pillows, towels, kitchen towels, cookware, dishes, and silverware. "Do we need a shower curtain, I asked?" "No, we're going to hope they can do a walk-in shower for you with a glass enclosure, Uncy said." Okay then. "Uncy, I asked, should I feel guilty that you're paying for all of this for me?" "Not hardly, Daniel, he said. The trusts and dividends connected to the trusts, are to take care of you three heirs for life. That's what we're doing. I was serious about taking the allotment check for repairs that you were given and donate it to your parish. We will also take on the responsibility of any repairs and maintenance that are needed for the cottage going forward." "Ok, I said, well thank you very much. I certainly appreciate it, Uncy." He just grinned at me and said we'd best head for home.

When we got home, Aunty had a rather perplexed look on her face. "Where have you two been?" "Well, said Uncy, we've checked things out, decided what needed to be done, taken steps to do them, and made the necessary purchases in preparation for Daniel's move. When's lunch?" With that Uncy went upstairs. Aunty looked after him for a moment, turned to me and said, "What has gotten into him?" "I'm not sure, I said. He seems to be in charge right now." "Good. He needed a project like this. It's good, Daniel. It's all good. Let's go find lunch." We went in the kitchen and Aunty got out a fresh loaf of her bread, some deli meat and cheese and condiments. I grabbed plates and knives and glasses to fill with cold milk. I asked if there were chips and she just smiled and threw me the bag. She knows I must have my chips! Uncy came down in time to join us for a sandwich. She looked in the fridge and found some macaroni salad and grabbed some forks for us. Great lunch! "Daniel, she asked, what do you have in store for settling in? Do you need to go to the church every day or what? "I don't think so. I'm going to go in this afternoon and set up my email and change the voice mail on the phone. I want to call both Fr. McMurry and Bishop Cornell and let them know what we're doing with the cottage. I know that there is an on-going prayer list on the desk that Fr. James left for me. Also, I would like to clean and rearrange the office to be more accommodating to my needs. I also want to draft a letter to all of the parishioners advising them of these changes and inviting them to respond with any questions that might have. I don't know how he was handling walk-in confessions. I need to try and figure that out as well. "Aunty, perhaps you would read through the letter I draft to be sure it looks good?" "Of course, Daniel. I'm happy to, she said." "Well, after we clean up, I'm going to head to the church. That way I can be home to help get dinner ready. What are we having?" "Daniel, I swear you're always hungry! We are grilling steaks and corn on the cob. I need you home by no later than 6pm to share in the cocktail hour and get the stuff ready for Mexican street corn like you always fixed." "Done, I said. I'll be here!" I cleaned up the island, loaded the dishwasher, kissed aunty, and headed to the church.

I got to the church and went into the office to see what I could find. I called the number for voice mail to get the messages and wrote those all down. There were three and I responded to each of those. I called Fr. McMurry and brought him up to date and then called the Bishop and did the same. They both seemed appreciative of getting the cottage cleaned up and fixed up as they were fully aware of its condition. They were also appreciative of the donation back to the parish. I told them my thoughts on coming into the office every other day and asked if they had any idea how Fr. James had handled walk-in confessions and such. They didn't but suggested that I post church hours on the door(s) and consider finding a parishioner that might like to work in the office. Fr. James had turned that idea down each time that it was broached. I thanked them for their thoughts and ideas and told them that I would stay in touch. I found the prayer list and made a copy to take with me. I also planned on going to visit the shut-ins. I typed up a notice to put on the front door with hours and my cell phone number. I drafted a flyer to put on the church bulletin board asking if anyone would be interested in working 3 days per week, 4 hours per day, answering phones, and helping with other church office matters. I was told that I could hire someone for 15 hours per week, minimum wage, and that the payroll would be handled through the Archdiocese of Boston. I had reminded the cardinal that I had donated my stipend back to the church if that would help pay for secretarial assistance. I found a listing of all the parishioners and took a copy so I could create a mail merge with aunty's help.

I headed home and got there in time to help set up the grill. Uncy had already made a pitcher of gin and tonics for dinner and aunty had the steaks resting ready to grill. I made up the mix to press on the corn to make street corn after it is grilled like we all loved. I spread mayonnaise on each dry ear and then sprinkle cotija cheese, chili powder and cilantro on the ear. We all got our gin and tonic and I brought them up to date on what I'd found. Aunty said we would put the letter together after dinner. They were happy to hear that I would be allowed to have some administrative help in the office. We poured our drinks and took the steaks and corn out to the grill. It was a lovely evening, so we enjoyed our beverage on the patio. Uncy cooked the steak and I turned the corn so that it would cook evenly. Aunty had already set the island so we could eat in the kitchen like we love to do. She had made a chocolate pie for dessert that was calling to me. I took the corn and smeared the deliciousness on it. There! We were ready to eat. It was delicious. The perfect meal.

Uncy said he would clean up so aunty and I could go do the letter and get it sent out. I had a rough copy of what I wanted and the parishioners email addresses which was the most difficult part. Aunty said once we had them loaded that she'd do a thumb drive, so I'd have them going forward. She transcribed my letter into a lovely missile for sending to everyone, pushed the right buttons and it was done. "Daniel, where did you get the list from?" "It was on the church computer, I said. Oh my gracious, I could have downloaded that and we'd have had the list. I'm sorry Aunty." "It's ok, Daniel. You'll remember that the next time we have a project." Yes, I certainly would. We went and cut the pie and made coffee. I told them that I planned on being an early riser so I could start running again. I've missed it terribly as Boston isn't really set up for priests to run. A little church humor.

Daniel was up early, had his run, showered, dressed, and was waiting for Uncy by 6:15am. They gulped down coffee and headed to their meeting with Steve the contractor. Steve and his crew were already onsite and had surveyed what needed to be done to the structure. They went inside and Uncy showed them what he thought might be a workable floorplan. Steve walked through and told them that the only problem was the electrical panel. It needed to be upgraded to be able to carry the load of newer appliances and modern technology. Agreed. Uncy asked when they would start and Steve said, "We just did." Uncy asked how long the project would take and Steve said, "I think we can knock this out in 3-4 weeks given no additional surprises or problems." Everyone agreed that this was an acceptable plan. Uncy wrote a check to Steve for 50% of the work with the balance to be paid when the work is complete. David looked at Daniel, smiled, and said, "Want breakfast?" "Yes, I thought you'd never ask." We were off to find pancakes.

The time spent with the parents was wonderful. Also, Daniel was able to connect with David several times for tennis or a round of golf. He took Mary and the children to lunch one day so they could visit. Mary was taking a couple of classes each week to get her high school diploma rather than a G.E.D. She felt it would eventually open more doors for her. She was still quiet and rather secretive, but she was also blossoming into a beautiful, confident woman.

The remodel was on schedule and it was going to be beautiful. A nice lady named Dinah answered the plea for administrative help, and I hired her right away. She's been cleaning the church for several years now for no pay. She is a dedicated member of the parish and believes in volunteering. She was, however, thrilled that this job would pay. She had been a schoolteacher for years but had taken an early retirement due to being diagnosed with breast cancer. She had, God be thanked, been cured but had decided not to return to work. She cleaned the church twice weekly and if she remembered correctly, had done so for the past eight years. She and I looked through the office, found the check books and the bills that needed to be paid. I gave her the key to the post office box so she could collect the mail. She would answer phone messages or a ringing phone, set up meetings for me as needed, pay the bills, and leave the checks for me to sign. We would, together, do weekly announcements and mass itineraries. Dinah helped me find Fr. James' notes that listed his sermons for the past six months. This was helpful to me in selecting scriptures and subjects for my sermons. I met with the choir and we discussed the possibility of a musical performance for parishioners quarterly. I find it is a wonderful injection into the congregation and is even better if it comes with a good potluck dinner. I need to do some online searching, I guess. Years ago, I recall a beautiful song that was performed by the church choir at Easter time. It was called "Life in Jesus' Name". I remember the lyrics from the first verse:

Sin abounds on every hand
Bringing death to every man
There's no life, there's no hope, or so it seems
Jesus came to give you life
To bring you hope, remove sin and strife,
Just believe and have Life in Jesus' name

I just feel that if I can pull something like this together that it will inject hope and renew faith in this wonderful parish that I've been gifted with. Perhaps David can help me. He's a natural born researcher.

# David And Alicia

I received a text from my twin asking that I research a Christian musical for him. I responded with an "A-ok" and marked it on my calendar to handle later. The inn has been constantly full for the past two weeks and even with Mary's help, Alicia and I didn't seem to have a moment to themselves. As soon as this boom is over, I think we should take a three- or four-day getaway. Perhaps Debra could come and watch the inn for us. I need to call her and plant the suggestion.

Alicia came in with a hot cup of coffee and a scone for me. We sat and enjoyed our goodies and visited for a few minutes. She had a suggestion for dinner tonight, so I needed to check the larder and see if we needed anything to bring it together. It was a lovely, warm day and she felt like seafood paella in the garden would be delightful and I agreed. We have 10 guests with us so that would be two large paella pans full of deliciousness. I went through the pantry and the refrigerator and found that I had what I needed. I pulled out shrimp and chorizo to thaw but would need to go to the market for calamari and clams. "Alicia, do you have anything else that we need from the market? I don't want to go there for two items." "I'll make a list, she said, and have it for you shortly." Alicia went back to her cleaning chores and I went back to my bookwork. The inn has been showing a profit steadily for the past five months. Aunty and I have gone through the numbers and are feeling very positive about our choices. My cell was ringing and was announcing my twin as the caller. "Hello brother, I said." "Hello back to you, replied Daniel. I hated to bother you because I know you're very busy with guests, but I was wondering if after you've fed everyone dinner, say 8pm, if you and Alicia could spare me an hour?" "Certainly, Daniel. Do you want to meet here or what?" "Well, if you can get away from there, I'd be happy to buy you a beer or a nightcap. Your choice." "Beer. Our favorite pub at 8pm. See you there." I couldn't help but wonder what was going on as I disconnected the call.

I found Alicia, kissed her, and told her I'd be back in about an hour. She gave me her note for items she needed, and I was out the door. There is a wonderful fish market on the docks in Edgartown, so I went there to get my calamari and clams. They also had some beautiful head-on shrimp that I got to go with the ones that were thawing. This would indeed be a feast! I stopped at the market and got all the things on Alicia's list and then headed home. We unloaded groceries, fixed lunch for the guests, and went about the remaining chores with the promise to meet in the kitchen at 4pm to begin preparation of dinner. I had some yardwork to do so I went out to begin that task. Our gardener greeted me, and we discussed what he needed to do in addition to my task. I like to keep up the immediate garden area and patio that is adjacent to the kitchen and porch area. Granny had planted a beautiful array of flowers that were still blooming each year. I felt she was close to me when I was working in that area. I still miss her and gramps every day. My mother had loved this house. When she was young, she would come to visit with her granny, and it was kind of a haven. She and her mother were not close. From all I've heard and read, Grandmother Rebecca wasn't close to anyone but herself. I finished up my work and went to grab a quick shower before joining Alicia in the kitchen. I dressed in a pair of chinos and a white linen shirt that hangs loose. It is such a comfortable outfit. I'm a big guy, so comfort is foremost in my thoughts. I was brushing my hair when I noticed some gray in the front. Gray hair! I'm just a baby. I certainly don't need gray hair. I'll check Daniel's head tonight and see if he has any. I went to the kitchen and showed Alicia my hair. She laughed until she cried. "You silly boy, she said, what's a little gray hair. You look distinguished." "I don't think so, I said, it makes me look old." "You'll just have to get over it, she said. I'm afraid that trying to wash the gray away only makes it come in stronger." We started prepping for the dinner. I cleaned all the seafood and Alicia started in on the vegetables. I kept an eye on the clock so at 5pm I'd go and light the charcoal on both barbeques. I stacked several bottles of white wine in a bucket filled with cold water and lots of ice. I set out the melamine plates and wine glasses, silverware, napkins, paper towels, and water glasses. I also filled a bucket with water and ice for the bottles of water and sodas. I set the red wines and corkscrews on the end of bar table. Salt, pepper, hot sauce, and miscellaneous condiments went on the end of each of the tables. There! That looks rather good. I believe we are ready. I went back into the kitchen and Alicia helped me bring everything out to the cooking area. While I got things started, she went back into the dining room area and suggested cocktails on the patio. She had set up all the different liquors, mixers, and beer along with cheese and crackers and nuts for a snack. All the guests were chatting away and seemed very content. A few mentioned that dinner smelled awesome. Each layer of the paella was emitting its own wonderful aromas. Alicia brought out two huge bowls of green salad for guests to start with. I began adding the different seafoods to the paella pans and by the time the guests finished with their salads, dinner was ready. By the time I had worked my way through the entire line of guests there were already return people wanting seconds. I guess dinner was a success.

After dinner Mary, Alicia and I picked up, cleaned up, checked on guests to see if they needed anything and then we went to freshen up to go meet Daniel. Alicia had set out cookies, pies, and pastries in the cooler and everyone knew where to find their snacks. There are also always cereal boxes, fruit, sandwich fixings and cups of soup ready to microwave for anyone that is hungry before they turn in for the night. Mary would be close at hand in case anyone needed anything else. We bid everyone a good night and headed to the pub. Alicia asked if I had any idea what was on Daniel's mind and I told her I didn't have a clue. We parked and went in to find Daniel, but we had gotten there ahead of him. It wasn't more than five minutes until he appeared at the door. He hugged us and sat down across from us with a big smile on his face. The first thing I asked him was if he'd discovered any gray hairs. He stared at me for a moment and then asked, "What? Why would I look for gray hair? I'm not even 26 yet." "Well, I said, because I found some in my hair today." I got up and showed him. He was laughing hysterically at my dilemma. I sat back down and asked, "So, what's going on? Are you okay?" "Yes, he said, I'm great. I want to tell you both a story. I hope to give you the shortest version possible so bear with me. Earlier this week I heard confession for a young woman. She was very distraught and tried her best to walk me through her troubles. After confession was over, she came back to my office and asked to speak with me privately. She, her name is Barbara McMillan, told me that she was a 24-year-old single woman from the greater Boston area. She had followed a boyfriend to Edgartown with his promise to marry her. Long story short, she became pregnant, told him, and he handed her enough money for an abortion and a bus ticket back to Boston. She had waited to tell him about the baby and by the time she did abortion was out of the question as she had felt life. Besides that, she is Catholic and was struggling with the thought of abortion anyway. She used the money he gave her to go to the doctor and get vitamins. She has been staying with a girlfriend that she met here locally but she needs to move soon. She came to me looking for help. She comes from an abusive homelife. She hasn't ever done drugs and detest alcohol because of her father and mother. She doesn't want the child but does want to know that she has secured a good home for the child. Do you have any questions or comments so far?" "I do, Alicia said, I'm quite sure I know why you're presenting this to us, and I appreciate the thought. How far along is she? What does she look like? What does she want in exchange for this child?" "All good questions, Daniel replied. As I said, she is 24 years old, slender to the point of gaunt at present time, strawberry blond hair, bright blue eyes, creamy Irish complexion, and really, the most beautiful mouth I've ever seen. She's about 5'4" tall and I would say minus the baby, about 110 pounds. She is less than a month away from delivery. She went back to the boy's house and obtained a typed release from any/all interest in the child, had it signed in triplicates, notarized, and gave me the papers. She is willing to do the same thing.

What does she want? She wants someone to pay for the hospital so she can have medical attention should she or the baby need it. She has been attending the free clinic for regular checkups. She also gave me those reports. The doctor at the free clinic suggested that the baby was already at more than 8 pounds. He is betting that it is a boy but of course, can't be certain. Oh, and she would like a bus ticket to the place of her choosing long as it isn't Boston. She is an intelligent young woman, is well spoken, and presents herself in a decent manner. From my personal observation, if I were interested in considering adoption of this child, I would have my sister do the necessary paperwork and handle the situation. Also, I would contact my personal physician and bring them into the loop and ask their advice. Further, if everyone agrees that this can be done legally, I would include a $10,000 check to the mother giving her a cushion to live on while she finds work and gets established." I looked at Daniel and shook my head. "I can't believe this has fallen into your lap. We've talked about this type of scenario and considered investigating it further. We're hopeful that if we get our minds settled and stop worrying that we'll be able to carry to full term so this one would have a brother or sister. Alicia, what are you thinking?" She was kind of slumped down in the booth and tucked in behind my shoulder crying softly. "Honey, can you talk to us?" "Yes, of course, I'm sorry, she said. We need to call Debra and see what happens next. There is, however, one thing that I insist on." We both said, "of course, anything." "She is not to be told who we are or where we are from. She is to know nothing about us other than the necessary things such as financial situation is stable, health is good, and we'll love and care for this child until the day we draw our last breath." Daniel told her, "Absolutely. I already conveyed these things to her, and she is looking forward to hearing from me or my lawyer. She doesn't know that the lawyer is the baby sister. She knows me, like they all do, as Fr. Daniel. She doesn't know my sir name. So, will you phone Debra tomorrow?" "No, Alicia said, I'm calling her right now." With that she got up and excused herself from the table. Daniel and I just looked at each other. Alicia came back about 15 minutes later and said, "Daniel, please call Debra first thing in the morning and give her all the information that you possess. She will put things together and overnight it back to us so we can get this done. Also, she agrees with the money to the young woman but believes that it should be $20,000 not $10,000. She said you can't do anything these days on $10,000. I don't know how to respond to that as my mother takes care of everything. Which reminds me. Are we bringing them into this conversation?" "I believe we need to, I said, especially given the need of funds. She has those purse strings tightly in her grip." Alicia just glared at me. We all decided we needed another beer and some soft pretzels to go with it. "When she came to my office the other day, Daniel said, I was so taken with her and her story. I didn't want to lose contact with her so she and I went to the store and got her a cell phone so she would stay in touch. Oh, and before I forget it, she needs to move from her friend's house sooner than later. I moved her to a nice motel and paid for 30-days for her." We just looked at him and shook our heads. He's such a nice man. We finished our beer and Alicia looked at her watch and said, "Let's go to the parents. They're still up and we need to talk with them." We all know better than to argue with Alicia, so Daniel said he'd follow us to the house.

The parents were watching TV when we walked up on the porch and knocked. Uncy came to the door looking very frightened. We assured him immediately that we were all fine but needed to talk to them. "Well, come on in, he said. Lucy, put the coffee on and get out one of those pies." We all started for the kitchen, but not before Jack latched onto Daniel's leg and hitched a ride with him. Man, somebody has got to teach this kitten not to do that. Aunty had pie, plates, and coffee cups ready for us. We all hugged her, and Alicia took the lead in bringing her parents up to speed. Aunty's eyes got very round as she listened. "Have you notified Debra of this, she asked?" "Yes, she is putting together the paperwork and sending it next day to you. She said that between you two you'd have all the necessary editing done and in place for signatures." "What else has been done, Daniel, she asked?" "Well, I got her a cell phone and I moved her into a motel just at the edge of town." "Did you promise her anything other than making inquiries, she asked?" "No, absolutely not." "Well, she said, I agree that this all sounds wonderful and I believe it is an answer to all of our prayers. I also agree that a distribution of $20,000 to this young woman to help her establish a new life is fair. Let's wait until we see the documents that Debra is putting together and then we can start tying up any loose ends. Daniel, did she already make arrangements with the hospital or do you know?" "I don't know, Aunty. I don't believe she said. We can call her tomorrow and ask and then decide. I don't know the doctor from the free clinic but perhaps he can be of some assistance?" "Yes, I agree. It's getting late now. Please let us know if you hear anything else and I'll contact you the minute the paperwork arrives. I'm going to bed now as I'm apparently going to be a grandmother very soon." We all just laughed, hugged them, and took our leave. Daniel said he was home so he thought he would stay. Alicia and I thanked him for his very thoughtful ways and that we hoped things would come together quickly.

## *Debra's First Client*

I had been working on the presentation letter to the D.A.'s office when this phone call happened. I got out the necessary reference books and began putting together the forms necessary for this private adoption between the young lady and David and Alicia. Daniel had sent me all the information that he had so it all came together rather quickly. I am going to put this in overnight mail to Aunty to review and file with whatever changes are necessary. Daniel and Aunty will act as the administrators of the adoption and obtain the young lady's signature on the paperwork. Aunty and Daniel will also have to be the contacts for the hospital. I hope that Daniel was able to reach the doctor at the free clinic. I reviewed my documents again and decided that they looked correct. I called UPS to pick up a next day delivery to Edgartown.

I have read through my letter to the D.A. about forty times now. I think it looks good, and I'm going to go ahead and post it today. I need to call Aunty so I can make the arrangements to either purchase or lease a car. I'm finding taxicabs and uber to be a pain. I'm just not a girl that likes to stand around and wait for something to happen. I might as well call her right now. The cell was ringing, and she picked up, saying, "Just the girl I needed to talk with." "Hi Aunty, I said, or should I call you Grandma?" We both laughed over that idea. Aunty, I am waiting on UPS to pick up the docs and then they're coming your way. On another issue, I need to get a car. How do you want me to proceed? "Do you want to purchase or lease, Debra, she asked?" "I'm leaning toward a lease so that I can just automatically update every 3 years. What do you think of that idea?" "I think that is a sound idea. What kind are you thinking about getting, she asked?" "I really don't know. Would you think I was awful if I said something sporty and cute?" Aunty laughed and said, "No, not at all. You are young and adorable. You should have something that reflects that. With your beautiful chocolate curls and green eyes, I think something in a gold metallic would be right up your alley." "Ooh, that sounds perfect, Aunty. Ok, I'll go to the Mercedes dealer this afternoon and see what they have available. I'll just have my people call your people. I love you. Talk to you soon." I decided to go shower and dress and get a cab or uber to the dealership. Why wait?

I arrived at the dealership and was bombarded by salespeople which is one of my biggest beefs with any organization. I eyeballed all of them and picked the absolute best looking one to act as my helper. I told him I wanted a sportscar, that I wanted to lease it, that I wanted it to be close to a gold metallic in color. He showed me a couple of models, but I selected the pretty one with the soft top. They had a black one, a silver one, and a solar beam yellow that was right up my alley. "I'll take that one, I said. Here is my aunt's phone number. She handles my families' financial matters. I'll wait while you make the call as I would like to take the car today." "Well, ma'am, he said, I will need a little more time than that. We have to service the car and do what we call a make-ready before it can be taken off the lot." "Can you deliver it to me tomorrow then, I asked?" "Certainly, he said. I'll call your aunt and get all the paperwork in place and call you to confirm a time for delivery. Will that work?" "Yes, that's fine. Do I need to sign anything before I leave?" "No, I'll have the paperwork ready for your signature tomorrow when I deliver. Shall I call you a cab or would you prefer uber?" "Uber is fine, I told him." I called aunty when I got home and advised her of my choice, the price, and so on. She said that he had just called, and she had sent him what he needed to complete the transaction. There! I have a car!

# So Many Changes

Aunty received the paperwork from Debra and advised Daniel that everything looked to be in line and ready for signatures. "I can call her and see if she is available and let you know." "Yes, Lucy said, that is perfect. If she is available today, I could meet you at the office at say 3pm?" "Ok, I'll get back to you. I called Barbara and got her voice mail. It wasn't two minutes until she returned my call. "Barbara, I said, I have a couple that want very much to help you and to adopt your baby. The paperwork is all drawn up and could be signed this afternoon if you are available?" "Yes, she said, that would be fine. Will you pick me up or should I try to get transportation?" "No, I of course will pick you up. Actually, if you're available now I could come and get you and we could share a bite of lunch first? Also, I know that the doctor at the free clinic has spoken to the hospital so we might go by there and see what they have to say." "Ok, she said. I need about half an hour to tidy up and then I'll be ready. In thirty minutes, I'll be standing by the office door." "Ok, see you in half an hour." I called Aunty and told her what we were going to do. She agreed and said she would see us at 3pm. "And Daniel, don't forget that you're not to call me aunty and you're not to divulge your sir name. Let's just pretend we're just meeting." "Got it, I said. Thanks for the reminder."

I arrived on time and Barbara was waiting for me. She was dressed simply but looked very pretty. "Hello, she said. Thank you for all that you're doing for me." "No problem, I'm just happy to be able to help you on your journey." We chatted about news, the town, and had an enjoyable meal. She was open about her upbringing and said she had a real interest in relocating to a small town near Chicago. "It would get me off the east coast where I could start fresh. She named Des Plaines, Illinois, where there is a good community college that she'd like to attend. "If I can find a job and save money, they have an online class that I could take, and I could use the computers at the library. I could make something out of myself." I told her I thought that was a great idea. We headed to the hospital to see what we could find out. When we went inside the hospital lobby, we asked to see the person in charge of the maternity ward. We were asked to wait while they would see if the person was available. A person came out and escorted us to a conference room where we were joined by the administrator. She told us that she had been notified by the doctor at the free clinic and understood that she needed to be able to give birth in a hospital environment. I told her that we were working with a local attorney to handle the adoption and that their office would satisfy any costs incurred. She made a few notes and then gave us a stack of paperwork that needed to be filled out. "Perhaps, she said, your attorney would oversee the completion of this paperwork and then get it back to us as quickly as you can." We thanked her for her time and took our leave. We had about 45 minutes before our meeting downtown. We sat in the car looking through the paperwork and I noted that Barbara was having difficulty reading through it. "Are you alright, I asked." "Yes, I just don't read very well so it takes me awhile to read it and understand it. I have something called dyslexia." We drove downtown and found a place to park close to the office. We went in and introduced ourselves to Mrs. Adler. She showed us to her office and went through the paperwork that had been drawn up by a local attorney. She told Barbara that a nice young couple wanted very much to adopt her child. They are well-off financially and very established in the community. They preferred to remain anonymous she told her. They want to help you through this journey and have prepared a check in the amount of Twenty Thousand Dollars. I need to know where to deposit those funds. Further, you had said you wanted a bus ticket to an unknown destination. "Do you now have a destination in mind, she asked?" Barbara told her she did and why she had chosen that town. "Will you excuse me for a moment while I make a quick phone call, she asked." She came back in the room a few minutes later and told Barbara that the couple would like to do something for her that they hoped would help her in the immediate future. "They would like to pay your first 2 years of tuition following you making application and being accepted to the school of your choice. Also, they would like to secure a furnished apartment for you to live in near the campus and would pay for a one-year lease. All of this would be handled through this office. You would need to make application online at your earliest convenience so we can try to bring all these loose ends together. Would this be satisfactory with you?" "Yes, of course, she said, but how can I make application or anything from here?" "I'll help you, she said. Let's just get the paperwork signed and get the hospital secured and then we'll take care of the rest of this. These people are wonderful people who will love and care for your child as their own. They just want to help you on your journey." Barbara signed all the paperwork that was put before her. She also gave Lucy a document that she had drawn up and had notarized saying she relinquished all rights, forever, to this child. She had one signed by the father also. Lucy didn't need these as the stipulations were clearly written in the adoption paperwork, but she took the papers from the young woman as she knew they were very important to her. "Father Dan, unless you have other questions or concerns, I think Barbara and I can handle this from here. I will drop her off at the motel when she and I have finished." "Great, I said. Barbara, if you need anything you let me know. You have my private cell phone number." "Thank you, Fr. Dan for everything you've done for me. I can never thank you enough." She impulsively stood and hugged me, and I simply hugged her back. "You take care, I said." I left the office feeling very emotional as this was my first real important interaction with someone as a priest. I will keep her in my prayers.

Lucy and Barbara filled out the online application for the community college Des Plaines. She was to have a response within 48 hours. "The response will come back to my email, Barbara, and then I'll call you on the cell Fr. Dan got you. If the application is approved and accepted, I will transfer money to the school for your tuition and we will secure an apartment for you. Then a monthly amount of money will be posted in your bank account to cover books, transportation and incidentals needed for school and whatever utilities need to be paid separate from rent. Is that okay?" "Oh yes, perfect. Thanks so much." "Then if you're ready to go I'll take you back to the motel. Do you still have some money, Barbara? "Yes, I do. Thanks for asking. The bank account information that I gave you is active. I've tried to leave Twenty-Five Dollars in it so it wouldn't incur costs or be closed. I opened it when I first moved here as I was waiting tables for a short time." "As you know, Lucy said, I can't transfer the funds to you until the child is born and the last paper is signed. I can, however, advance you some funds if you need it." "No, she said, I'm fine. The motel room has a kitchenette and Fr. Dan took me to buy some groceries, so I'd have enough to eat." "Ok, that's a good thing. Let's go then."

Aunty called me after she dropped Barbara off at the motel. "I think it went well, Daniel. We'll see if the application is approved and go from there. I can't think of any reason why it wouldn't be accepted. I've found 3 apartments near that campus that are all in good areas. So now we just wait." "Thank you for everything, Aunty. This was my first real mission as a priest and I'm feeling rather good about the outcome." "As well you should, she said. You were so helpful to that young woman. She really is quite lovely. I think she doesn't read very well and wondered if perhaps she needed glasses." "No, she told me she has dyslexia, and it takes her a bit to read it and then absorb the meaning." "Okay, well that makes perfect sense, she said. Thank you again Daniel for all your help."

# A New Family Member

"David, said Alicia, I don't want to go into a tailspin buying things and putting a nursery together until I feel positive about the outcome." "I agree, honey, but we need to get things in order. We can use the sitting room for a nursery for the time being and then figure out what to do as we go forward. I do think that we need to order furniture and think about clothing, don't you?" "Yes, of course. I'm just so frightened that something will go wrong." "It won't, honey. It is all going to be wonderful, he said. I'm sure of it."

A couple of hours later Alicia asked David about going to the baby furniture store to see what they have. "A great idea! Let's meet after we clean up from lunch. That should give us plenty of time before we start prepping for dinner." David was so glad that she had thought about it and decided to start getting ready. He was just sure everything was going to be okay. They cleaned up from the lunch serving and headed to town. They found a beautiful crib that would convert to a youth bed, a matching dresser, chest of drawers and small armoire (but wait, Gramps and Dad made all this furniture for us, and it is stored in the attic at the house). They got a changing table, a bassinette, a rocking chair, and lots of accessories. They told them to hold the items until they called and then deliver them. We then went to the local children's shop and bought everything we could think of in unisex colors and patterns in both newborn and 3-month sizes. We ordered diaper service and told them we would call them with a start date. There! That should take care of this baby that was moving into their lives very soon.

David called Daniel when they got home to see if he had heard anything new. "No, said Daniel, Barbara has been calling me daily to let me know how she is doing. I've told her when she is ready, I'll come and take her to the hospital. Between Debra's adoption paperwork and Aunty's support in getting everything in place the hospital has come on board without a problem. The doctor that works at the free clinic is also on-staff at the hospital which just eliminated any problems arising there. He has been paid his normal fee and will continue to see her at the clinic and then attend at delivery. Also, the school in Des Plaines has accepted her enrollment application and Aunty has secured a 1-bedroom, furnished apartment about 3 blocks from the campus. I assume that Aunty brought you both up to speed with what all would be done for her?" "Yes, she called us, and we very much appreciated and agreed with all her decisions. She said *that the young lady seemed pleased and appreciative as well." "Yes, Daniel said, absolutely. She had no idea that she* would receive this kind of assistance. The young man gave her $350 for the abortion and $50 for a bus ticket. She had been waiting tables in West Tisbury from the time she arrived here, so she added that money to her bank account and that is how she has been managing on her own. Aunty said that she still had $25 in the account, so it was beginning to look bleak for her." "Dear Lord, said David, I can't even begin to imagine what she has gone through." "Nor can I, Daniel replied, nor can I."

## *Meanwhile In Boston*

I received a call early this morning from the D.A.'s office asking me to come in and interview for a ground-level position that was opening up. I took the information and readied myself for the interview. The same lady that had taken my information for the temporary job greeted me and escorted me to the office of the Assistant District Attorney. She introduced us and took her leave. The Assistant D.A. came right to the point saying that they were extremely impressed with my school grades, my scores from the board and the letter that I had sent with my credentials. I thanked her and inquired further about the position that was available. "Well, she said, when we bring a new lawyer into our fold, we make sure that they get as much education as possible about what we do. You would do extensive research, acting primarily in the capacity of a paralegal. We normally have our new staff member work for at least six to twelve months in that capacity before reviewing their qualifications and skills for going forward with our office. We have an annual starting salary of $55,000 plus health insurance benefits. We are prepared to offer you this position immediately. Do you have any questions?" "No, I don't believe I have any questions for you. I would like to thank you for your time and taking this interest in my application. I believe I'll take my qualifications and skills elsewhere. Thank you." And with that, I left. I walked out of the building with my head held high, feeling good about my decision. I drove home, went in search of my neighbor to see if I could buy him dinner, and went home to find something more comfortable to wear for my dinner date. My date came to my door about 40 minutes later looking dapper and ready to go out on the town. We chatted while we were walking to the café. We shared a delightful dinner, split a dessert, and got a cab to take us home. "I wanted you to know that I'll be moving back to Edgartown and that my aunt and uncle will be putting the house on the market to sell. I hope that you'll call me and tell me you're going to come to Edgartown to see me. My brother and sister-in-law own an Inn and will always have room for you." With that I hugged him and bid him good night. It was close to 9pm but I knew aunty would still be awake, so I called. She answered right away saying, "Are you ok?" "Yes, I said, I'm fine. How are you?" "Oh, we're good. Just watching some silly program and waiting for you to call." I laughed and said, "Well, here I am. Aunty, could you take a couple more things onto your already very full plate?" "For you, anything. What's up?" "Well, I would like you to first direct a moving van to the Boston house so that I can oversee the shipping of the furnishings here. Next, I would appreciate your securing me an apartment, perhaps unfurnished so I can use some of the pieces here and then purchase whatever is needed beyond that, and next could you please put this mausoleum up for sale because I'm coming home. Aunty, are you crying? What's wrong? Are you okay?" "Oh, Debra, you're simply an answer to my prayers. I love you so very much and can't wait for you to get here. Are you sure you want to oversee the moving people?" "Yes, ma'am, I have a huge stake in the stuff that's here and I want it to arrive intact. Which brings me to the other question, arrive where?" "I'll worry about that, she said, while I have them on the phone making arrangements. I'll keep you posted. And, Debra, should I plan to move to the outer office?" "What, oh, well, no. Just wait until I get home and we'll walk through this. I love you. Goodnight." I hung up smiling to myself. Aunty and I would have a great time putting things together and hopefully this would take some of the burden off her. Afterall, she was going to need time to be grandma.

Aunty called early letting me know the schedule for the moving van. They would come to the house in a team to pack up all the dishes, flatware, kitchen, linens, and other breakables first. They would send one truck to load the items that I wanted for my apartment or to go to the Inn and another van that would load up items for storage. Aunty told me if there were items to go to charity to mark them accordingly and we'd deal with them later. The packing team was arriving at 8am on Thursday which was just two days from now. This woman doesn't mess around! I grabbed some toast and jam and got a pad of sticky notes to start marking things. I knew that I wanted the bedroom suite from the room that I was sleeping in. It had been my dad's room when he lived at home. Gramps had made the furniture and it was solid looking, but not masculine. It was perfect. I marked all the linen for that room and the bathroom for my van as well. I went downstairs and marked the tallboy in the foyer to go with me. I didn't know yet what I would store in it, I only knew that I couldn't part with it. I looked at the dining room furniture and thought my heart would break. It was much too much for me and the Inn already had a beautiful set. Granny was so proud of her dining set and the buffet was full of her treasures; some of which my mom had given her as gifts over the short years they spent together. I called Alicia and David to see if there was a chance that they could squeeze the buffet and its contents into their place. Also, all the linen from the guest rooms and kitchen. No hesitation from those two. "You bet, they said! Consider it done." I called Daniel and asked him if there were any pieces he would like for the cottage or the church basement. After a few minutes of thought he named off the dining room set, the chairs from the den and the bedroom suite from the grandparents' room. "I had chosen a bed, but I'll cancel it. I would be honored to have our grandparent's bedroom suite as my own. The comfy chairs and dining room furniture I'll put in the church basement. Aunty will need to mark those as charity items." I marked the items for Daniel and for David. I included the linen from the grandparents' room for Daniel as well. The kitchen was going in my van and there was a Queen Anne divan and chairs in the formal living room that I also wanted. I went through all the bathroom linen closets and butler's pantry to see if there was anything tattered or soiled that needed to be discarded. Nope. Not in my granny's house. Well, I think I'm ready for the packing people. I'm glad they're doing it because it is a big job.

The doorbell rang and I went to see who was calling. Harold was standing on my stoop with a beautiful bouquet of flowers and a big smile on his face. "Debra, I just felt you were busy getting ready to leave and I didn't want to miss seeing you one more time." "Well, come in Harold, and we'll make some coffee or tea and visit for a while." We made a fresh pot of coffee and I put some cookies out to go with it. "I hope, I said, that you'll come and visit us in Edgartown. The whole family adores you and we don't want to lose touch." "Well, I'll just have to plan a visit then. Listen, I know you're very busy, but I was wondering if you could help me with my will before you leave? I have one, but it is old, and it needs to be updated." "Of course. After you finish your coffee go and get it and I'll have a look at it later and make some notes. Can you join me for breakfast in the morning and we'll make the changes you want and get it finalized?" "Oh, Debra, that would be perfect, he said. Thank you so much."

Harold went and got his will and brought it back to me. He had some notes on it which would help me sift through it. We agreed on 9am tomorrow morning for breakfast burritos which I would have the neighborhood Mexican restaurant make up and deliver. I continued my journey through the house and decided that I should go check the shed and the garage and see if there were things there that needed to be kept in the family. I found the keys to the shed and was remembering that I used to follow gramps out there when I was little. All his tools! These all needed to go to David. I went out to the garage and I felt my breath catch as I opened the doors. Granny's car was sitting there. All the yard tools were lined against the far wall. I needed to call Aunty to see how she wanted to handle these items. She said that she had totally forgotten about granny's car and would have to figure that one out. "I really think that all the tools and yard tools should go to the Inn. There is plenty of room in the coach house for those items and in time David will find them useful I'm sure, she said." I told her I would earmark the tools for the van and then secure the garage and retain the keys until she had a decision. "I've got my van about full. I'm not certain that we can get all of Daniel's and David's items into the van with my things. We may need another truck." "Do you just want to relocate the house to Edgartown, sweetheart, Aunty asked?" I laughed, but it was a consideration. "Aunty, do I have an apartment yet or have you had time to look?" "Well, my darling, I went on a tour with our agent and I didn't like any of the condos. They are too small and way too many people around you. You would be screaming for privacy. I did, however, find the perfect house and I think you'll love it. It is within walking distance to the village on a quiet lane. It has 3 bedrooms and 3-1/2 baths and is 2100 square feet which should work perfectly for you. You need to accommodate house guests as well as the possibility of growth in the future. It has the perfect kitchen for someone that doesn't cook at all. The upstairs has a beautiful room that would serve as an office or you could convert the downstairs guest room into your office. Are you taking gramp's desk?" "Oh, my goodness, the desk! I need to mark it! Thank you, Aunty for remembering. I agree about the too many people. Go ahead with this house. It sounds perfect. I've captured quite a bit of stuff from here that I want so I need the space." "Done. When will you be here?" "Well, the packers arrive Thursday, the two vans on Friday, and I'll plan to follow them and be home on Friday evening. Do you think the two vans will be enough?" "No, I ordered a third, but it will be half the size. We'll use it for the storage items. Can't wait to see you. Safe travels. We love you."

# *Father Dan*

Daniel was working in his office when his personal cell rang. He saw that it was Barbara calling and hoped everything was alright. "Hello, how are you, he asked?" "Fr. Dan, I need to go to the hospital now. My water broke and the pains are about 10 minutes apart." "I'm on my way. Stay put." He was out the door and headed toward her in a flash. Luckily, she was about 5 minutes from him, and they were about another 5 minutes from the hospital. He arrived at the motel and pounded on her door. She had her overnight case and was ready. He could tell that the pains were coming closer together. Dear Lord, please let us get to the hospital on time. "We will be there in a minute. Just hold on, he told her." They arrived at the hospital and the nurse came out with a wheelchair. "We've got her, she said." He squeezed her hand and told her he'd be in the waiting room. He walked outside so he could phone aunty without being overheard. "Aunty, we are at the hospital. She's in hard labor so I don't think it will be long. What do we do now, he asked?" "I'll let David and Alicia know but the plan is that the baby will be held for an additional day following Barbara's release. That will give us the time needed to get her on a bus before your brother picks up the baby. Stay in touch, please." "Will do, he said."

He paced, he prayed, and he paced some more. It seemed an eternity, it was less than two hours. The doctor from the free clinic came to the waiting room to let him know that Barbara was doing fine and that she had delivered an 8-pound 14-ounce screaming baby girl. "They are both doing fine. We have, of course, separated the baby from the mother. Do you wish to see either of them?" "yes, both please."

The doctor told him to follow him to where Barbara was being held. "She came through this like a champ. No problems at all. We will release her in the morning. Will you be picking her up or someone else?" "Either I will, or Mrs. Adler that is handling the adoption will. I'm not sure which." Daniel went in to see Barbara. She looked exceptionally beautiful. She is a pretty girl anyway, but right now she was glowing. "How are you, I asked?" "I'm fine, Fr. Dan. Thank you for staying with me. The doctor says that the baby is healthy and that is a huge burden off me. I know that she will be a blessing to her new family. I'm to be released in the morning by 10am. Is there a chance that I could get a bus tomorrow and be on my way?" "Yes, of course. I'll call Mrs. Adler to take care of the arrangements. Is there anything else we can do for you?" "No, I'll be fine, Fr. Dan. I'm not at all sad about giving the child up for adoption because I never wanted it to begin with. I hope that doesn't sound too harsh, but it is true." "No, I believe I understand your reasons, he said." They prayed together and he told her that he'd see her in the morning. He walked back down the hall to find the doctor so he could see the baby. The nurse took him to the nursery area and brought the baby to the window so he could get a glimpse of her. She was beautiful! She had a head full of strawberry blond curls, fair skin, and was perfect. He would have sworn that she opened her eyes and looked at him but of course, she was too young for such a thing. He thanked the nurse and started for his car. He discovered that the tears were streaming down his face. My niece, he thought, that was my beautiful little niece. He called aunty who was at David and Alicia's and put the call on speaker. He brought them up to date and knew that they were so relieved and excited. "Have you chosen a name, he asked?" David replied, "Yes, we have. Her name is Amanda Kay Donaldson."

# David's Tribute To His Mother

Alicia and I met Aunty, Uncy, and Daniel at the hospital 24 hours after Barbara's release not fully knowing what to expect. The doctor came out to greet us and asked that we join him in the conference room down the hall. We were so nervous; scared. Had something happened? Had she backed out? Was the baby ill? Daniel introduced everyone to the doctor, and he apologized for causing any upset. "Everything is fine, he said. Barbara was released yesterday, as you know, and she is on her way to her new life. The baby is a big, fat bouncing baby girl who likes to scream until someone picks her up. Good luck with that." Everyone laughed at the thought with memories of Debra's first months on earth. "The head nurse and I, he said, thought that Mr. and Mrs. Donaldson might like a quick 24-hour training session inasmuch as you don't have other children to lend you prior experience." "I think that is an excellent idea, said Alicia. I babysat a lot during my teenage years but certainly am out of practice." "Well, he said, if you all would like to meet your baby girl the nurse has her in a private room off the general nursery." We were all a bit shaky, but we walked together to just outside the room. Aunty told David and Alicia to go ahead and they would meet her after they had a few minutes of time alone with her." Alicia was crying softly, and I was trying to hold back the tears. The nurse opened the door with a big smile on her face and took us to a big, overstuffed chair next to a rolling bassinette. The nurse lifted our daughter out and handed her to Alicia. She was without a doubt, the most beautiful child we had ever seen. She snuzzled into Alicia's arms as if that were exactly where she belonged. She had beautiful dark strawberry blond curls, very milky fair complexion, and great big eyes that were so dark you just knew they were going to turn brown like her namesake. Alicia handed her to me, and she stared at me for a moment before getting comfortable. She was so warm and comforting. The nurse told us that she would be available for the rest of the day if we could stay and work with her. "Yes, we both echoed. Thank you so much." Alicia told me to go get the parents so they could meet their granddaughter. I stepped out of the room to tell Aunty and Uncy to come and meet their granddaughter. They were both looking very emotional as they came into the room. Alicia got up so they could sit in the big chair and hold her. The nurse couldn't help grinning as she watched all of them dote on this child. What a lucky baby girl this was to have gotten this family to raise her. Daniel came in and acquainted himself with his niece. He also blessed the family and this child, and we all prayed together as a family asking for God's guidance and love. Alicia told her parents and Daniel that they were spending the rest of the day at the hospital. Everyone took turns saying goodbye to little Amanda. The nurse briefed us on what they needed to accomplish by the end of the day. They learned to feed her, change her, rock her, swaddle her, and were told all the problems that might occur, so they'd be watchful. "Did you purchase a bassinette, the nurse asked?" We told her we had. "Well, plan to keep her in your room for the first 3 months. You'll hear her every movement which is important. If you have questions or fears, all you need to do is call the direct number to the nursery and one of us will help you." The nurse gave us several pamphlets to read through while she got things ready. We both bathed baby Amanda, and took turns feeding her, burping her, and rocking her. We learned quickly that you didn't have to strain to hear her if she wanted something. My word but that child can scream! Amanda did not like being swaddled at all. She resisted with every ounce of her being and screamed bloody murder until her arms were free. We looked at one another and laughed again reminded of Debra as a baby. This is just very strange. It really did feel that this child was a perfect fit for our family.

We finished up our crash course at just before 10pm. We were instructed to pick the baby up by 10am tomorrow morning. We were to arrive with a bottle for her to travel with, clothing to be dressed in, and the proper type of car seat for her to ride in. We went home feeling exhausted but exhilarated. We were parents! We were so excited that we could hardly sleep at all. We hadn't even worried about the Inn and our guest. We had asked one of Alicia's girlfriends to come and watch the Inn, along with Mary, for at least 10 days while we acquainted ourselves with our new routine. She was sleeping at home but was on-site from 5am to 10pm daily. Mary was available to help after hours if needed.

We were up at the crack of dawn, had coffee and a pastry and headed to the hospital. We were standing outside the nursery window at 6am when they pulled back their drapes. The head nurse, Mrs. Griffin, was there and laughed when she saw us. She signaled that she'd be with us in a moment. She came to the door to let us in. She pointed to the bassinette telling us to ready our daughter for travel and she left. We were kind of nervous but more excited. She was screaming until we peeked over the side and then she just stopped and kind of stared at us. We picked her up and cuddled for a few minutes before changing her and getting her dressed to go home. She was all set, and the nurse came to push Baby Amanda and Alicia in a wheelchair to the front of the hospital. I went and got the car to get them loaded. The nurse helped us to place her in the car seat so that we were totally comfortable with how it worked. Alicia sat in the back with the baby and I drove about 3 miles per hour home. We arrived at the Inn and were greeted by Alicia's friend, Julie. The guests that were up all gathered around us to meet the baby. We excused ourselves and headed for our quarters so she would have a chance to get familiar with her surroundings. Alicia had hung a beautiful musical chime above the bassinette for Amanda to listen to. It was such a comforting sound that we just knew she'd love it. It created shadows on the ceiling which seemed to fascinate her. I had been worried that it would frighten her, but not this child. She had taken a little bit of formula on the ride home and now was content to rest. We changed into some comfy clothes and Alicia snuck out of the room to go fix us an omelet. We were both starved. I read through some of the pamphlets that the nurse had given us and then set about reading through the family history that Barbara had supplied Aunty with. She was an only child born to Irish parents in the lower east side of Boston. Both were factory workers and neither one had graduated from high school. Both, it seemed, had a drinking problem but neither one had ever been arrested or incarcerated for any drug or alcohol offense. Barbara's grandparents, on both sides, were deceased by the time she was born. Her parents had not been helpful in answering any questions that she may have had. Barbara's boyfriend, the child's biological father, was a resident of West Tisbury. His father's family went back several generations in the community. His mother's family had come from Edgartown. His maternal grandmother was from a family that was well-known, and his grandfather's family was still active in the community and, we knew him. I would discuss this with Aunty and Debra when she gets here.

Alicia came in with our breakfast and we both ate hungrily. Just as I was drinking the last of my coffee the baby woke up. Alicia got to her before the screaming started and fed and rocked her. She was soaked through, so we gave her a warm bath and got her fresh clothing. "I think we need to double that diaper David. What do you think?" "Yes, I said, I quite agree. Also, perhaps we need to be sure the rubber pant that fits over is sitting correctly." "Yes, Alicia said, we need to be sure this child is covered correctly." Alicia and I called the parents to see if they wanted to come and bond with their grandchild. They said they were right around the corner and would be there in two minutes. I was sure they were kidding but apparently not as they were in the foyer. Too funny. They stayed and rocked and talked with Baby Amanda for about an hour. They brought clothing, toys, mobiles, bottles, formula, and who knows what else. They were simply over the moon over their granddaughter. I went and fixed us some lunch and we ate while the baby slept. We were told she would sleep about 20 out of every 24 hours for the first month or so. We'll see. I took our dishes back to the kitchen and was cleaning up when I heard Baby Amanda screaming. I ran back to our quarters in time to see Alicia picking her up at which point she ceased screaming. "Do you think something is poking her, or scaring her and that is why she screams?" "No, I said,

I don't. I think somehow that Debra has overtaken this child's body. Don't you remember? That's exactly the way Debra acted for the first 3 or 4 months of her life. We all thought we'd go nuts. Worse, she hated mom and dad. She glared at them like they had 7 heads." "Oh, she said, I guess I do recall some of that. Oh dear, I hope she doesn't treat us like that. She seems to like us already." "Yes, don't worry, I said. It is obvious that she already adores you the same as I do."

# *Debra's Headed Home*

The packing people arrived at the stroke of 8am just as promised. There were 10 of them and they disbursed locusts with boxes and tape in hand. The person in charge of them told me he had been assured that I had everything clearly marked. "I do, I said. I don't think there will be any confusion there. Will you complete this task today?" "Yes, yes, of course, he said. We should be done no later than 2pm." "And how many people, I asked, will accompany the truck drivers to help load?" "Each truck will have a driver and a helper. Rather than having people running over the top of one another, the front truck will be the one designated for your items. The other two drivers and helpers will assist with loading that truck and then they will do the truck for Fr. Daniel Donaldson and Mr. and Mrs. David Donaldson. The third truck is considerably smaller, and they will load all the items marked for charity into that van which should completely empty this house of any contents. At that time, all trucks will embark on their journey to Edgartown. We will arrive at 8am on Friday and will be on the road no later than 2pm so we can make the 5pm ferry. We will not deliver until Saturday. The crew of packers will meet up with the trucks on Saturday morning prior to deliveries. It will be late when we arrive, and our people will already have put in a long day. We will be at each location beginning at 8am on Saturday morning, the packers will unload boxes that house lamps and miscellaneous appliances and will be sure that all the other boxes are in the rooms that they belong in, and then leave on our journey back to Boston. Your aunt, I believe she is Mrs. Adler, has already paid for everything so the only loose end would be any gratuity that you might deem appropriate for the packers and the drivers and helpers." "Ok, I said, well thank you so much for going through the entire scenario with me. I will stay out of the way while you're all working." I went and called Aunty to ask how she wanted me to handle the tips needed for the packers today. "Do you have $1000 cash on you, she asked?" "No, do you, I replied? Sorry, I didn't mean to be flip. I guess I'd best hightail it to the bank and get some cash. ATMs won't give me that much at one time. I know that because I've tried in the past." I felt her smiling through the phone. "By the way, how is my mother's namesake?" "Oh, Debra, you are going to fall in love, she said." "Well, I can't wait to meet her. See you all Friday evening. Love you both."

I went to the bank, got the cash, stopped, and got me a pizza for dinner, and headed home. The packers were about two-thirds done with the job from what I could see. I must say, they don't mess around. They don't visit, except when they're on break, and they don't rest at all. Interesting. I did a walk-through to be sure that everything was packed and that nothing was left unattended. The head of the packers (I don't know why but I found that to be funny) came and announced that they were finished. I thanked each of them and gave them an envelope with a crisp $100 bill in it. I didn't tip the head packer as I didn't find it appropriate. He was in a supervisory position and I'm sure he's paid accordingly. I went in search of a bottle of white wine to go with my pizza and headed to the den so I could relax and watch TV until bedtime. I drank about half of the wine and ate all but two slices of the pizza. At this rate I'll be a butterball soon. I watched a movie and then most of the news before heading to bed. I have a ton of shopping I want to get done tomorrow before leaving Boston and heading home.

I was up early, grabbed breakfast and headed out to do the last-minute shopping and other tasks that needed to be attended to. I started at the mall. They have a wonderful baby shop and I think I bought most everything that was for a girl. They promised to wrap it all and have it ready when I returned just before 4pm. Next, I went to a boutique that I remembered granny saying that my mom just loved. I went in and looked around and could certainly see why she had loved it. They had a beautiful array of clothing for most every occasion and every figure. The sales lady came over and introduced herself and started a room for me. I told her that I wanted 3 spring/summer dresses suitable for the office and perhaps either blazers or cardigans to go with each one. I also requested 3 business suits in black, charcoal and navy, either two piece or three piece and 6 blouses that could be used with any of them. She started pulling those items and I tried on what she brought me. The dresses were so cute and comfy that I told her I would like her to find 3 more of them. They have a shoe department in the boutique, and she found me 6 pairs of two-inch pumps or sandals that would work with any or all the outfits. When I finished trying on everything, I asked her if she would be able to double the order for fall/winter attire and ship that order to me. "Certainly, she said, I'll be happy to. May I inquire where the order is to be shipped to?" "Of course, I said, and gave her the address." "Miss Donaldson, are you by any chance, she asked, related to Lorraine or Amanda Donaldson?" I smiled before responding and said, "Yes, Lorraine was my grandmother and Amanda my mom. Did you know them?" "Yes, she said. I own this boutique and have for more than 35 years. Your grandmother used my services over most of those years and your mother for several before she passed. I'm sorry. I didn't mean to bring that up." "No, no, I said, it is fine. It was a long time ago and I was very small, but I still have my memories and all of those that people continue to share with me. It actually makes my heart incredibly happy when she is remembered by someone." "Oh, Miss Donaldson, she said, your mother was a most gracious lady. She had impeccable taste and was such a pleasure to work with. She knew if I didn't have it that I would find it for her. Whenever I think of her, I always know how much I still miss her." I couldn't contain myself. I reached up and gave her a big hug and told her thank you for her kind words. I paid for the entire order and told her I would look forward to working with her in the future. I left feeling better than I'd felt in a very long time. I finished the rest of my errands and went and picked up all my baby gifts for my new niece and headed home. I was absolutely starving! I had forgotten to eat lunch and I'm sure

I was close to fainting. I packed everything into the trunk of the car and went in search of Harold. Surely, he would have dinner with me.

The trucks all arrived right on schedule and the loading began. It seemed like they were finished up in no time. I called Aunty to ask if she'd decided about Granny's car. She said she hadn't and just to be sure the coach house was locked up tight and that the outside lights were all in working order. I told her that Harold was going to keep watch until it sells. "Remind me, she said, to send him a nice gift certificate or something useful like that as a thank you." I assured her that I would remind her. "Ok, I said, I'll be right behind the vans headed home. See you tonight. I love you both."

I went to check on the person who appeared to be in charge and he assured me that they were doing a walk through now to ensure that nothing was missed. "We will be ready to pull out within the hour, he said." I reminded him that I would be following them and asked if he needed any of the addresses for deliveries or directions. I also reminded him that either my aunt or uncle would be at my house, my brother and sister-in-law at the Inn and my brother at the cottage behind the Catholic church. "Yes, thank you for the reminder and no, ma'am, he said, we have all we need." Ma'am? Who does he think he is?

I went out to check on the coach house to be sure it was locked. I checked all the outside lights and called Harold to tell him goodbye. I put the last of my personal stuff in my car and was ready to pull out following the final van. We were right on schedule and it should be an easy ride to the ferry docks. The traffic was minimal at that time in the afternoon and the trip went very nicely. We arrived about 40 minutes before the ferry would arrive. I got my ticket, parked, and walked over to the café to get a snack. A couple of the drivers came in to do the same. I selected a black coffee and a Persian pastry and headed back to the car. I sifted through emails and text messages and before I knew it the ferry arrived. Within 15 minutes we were loaded and on our way home. I sent a message to aunty to double check the best way to my house and she texted me right back with the directions. I had already decided that I would take the lead to my house.

There was a wreck on the highway going into town which is always upsetting to me. ***Too many memories***. I followed the directions that aunty gave me, and the truck stayed right behind me. All the lights were on and welcoming as we drove onto the most beautiful circular driveway I'd ever seen. Oh, Aunty, I thought to myself, you did a great job! Both Aunty and Uncy were waiting in the doorway for me. I was so happy to see their smiling faces and get the best hugs and kisses ever. They are absolutely wonderful people and I love them dearly. Aunty took control of the driver and where things were to be taken to. I went with Uncy to do a walkthrough. "Oh, Uncy, I said, it is simply magnificent." "Yes, he said, I absolutely agree. Your aunt decided only the best for her baby girl." Each room was flooded with natural sunlight through beautiful windows that were trimmed in black. The window in the dining room was a work of art. It was a total of three windows with stained glass transoms above each of the three windows. The window at the far end of the living room literally took my breath away. It went floor to ceiling about 12-feet wide and the window created a circular effect with 4 columns running vertically the length of the window. But the star of the show was the master suite. The headboard for my bed that I had brought with me was a ceiling to floor window that looked as if it had been cut out of the wall in a pattern of vertical ribbons. Exquisite! I believe I was drooling by the time I finished my tour. Uncy just laughed and hugged me and said, "Your aunt has wonderful taste when it comes to spending money." "Well, hallelujah, I said!" Within 3 hours the movers had everything in place and the packers had shown up on schedule to unpack everything that they could. Aunty had an envelope for the drivers and the packers along with her thanks. She phoned David and Alicia to be sure their truck had arrived and that those pieces were in place. David assured her that they were. She then phoned Daniel who was whooping and hollering so apparently his had arrived safely as well. His contractors were awfully close to being finished with his restoration and I'm sure he was anxious to move in. Uncy asked if I was ready to head to their house to stay until she had everything in its place. "Yes, I replied, I'm ready, hungry, and tired. But first I have to stop at the Inn to meet my niece and unload my car." Uncy was laughing at the thought. I'm sure he figured that there was a boatload of stuff for that baby girl. They headed home and I headed to the Inn.

I got to the Inn and went in search of David and Alicia. I found all three of them in the kitchen where they were cleaning up from the dinner hour. Mary was helping clean and came to give me a hug. Alicia handed baby Amanda to me and I just melted. She is the most beautiful child I've ever seen. She seemed content for me to hold her, so I dispatched David to go get everything out of my trunk. He just laughed and went about his task. I caught up with how Alicia was feeling, how the baby was doing, and so on. They seemed to have settled in very quickly. I think they were meant for this role as parents. David came back in laughing and trying to balance all the packages that he'd gotten out of the car. "Did you buy the store, Debra, he asked?" "Pretty much, I said. I was sure that she was running around naked and had nothing to play with, so I had to take charge." Alicia started opening all the presents and they both exclaimed joy over each of the items. Alicia said, "Debra, she won't need clothes until she starts school!" "That was the general idea, I said. Ok, well, here is your daughter. I must run. I'm tired and I need to get to the parents before they lock me out. I'll see you all tomorrow. You simply must come and see my house! It is magnificent!" With that I was out the door and headed home.

I drove up to the house and Daniel came out to greet me. It was so good to see him! I love him so much and he just makes every one of my days brighter. He helped unload the car and we went in to pester the parents. Aunty had coffee and pie and goodies or sandwich stuff whichever I was wanting. Hello! I'll just eat it all! I made myself a sandwich, grabbed some of the chips before Daniel ate them all and then a piece of Cherry Pie ala Mode. Yum. The parents caught me up on what was going on in town and with them. I told them that I wanted to go over to my house early tomorrow morning and put things away and get a feel for where I was living. Daniel asked if he could go with me? "Will you help or just supervise, I asked?" "No, I'll help. I know stuff, he said." I just rolled my eyes at him and told him fine. "Aunty, would we be able to go to your office on Sunday after church?" "Yes, of course. But, Debra, she said, it isn't my office. It's our office." "Well, I said, we'll see. I have some ideas and I'm not sure how they are all going to play out yet. Let's just do a look-see for now. Uncy, you have a birthday coming up in the next couple of weeks. A rather important one. I believe that 75 is looking you in the face. Have you decided what you would like to do to celebrate?" "Well, my darling baby girl, I have not. 75 is not in the least of any importance to me. If your aunt were to say, "let's go away" then I would give that some consideration. "Well, Aunty said, let's go away!" "Oh, he said, well alright then. Where do you want to go and how long do you want to be gone?" "I'm uncertain about that at this second, she said, but I'll get back to you shortly. I am considering a cruise out of Florida to the West or Southern Caribbean. Perhaps a 5-day or 8-day cruise. Then we could come home and party with all of our children and granddaughter." "Ok, if that is what you would like to do, he said, then please make the reservations and pack my suitcase. Call me when you're ready to go." Daniel and I just stared at them. "Really, I said, you're going on a cruise?" "Yes, Aunty said, I believe we are!"

I woke early and Daniel and I headed over to my house to unpack and try to find a place for everything. We stopped at a diner downtown and had breakfast before starting in on our chore. The packers had done a good job of unpacking what they could and putting boxes where they belonged. Daniel started on linens for kitchen, bathroom, and bedrooms. I started on the kitchen items. There were lots of cabinetry in the kitchen and a walk-in pantry. I placed all the kitchen gadgets in the pantry rather than on the countertop. I don't personally use them, but they looked nice. I got the cookware stored away in the island which also housed the gas cooktop. By noon we had most of the miscellaneous boxes unpacked and put away. Daniel went and got us deli sandwiches and cold milk for our lunch. I'll grocery shop later today and stock the cupboards, fridge and freezer. We ate our sandwiches and visited about the adoption and Daniel's involvement with the young woman. "I'm a little concerned, he said, that some of the biological father's family are still very active in the community.

It's a small town and we have our share of gossips. The addition of a baby in David's home when everyone is aware that she wasn't pregnant, and the absence of his very pregnant girlfriend might give cause for speculation. I guess we'll just pray that this isn't the case. If it is, we'll deal with it." "Wow, I wasn't aware of this. It is rather unnerving, I said." "I agree, said Daniel."

We got the beds made, the bathrooms put together, the kitchen was done as was the living room. The tallboy fit into my foyer as if it were made for it. I still don't know what will go in there, but I'll know it when I find it. I asked Daniel what he was doing for dinner? "I don't have plans, he said, but it needs to be an early night so I can review my sermon for morning mass. Why, what do you want to do?" "I thought perhaps we could go get dinner by the pier and then take a walk before calling it an evening." "Oh, well that sounds perfect, he replied. Did you have a place in mind?" "The Seafood Shanty. Do you think we can get in without a reservation?" "I don't know. Let me give them a quick call and find out how busy they are. Done. Go change clothes and do something with your hair. I'm not taking a rag-a-muffin to dinner." "You can be so rude for a young punk priest, I said." He went to wash up and I went to clean up. We had a marvelous dinner and a very enjoyable walk. It was quite lovely to be able to simply stroll from my house to downtown. Aunty had done her job! A couple of my new neighbors were on their porch when we strolled by. They waved and we stood at the fence to introduce ourselves. They were so welcoming and lovely folks. This was going to be a wonderful place to live.

Sunday mass was beautiful, and it made my heart happy like always. The parents and I went for lunch following the service and then to the office. Aunty had some things to attend to and I was looking around at the office and the way it was laid out when Uncy asked me, "What are looking for Debra? Can I help?" I told him that I really didn't know what I was looking for. "I keep going back and forth with what I want to do, I told him. I thought about applying to the D.A.s office here but I don't think I'm a good fit for that. I thought about hanging out my shingle as a Criminal Defense Attorney but

I'm still on the fence about that one too. I know that I don't want to do the DUIs and ambulance chasers. I believe that I'm trying to find a way to combine Estate Planning, Public Interest, Real Estate and Bankruptcy law all practiced out of one office. I have the credentials and the license appropriate for any or all the above." "I don't know a lot about all of this, David said, but my head tells me that this might be too much. What about Estate Planning and Real Estate law to start with and see where that takes you? I've heard scuttlebutt about Public Interest law, and I believe a great deal of it ends up pro-bono." "Yes, I believe you are right about that. I wish that Uncle Judge Henry were still alive. He was such a valuable commodity to all of us." "Yes, I agree. Your mom adored him and he her. Well, what do you think?" "I think you are correct. I believe that there is a correlation between the two that will work nicely in this community. Do you know anyone that makes signs?" He hugged her and told her he was sure they could find someone to handle that task.

Aunty joined them and they brought her up to speed. She seemed pleased with my ideas for launching a career here in Edgartown. "Debra, how much staff are you going to be hiring, she asked?" "What? Oh, I thought between you and me we could handle it. Is that not going to work?" "No, she said, it won't. I want to retire. I want to travel. I want to be grandma. I don't want to be a paralegal or an administrative assistant. I've been those things. I'm 67 years old. I want to do something fun." "Oh, I said. I see. Well, in that case then I would say a paralegal and a receptionist. Will that work?" "Yes, I think that is perfect, she said. I've already instructed Patrolman James to move out of the office and he's pretty much out from what I can see. David, we need to paint and lay new flooring. The bathrooms need to be brought up a bit too. I really think that the conference room could be walled in half and the new space would work for your paralegal. What do you think?" "I think, David said, that I'd best get to work so this will be done before our cruise ship leaves port." I went to look at the conference room and her idea seemed sound. I wanted to rearrange my office so I was glad we were painting because that would be the perfect time to orchestrate that matter. I made note to call the local temp agency in the morning and see if they had any candidates for full time employment. "What do you say to swinging by the Inn to say hello and then going out to dinner? Did you already have dinner plans, Aunty?" "Nope, I think that sounds wonderful, she said."

I called Daniel when we got to the car and asked if he could meet us for dinner. "Yes, he said, that will be fine. Any thoughts where we're going?" "Yes, the Seafood Shack. I love that place. I'll call you when we head that way." We had about an hour or so to visit with baby Amanda which would free Alicia and David up to wait on their guest. They had such a cute little contraption that they affixed on themselves to pack the baby around with them. They all looked very content with one another. Aunty was over the moon for the baby. She and Uncy had hoped to be grandparents and it seemed all their dreams were coming true. I looked at the pair of them and thought them both to be in good health. I simply didn't know how I could survive without them. I reminded myself though that they were 67 and soon to be 75 years young and we needed to take some of the burden off them. I called Daniel back and asked if his remodel was done or close to being finished? "Yes, he said, he has another day or two at the most and I'm ready to move in. Why?" "I think we should inquire whether he could redo the office bathrooms, build a half wall in the conference room, paint the interior, and lay new flooring. Aunty has assigned Uncy to do this, but I think it's way too much for him. What do you think?" "I absolutely agree! I will call Steve right now and give him the head's up. Thanks for thinking of this, he said."

Monday morning came quickly, and I headed to the office to see what I could do about a staff. Steve, the contractor, had already called me and said he would put his other crew on the office today if that worked for me. I told him I'd meet him there. I called the temp agency to see if they could help me out. "We have a lovely lady that would suit your needs for a receptionist and is more than capable of handling secretarial duties as well, she said. We don't have a paralegal, but I'll call over to the courthouse and see what ideas they might have. I'll get back to you." The lady that she was sending me for the receptionist position would come to the office on Friday to apply and interview. The contractor said he'd be done by Thursday afternoon. They had already torn the flooring up, had the bathrooms stripped out and had built the wall separating the conference room into two rooms. The carpet in that room was still like new so the workman asked how I wanted the conference room laid out and they set the whole thing up for me in a matter of minutes. There was my dad's desk that was stored in the back room along with a couple of his file cabinets and bookcases. I would have those moved into the new office for the paralegal. I called the sign maker, and he came by to gather the information and told me he's have the sign ready by Friday. I told him I wanted a font and color that would be easily read, and it was to simply read, "D.L Donaldson, Attorney at Law on the first line and then one pitch smaller that would read Estate Planning and Real Estate Law". I walked over to City Hall and filled out my paperwork for the city license that I would need. I had already applied for an Employee Identification Number from IRS, so I think I was about set to open my doors. I walked over to the newspaper office and put in an ad with my name and credentials. I called the utilities and had them changed into my firm's name. I called Aunty with my concerns about having a bank account for my firm's needs. She said she had already called the bank president and that he'd be available whenever I made my way over to visit with him. I thanked her and then walked to the café on main street for a bite of lunch and then walked over to the bank. He acknowledged me as soon as I walked through the doors. We visited a little about the plans for my business and then he gave me the paperwork that I would need to fill out. He told me that I would need a business checking account, and a trust account for housing client deposits. He suggested that I might want a separate account for processing payroll and payroll taxes. He told me that he would order the check stock necessary for processing the three accounts. Aunty had already transferred one-hundred thousand dollars to my business account. I thanked him for his help and walked back to get the car. I just remembered I needed computers, printers, paper supplies, and everything else for running an office. I have my laptop, of course, but I wanted a desktop computer for the office. It was apparent from what was left in the office that Aunty had told Patrolman James to take everything with him for his new office. He was a thriving Private Eye and had two people working for him! My dad would have been so immensely proud. I got everything ordered and they set it up to be delivered Thursday afternoon. My cell was ringing, and I found that it was the lady from the temp agency. "I have found you a paralegal, she said. The courthouse has been using her as a temp while she finished up her schooling which she has now completed. She can interview on Friday, say two hours after your receptionist interview." "That's perfect, I told her." I found that I was positively exhausted, locked up and went home to sleep in my own house.

# A New Lawyer In Town

It seemed that it was only yesterday that I had hung up my shingle, but it has been three months! Aunty and Uncy are gone on their cruise, Daniel looks more priest-like daily, and David, Alicia and baby Amanda seemed very content. I was so lucky with the two ladies that the temp agency found me. Melinda, my receptionist, is a jewel. She is just 40 years old, single, has work ethics second only to my mother, and is fabulous at everything she is given to do. Tina Marie, my paralegal, is also fabulous. She is 22 years old, also single, and smart as a whip. I've asked whether she is considering continuing her education to be a lawyer, but she says no. She is quite happy editing my work. Since opening my doors, I've acquired a real estate firm that has commissioned me full time and taken on three new estate planning clients. When you add Brice and Bradley/Donaldson trusts to that we have a very full plate. I've been invited to David Donaldson's for dinner tonight. I have no idea why, but it is a free meal. I locked up and walked home so I could freshen up before heading to the Inn.

I noticed Daniel's car in the driveway when I got to the Inn so we're apparently having a sibling meeting of some sort. A very unusual situation for the Inn, they had no guests. Alicia had set the dining room table for dinner for the four of us. We offered to help but she said Mary already had everything done. She led us to the den to have cocktails and appetizers while we visited. Both appeared a little bit nervous. Finally, I could not stand it any longer and asked, "What is going on?" David took the lead and said, "We would have preferred that the parents be here also, but we'll just have to bring them up to speed when they return. Alicia has been so busy with baby Amanda and me with the Inn and the guests that we hadn't noticed any changes in our daily lives. Yesterday Alicia announced that she had a doctor's appointment and that baby Amanda, and I needed to go with her. It seems that sometimes when your mind is on something else you cease to worry about things that otherwise were consuming your life. Alicia is about 4-1/2 months pregnant, with twins. She hasn't been ill, she hasn't had any pain, and it appears that everything is going along quite nicely. We are a little bit nervous about having three children 8 months apart, but we are sure that we'll have lots of help for the next 20 or so years." Both Daniel and I just sat there staring at them. We did not say a word and neither of us had moved. Finally, David asked, "Did you guys hear what I said?" Daniel recovered first and went to hug his brother and sister-in-law. I followed suit, but still hadn't found my voice. Daniel asked, "what are you going to do with the Inn?" "Yes, I said, that is an excellent question?" "That's all you two can come up with, David laughed, after my news you're only concerned about the Inn?" "No!" We both said simultaneously. Alicia laughed until she cried. We finally found our brains and asked the appropriate questions. Alicia said, "In answer to your question, we've decided to eliminate the business and just use the house as a single-family dwelling. Do you think the entire family will be okay with that decision?" I told her that I didn't think it was any of the family's business one way or the other. "It's your house to do whatever you wish with." Baby Amanda was screaming because she was being ignored. I told Alicia that I couldn't imagine any child screaming like that. Everyone burst out laughing and I'm still unsure why.

David had made a huge pot of beef stew and Alicia had made her mom's wonderful biscuits to go with it. We all ate until we thought we'd bust and then all of us helped to clean up the kitchen. Alicia went to get Amanda ready for bed and we all had coffee and a liqueur while she took care of that. When she came back to the den, she asked me to walk upstairs with her. When we got to the top floor I was really taken back to another time. I had forgotten that a hallway between the rooms had been created and two extra baths to accommodate all the guest. Alicia thought that the front room could easily be converted into a master suite as there was a bath right next door to it. The other three rooms she thought could be one for Amanda and one for the twins. The third room could either be a playroom or a guest room. "What do you think?" "I think it is perfect." I hugged her and told her how happy we were for her. "Are you worried at all, I asked?" "I'm not, she said. I really believe that God has this wonderful plan for us and now we just need to relax and enjoy it. David will have to get a job to support our family but I'm hoping that he can wait at least one-year. Mary has agreed to stay on for at least another year as I'm going to need help." "Yes, you most assuredly are.

The parents got home, and David and Alicia shared their news. Alicia was already huge so there wasn't much need to tell them anything. The parents were over the moon with the news and incredibly supportive of the kid's decisions to shut down the business and convert the house to a single-family dwelling once again. Uncy reminded everyone that Amanda's grandparents had filled that house with children a long time ago. The contractors had already come and drawn up plans for the remodel. The quarters that were being used by David and Alicia at present would be converted back to a study. Alicia didn't want a live-in nanny but was very much in favor of a fulltime person during the day. She felt like Mary wasn't really ***that*** person. However, she didn't want anyone to help with the babies except David for the first year. "I want us to have a chance to bond with our three children before he looks for work and I look for someone to help me around the house." We all agreed with that decision.

# Perhaps A School

I was so grateful for Dinah. She kept the church office running like a well-oiled machine. Between us everything seemed to run smoothly. I had approached Bishop Cornell with the idea of a parochial school, and he was giving it consideration. There was plenty of land next to the church to construct a school. I was also working with the choir to have quarterly musicals and potlucks to inspire our congregation. It was a busy time, but I had never felt so complete. It was a blessing to be able to stop by the parents and visit or stop at the cemetery to shed necessary tears with my mom and dad, or to visit with my twin and his family or my baby sister. What more could I ask for?

It was a quiet afternoon when a burly man walked into the church. I was working at the altar changing out some plants when he arrived. I inquired whether I could help him with something, and he said he wanted to speak privately. "Well, there's nobody else in the church other than God and his saints, so this is about as private as we'll get, I said. What seems to be the problem?" "No problem, Father, just some questions, he said. My son knocked up a gal awhile back and it appears that she and the kid have left town. I wondered if you knew her whereabouts?" "Why would I know this woman's whereabouts, I asked?" "Because, Father, she came running to you when he threw her ass out." "First of all, I said, I would appreciate your keeping your language civilized in this place. Second, I have spoken to many people needing my help since I've been here, and none of them are any of your concern, sir." "Yeah, he said, well we'll just see about that." He started to come toward me, and something made him think again.

"You need to leave, sir. And in the future if you want to enter the Lord's house you will do so quietly and with respect. Otherwise, I will contact the local authorities to escort you off the property. Do we understand each other?" "Oh yeah, he said, we understand each other just fine. Just know that I'm not done with my questions and you'll be coughing up the answers." He started to turn to walk away but not before shaking his fist at me. I waited until he left the church and then I phoned my uncle. I told Uncy what had transpired and asked if he had any suggestions. "Are you okay, he asked." "Certainly, I said. I was ready to knock him on his backside if he came any closer." Uncy laughed at that and then said he would phone the precinct and they would dispatch someone to the church. "I will be there shortly, he said." Uncy and the police showed up at about the same time. I gave them the gentleman's name and told them what had transpired. I also told them that he had, in fact, threatened me and that I was concerned for my own safety and the safety of my secretary and my parishioners. The policeman told me that they would be paying the gentleman a visit and that they had already filled out the paperwork to be signed for him to stay clear of me and the church. "Thank you, I said. I'm not necessarily afraid of him, but I don't trust him at all. I'm uncertain what he wants but I'm sure he means to make trouble if possible." The policeman said that a patrol car would come by the church every 15 minutes day and night and if they saw anything that seemed inappropriate, they would be on it. "If you get any phone calls, or messages of any kind from him, please let us know immediately, he said." Uncy and I walked back to my office to continue our conversation. "Daniel, Uncy said, this is not to be taken lightly. I realize that you and your siblings are all black belts in Karate and are all excellent shots with both pistols and rifles, but that is when you're in control of the situation. We are not in control of this asshole." "I agree Uncy. It truly rattled me at first and then just genuinely offended me. He's ignorant as well as uncouth. Not a great combination." "I think, Uncy said, that the police will pay him a visit. That will let him know that we're not putting up with his threatening manner, but it can also send a different message which is what worrying me. I think for at least a couple of weeks you might tell Dinah to stay away from the parish.

You need to let your superiors know what is going on also. Also, you'll stay at the house until this is under control. I'm not suggesting that you act in a cowardly manner, just a smart one." "I agree Uncy. Thank you for always being there for me."

## *Waiting On Babies*

Alicia was pretty much a couch potato. Mary and David were handling all the daily chores and most of the care of Amanda. The doctor had ordered her to stay off her feet as much as possible. The focus was to carry the babies as long as she possibly could which would insure a good birth weight for them. Alicia was not quite half-way through her third trimester. They had gone back and forth deciding whether they wanted to know the sex of the babies. On one hand they wanted to be surprised and on the other they wanted to try and be ready for them. Finally, they decided they had to know so they could get everything ready while Alicia was still able to get up and around. Two baby girls! Just think, a houseful of teenage girls! Our lives would never be normal again. Baby Amanda, who had just turned 8 months old, was up on her feet and walking all around holding on to the furniture. Alicia was more concerned than ever about trying to manage a toddler and two newborns even with David's help. She decided to call her mom and see if she would bring pizza for lunch. Lucy laughed and told her she'd see her shortly. She arrived with a sausage pizza that was guaranteed to give Alicia terrible heartburn. They ate their lunch and Alicia poured out her concerns. "I'm just not sure we can do this. I'm concerned that Amanda won't get the attention that she needs while trying to hover over two newborns. What do you think?" Lucy told her that in case she'd already forgotten, newborns sleep about 20 hours a day. That would give her plenty of time to play and nurture Amanda. "My concerns, Lucy said, aren't the babies. It is your husband. He is a wonderful, dedicated man, but he needs to get a job and do what the man of the house is meant to do. I really think we should hire a live-in nanny to help with the children and to act as a housekeeper. Mary's interest is starting to blossoms and I don't think you'll have her here much longer. She also wants nothing to do with being a nanny. I also think that about six-weeks after you give birth to the girls that you need to be up on your feet doing productive things each day." Alicia was crying and Lucy felt badly, but also knew that she was right. Finally, Alicia said, "You are right, mom. Will you help me to hire someone as soon as possible? Even though I've still got about 4-6 weeks to go full term I'm not sure that will be the case. I need someone to be with Amanda if I have to be away for more than overnight." "Yes, Lucy said, I'll get on with finding you a live-in. In the short term, just concentrate on staying quiet and healthy so you'll be ready to give birth to these two wonderful little girls." "I love you, mom. Thanks for always knowing the right answer."

After Lucy left Alicia filled David in on their conversation. He was surprised but pleased over the decisions. "I have looked in the paper a couple of times and I think with my business degree that I can find some type of work that will make us a living and be inspiring at the same time." "What would you like to do, she asked?" "I think I would like to sell real estate. I love our hometown and I think I could do a good job of selling it. If not real estate, then my next choice would be working for a title company handling closing paperwork." "I know you'll be wonderful at whichever one works out for you. I would like you to hold off until these children make their entrance and then you'll be able to start your search."

# Never A Dull Moment

I had spoken to Fr. McMurry and the Bishop and brought them up to speed on what was happening. I was genuinely uneasy and a little bit angry. My beautiful cottage was finished, and I wanted to move into my new home. I decided to swing by the precinct and see what they had to say about the fellow. I spoke with the patrolman that had come to the church when the incident happened. He said that they had been called a couple of times for him being drunk and running his mouth in a bar. I asked the policeman if he would accompany me to go and seek out the young woman's ex-boyfriend. "I think if I can convince him that I can be of no help to his father and his inquiries that perhaps we can bring this mess to a close." The patrolman felt like this was worth trying. They couldn't just keep driving by the church forever in case something occurred. They went to the young man's apartment and found him home. I introduced myself to him and he seemed genuinely confused. "Why are you here, he asked?" We reiterated the story to him about his father's visit to the church. "Are you serious, he asked? I had no idea." "Well, I said, he seemed to know that she had come to the church to offer her confession. She and I talked, and I certainly was sympathetic toward her. But that was the extent of it." "I'm really sorry, Fr. Dan, I'll speak to my father, he said, and set him straight. This is ridiculous. She is long gone. I knew she would never have an abortion because of her faith, but I felt like the money would help her out a little. Barbara came to see me and wanted me to sign a paper and we had it notarized. She said that she had found a family in Boston that wanted the baby, and she was giving it up for adoption. I knew she had left town. I'm so sorry that my father was trouble to you. I will talk with him." I felt very relieved when we left him. It was obvious to me that Barbara had covered her tracks and led them far away from Edgartown.

I stopped by the office to see Debra while I was already downtown. She was busy but seemed glad for the interruption. We visited about her business and I brought her up to speed on my situation. "I'm moving to my cottage and putting this all behind me." "Good for you, she said." "Hey, Pixie, you want to go to dinner tomorrow night? My treat." "Where, she asked?" "How about the Atlantic Fish & Chowder House?" "You're on, she said. Pick me up at 6pm." "Will do. See you tomorrow little sister." I stopped by the parents and brought them up to date on my visit with the ex-boyfriend. "Daniel, Uncy said, I think that was a brilliant move. I'm so glad that this is behind us." Me, too, I said. I want to gather my belongings and move to my new cottage. Do you think that'll be ok, I asked?" Uncy thought for a moment and said, "Daniel, let's wait a couple more days to ensure that he or his cronies don't surface again. Your aunt and I will just rest easier if you'll be willing to do that." I told him of course. No problem.

I was johnny on the spot to pick up Pixie for our dinner date. She looked beautiful as always. We walked over to the restaurant and had a delicious dinner and even better conversation. It felt like we'd not seen each other forever. We've always been best friends and we tend to miss each other when we get busy and out of touch. Sometimes I feel closer to her than I do to my twin. David has always totally belonged to Alicia. Even as small children they were inseparable. We walked back to Debra's house and just as I was seeing her to the door, both our cells rang. She answered first and I heard her say, "We are on our way." "What, I asked? What's wrong?" "We are having babies, she said. David said to meet him at the hospital." We took my car and drove to the hospital. Debra phoned the parents to see if they were also on their way. We found David pacing in the lobby area. "They've told me to stay out here while they are getting things under control. I'm so scared, he said, and promptly broke down." Lucy went in search of a nurse or doctor to get some information from. About that same time the doctor was coming out to talk with David. "Everything is fine, he assured us. We are going to get her into a labor room to see how she does, but it may be that we'll do a C-section if she's having difficulties. You are welcome to join us David in just a few minutes. The nurse will come and find you. The rest of you, there is a cafeteria that is open 24 hours so you may want to wait there. I'll let the nurse know that you're all in the area." David waited for the nurse to come and get him and told us that baby Amanda was with Carol, the new live-in nanny. "Thank God you found her when you did. I don't know what we'd have done otherwise, he said." The nurse came looking for David and the rest of us headed to the cafeteria. We were sure it would be a long night as we waited for the arrival of our new babies. David and Alicia had told all of us that the babies were girls. They had chosen Arianna Lucille for baby #1 and Adelina Lorraine for baby #2. Arianna would be called "Ari" and Adelina would be known as "Addy". They were sure that Amanda would either be Mandy or Amy as she got older. They found a deck of cards in the cafeteria and played rummy while they waited. It seemed forever but about two hours later David came down to find us announcing that his daughters had arrived. "Everyone is healthy and beautiful. Alicia did such an amazing job. She managed to give birth naturally and I'm just so proud of her. The girls are both over 6 pounds so their stay here will be minimal." We all were laughing and crying and hugging one another and Daniel prayed with and for us thanking the Lord for watching over our family. We followed David so we could go see our Alicia and the girls. She was in a private room with two bassinettes close around her. She looked gorgeous but also very tired. We told her we just wanted a peek at the girls and then we'd leave so she could get some rest. "Mom, will you please go to Amanda. I don't want her to be frightened if she finds we aren't there." "Absolutely, Lucy said, we will all go to the Inn when we leave here. Don't you worry about a thing." David picked up the babies and gave one to each grandparent. David was beaming all the while the tears streaming down his face. "Alicia, she is so beautiful. Which baby do I have?" "Look on her wrist, Dad, and you'll see her name." He saw that he had Ari so Lucy had Addy. Everyone was commenting on how beautiful the girls were. Debra said, "Look at that head of hair that both girls have. Cold black just like their father. Ari's eyes are very dark, and Addy's are light colored. I'll bet you that Ari's eyes will turn brown like her dad's and Addy's will be bright blue like her uncle Daniel and her grandfather Tim. These girls are going to be real lookers. Good luck to you both with three beautiful teenage girls in the house." We all started laughing at the thought of that. We put the babies back in their cribs, hugged and kissed David and Alicia and headed to the Inn to be with Amanda. Our baby Amanda was now officially a big sister.

## *Something Is Going On*

There was so much happening with our family that it was like being tossed about in a storm. I was worried about Daniel even though the biological father of Amanda seemed on the up and up. David and Alicia were home with a houseful of screaming infants. All adorable mind you, but really loud! The parents were worried about something, but I hadn't yet been able to put my finger on what it was. Neither of them was talking which is always rather disconcerting. I was walking around my beautiful home while drinking my morning coffee trying to make a mental list on what still needed to be done. I decided that the mental part wasn't working and went to find paper and pencil. A dining room set. The room is absolutely stunning with the 3 stained glass windows. Never mind that the view is of my neighbor's house. The room is rectangular and good sized, about 16-feet x 12-feet. I was thinking that one of those benches along the underside of the 3 windows could be really pretty. Then a rectangular table, glass I think, with 2 captain chairs and 4 dining chairs. The banquet, I believe they call them, would accommodate 4 people with 6 more in the chairs. That was perfect. The far end of the room would accommodate a buffet in the same wood tone as the window casings very nicely. I had brought granny's everyday dishes but didn't have any china or flatware for guest. I need to add those to the list. Ok, then, that takes care of that room. My formal living room. I had the Queen Anne settees and 2 chairs that were granny's set up across from each other but need a coffee table to go in between and occasional tables to match that would go between the 2 chairs and on either end of the divan. I wish I'd been smart enough to have included the tables from grannies. The kitchen and my bedroom were set up perfectly. I was still dragging my feet on which room to set up as an office and which would be a guest room. Presently dad's desk was in the upstairs master suite and I'm thinking that is the best place for the office. The other bedroom is at the far end of the upstairs giving a guest plenty of privacy in case I needed to be in the office. I liked having my master on the main floor and I simply couldn't give up the window that is the star of the show. So, I have a desk, a credenza which doubles as a file cabinet, and a chair in the office. I guess a couple of guest chairs but for the life of me I don't know why. That leaves the guest room to furnish. So, I need a queen size bed frame, mattress, box springs, dresser, chest of drawers, two occasional chairs and a table to fit in between them. The bathroom was already furnished so I needn't worry about that. The powder room on the main floor needed some fun wallpaper but that could be a project for later. Ok then, I believe I have a complete list. I needed to drop by Aunty's and see how she wanted me to handle these purchases. Perhaps I can coerce her into telling me what's going on with them.

I arrived just as Uncy was headed out the door to run errands. He gave me a big squeeze and said he'd see me in a few. I went in and found Aunty in the kitchen. The house had a wonderful aroma of her fresh baked goodies. She put on the pot for coffee and we sat at the island visiting and snacking on her new cookie recipe. I told her about my list, and she told me to go pick everything out and arrange for its delivery. "What kind of china are you going to look for, she asked?" "I don't have a clue, I told her. Do you have any suggestions?" "Yes, she said. I do. Lenox is always a good choice particularly for young people. You can select the contrasting color you want but otherwise it is white with gold etching. They have a dark blue, a dark red, and I believe a black which is quite stunning. Westbury silverware is lovely, plain and a nice weight to it, and it comes in a complete set which you will want to purchase. Don't forget when you get your china that you need serving pieces as well." "Alright, well that should keep me busy for a while, I said. Aunty, you know that I never mean to pry, but I have a feeling that something is going on with the two of you. Are you alright? Are either of you ill? Is there something that I can do to help?" Aunty's eyes welled up with tears and she kind of turned away from me. "Aunty, please talk to me. I won't breathe a word of what you tell me to another living soul if you tell me not to, but please talk to me." Aunty seemed to take a deep breath, and then said, "Debra, I will eventually talk to the entire family, but for now let's keep this conversation between us. I've been diagnosed with Breast Cancer, stage 3. The doctors feel that with surgery to remove the tumor followed by radiation and chemo that I'll be fine. The tumor is in the right breast and they haven't found anything in the left breast, however they did find problems with the lymph nodes so additional testing will probably be necessary. Uncy is very upset and frightened as you might expect. I haven't said anything to the family because I wanted to wait until these tests were complete and we have a clear path for treating it. This has been difficult for me, particularly at church, as I've avoided confession for obvious reasons. I guess I'll have to deal with that when the time comes." I was listening but the tears wouldn't stop. I finally got up and went and hugged her and cried it out. "I'm so sorry, Aunty. I love you so much. I just know everything will be ok." And then, more tears. I promised her that I wouldn't say anything. She was having additional tests next week and was going to have a consultation with her doctor and then she would tell the family. "Debra, I want you to not worry yourself sick over this. I'm confident that the doctors will do what is best for me and that I'll be fine. I don't want your uncle upset more than he already is. I'm glad that you are home and taken the reins on the trusts as I really was a bit beside myself and a little worn out." I told her that I promised I would be strong for her and that I was there for anything that she needed help with. All she had to do was call and I'd come running. I gave her a hug and told her I was going to go shopping and see if I could scratch everything off the list.

I got out to my car and drove straight home. I walked into my beautiful house that Aunty had found me and fell on granny's expensive Queen Anne settee and sobbed my eyes out. I couldn't share a word with the family as I had promised her. I pretty much have no friends so I couldn't call anyone and share the horrible news. I am pretty much pathetic as I wallowed in my own self-pity. I went into the bathroom and washed my face and tried to repair the blotchy red skin from crying. Get it together, girl. This isn't about you. This is about the most wonderful woman you know, and she is being very brave considering the possible outcome. I checked in the mirror again and determined that I could be seen in public. I grabbed my purse and headed to the furniture store. I walked in and looked around on my own before a nice man came to offer his assistance. I told him that I loved the one table he had on the floor, but I wanted it rectangular rather than round. Would he be able to order that for me? He asked if I was interested in anything else before he went to check on that. "Yes, I told him, several things. I love those Captain's chair and I want two of them. Do you have something similar in a plain dining chair? I need four of those. I found a buffet and hutch that I really liked but I was worried it was too modern looking. I asked the salesman his thoughts on the matter and he agreed, however he had a beautiful wooden buffet that would match my window cases and a hutch that was the same wood with glass shelves. It would be perfect. I told him that I had Queen Anne and Louie XVI furniture in my formal living room but that there was an area in front of the bay window (I showed him a photograph) that was crying out for furniture. He found two beautiful Bradon armchairs by Astoria Grand in bone white and a silver and glass occasional table to fit between them. Perfect! He found me a coffee table and 3 occasional tables in that same collection to fit out the rest of the living room. Next, we looked at bedroom furniture. He suggested a sleigh bed in walnut with a plush mattress and box spring, and matching chest of drawers and dresser. I also selected a small armoire to finish that room. "Great! You've been very helpful. Please find out about the dining room table and then we can complete the order and set up delivery time." He went to check and came back letting me know that it was in another warehouse and they would get it and have everything delivered next Thursday if that was satisfactory? "Yes, make it late afternoon delivery and call me 30 minutes prior to them arriving, please." From there I went to the local department store and ordered my china and silverware. I ordered the Lenox china in the black and gold and got the matching serving pieces as Aunty suggested. They had the silverware in the store, but I asked that they deliver it along with the china. They said they could deliver Thursday as well, and I requested a late afternoon delivery with a phone call prior to showing up. While I was in the store, I went in search of table linen which I would store in the buffet. I found a beautiful salt and pepper set, napkins, placemat, table runners and a gorgeous artificial flower arrangement for the center of the table. While looking around I also found a beautiful wreath for my front door. I asked the salesperson to please add these items to my delivery order which she was happy to do. I had ticked off everything on my list and was ready to go home. I would order delivery dinner a little later. Right now, I just needed cold white wine, lots of cold white wine.

# *Changes For David*

The babies were all growing like weeds. Amanda, now officially called Amy, was almost 10 months old and the twins, Ari and Addy were two-months old. Carol was a Godsend and all the girls loved her. She helped with the children, as well as the cooking and shopping. Mary has finished up with her schooling and has met a nice young man. Her interests seem to be going in a quite different direction now. Alicia was getting her strength back and was starting to feel like her old self. We had hired a housekeeping team to come in and clean weekly. They also did the linen laundry which kept the beds and towels fresh. Alicia and Carol managed the other items between them. I had applied at a couple of the local real estate offices but hadn't heard anything yet. I went and talked with the people at the temp agency and they felt my best bet to get into the real estate market was to take the classes online, pass the final exam and be able to present credentials to the brokers. I signed up for the class and seemed to be busy every day studying and taking the various tests that were offered. The requirement is 40-hours of training and you can achieve that at your own speed. I was about halfway through the studying/tests so I felt another week or so should be adequate.

Aunty had called a family meeting for tomorrow night at 7pm. Strange time because normally she would always plan something around us all having dinner together. She had suggested that we leave the children with Carol and that the meeting would only be an hour or so. Alicia was acting very nervous about the whole thing. "I just feel like something is wrong, she said. I can't put my finger on it, but something is amidst."

We called Debra and asked if she wanted to ride with us, but she declined. Said she had something going on and would just meet us there. We arrived right before 7pm and found that Daniel and Debra were already there. Aunty had us set up in the living room and there was a carafe of coffee, one of wine and bottles of water. No cookies, no cake, no pie, just beverages. We were all wearing the same frown on our faces and were sitting across from Aunty and Uncy waiting for the shoe to drop. Aunty thanked us all for coming and said that she had some news that she wished to share with all of us. She began by saying that she had been diagnosed with Breast Cancer. Originally, she said, they told me that it was Stage 3, but after the biopsies of both the tumor and the lymph nodes was completed, they have pushed that to Stage 4. I'm having a radical mastectomy on the right breast on Friday. They will then begin chemo to try and insure no more threat from the disease. I will have reconstructive procedures following chemo if nothing else occurs. I want each of you to know that while this is a terrifying diagnosis, I feel the prognosis is a good one. I need each of you to do your part in taking care of Dad/Uncy while I'm in the hospital and during my recovery period. I'm sorry if you feel I've kept anything from you, but I didn't want any of you to worry needlessly. You may worry now." We all were crying as we jumped up to run over and embrace her. Uncy moved to avoid being trampled. Daniel sat beside her and prayed while the tears streamed down his face. Alicia was pretty much a basket case, but we all promised that we would do whatever was needed to help them through this ordeal. "I do not want any of you at the hospital. My husband will be there, and he will let you know whenever there is news that needs to be delivered. Daniel, if you could please take Jack home with you, I would be grateful. He needs attention and I'm not sure we're up to supplying it right now." "Of course, Aunty, I'll be happy to tend to Jack while you're recovering. In fact, I'll take him home tonight, so you won't have to be worrying about him." We all hugged everyone one final time and took our leave. Daniel stayed behind saying that he needed to get Jack's stuff. I made sure that Debra was okay to drive and then got Alicia into the car. She was sobbing as I shut the door. "I'm so scared, David. She's never sick, she's always there for all of us and now we can't do anything to help her." "Yes, we can, Sweetheart. We can do what she asked us to do. I have faith that she will be fine, and I believe she is in good hands." We drove home in silence.

# *Lucy*

I started getting Jack's food, dishes, his bed, and toys together to take with him. I poured a glass of wine and went back into sit with Aunty. We talked for a bit and we prayed together. I knew that she was more worried than she was letting on, but I respected her privacy. "Aunty, are you sure that I can't be there with Uncy while you are in surgery?" "No, Daniel. Your uncle needs to not have to hide his feelings or his fears and he can only do that when he's with me. We will be fine. What you can do is when you're given the time of the surgery is to pray, please. I need all the prayer that you can muster." "Are you worried about this radical surgery?" "No, not at all. My darling boy, my breast isn't much to write home about anyway, so we probably won't even miss it. Long as I'm able to remain with my wonderful family, I'm fine with whatever needs to happen." I gave her a squeeze and smiled at her attempt to humor. "Ok, I'll take my leave. You know how to reach me if you need me. Day or night. I love you Aunty. I'll go find Uncy to say goodnight." I went in search of my uncle. He was sitting on the back porch just staring at the darkness. I asked him if I could get him anything, but he told me he was fine. "It'll be ok, Daniel. She is the most wonderful woman I've ever met, and I just know she'll be ok. I'm counting on your mom to act as guardian angel over my Lucy." I hugged him and took my leave.

I wish there was something I could do to mend their hearts, but there isn't. They just need to get through this their way, together. I called Pixie to see if she was okay. She wasn't but said she'd share her wine if I wanted to come by. I drove up and she was sitting on her porch waiting for me with wine in hand. We just sat and hugged and tried to make sense of everything. She admitted that she had known for a while as she had forced Aunty's hand and made her talk and then she swore her to secrecy. It had been a long week!

# *Darling Lucy*

The week passed way too quickly, and it was time for me to check into the hospital. David hadn't spoken more than half dozen words in days. Whenever he started to speak, he would break down and run away. We drove to the hospital and got me checked in. The doctor came into talk with us saying that they would begin prep in about an hour. "The surgery, he said, would last about two hours. At this moment we don't expect any problems or complications. You'll wake up in the recovery area and will stay in ICU for approximately 24 hours. This is a precaution against infection and ensures that you're monitored 24-hours each day. You will feel burning in your chest area and it will be quite intense. When you feel the pain, I want you to tell the nurses so they can administer some paid meds. Don't try to be a hero. Let the pain meds and rest help you to recover. When you are returned to a private room we will talk about the surgery, my findings, and our next steps. You will remain in ICU for 24-hours minimum and 3-5 days in a private room. Ok?" "Yes, I understand." David held tight to my hand until they came to get me for prepping. He leaned over to tell me he loved me and hugged and kissed me. I told him he was the most wonderful man I had ever met and that I loved him more.

It was closer to 3-1/2 hours when the doctor came to find David. He told him that the surgery had gone well and that I was in recovery. "The tumor was large, he said, and so the decision to remove the breast and nodes was the best call. It will be several hours before she is fully awake, and it will be tomorrow before you can see her. Why don't you go home and get some rest?" David thanked him and left the hospital. He sat in the car for a long time before heading to the church. He needed to pray, and he needed Daniel. Daniel was in his office when David finally found him. Daniel took one look at his uncle and immediately engulfed him in one of his famous bear hugs. David took solace from his nephew's love. "Is she okay, Daniel asked?" David told him everything he knew. He also said he needed to call the other children but hadn't done so yet. Daniel told him to relax and he'd fix him a cup of hot tea and they would call the other kids. David drank his tea and they called David and Alicia and Debra and brought everyone up to speed. David told Daniel that he needed to pray but the words weren't coming. Daniel assured him that God had heard his heart which was far more powerful than words could ever be. They went together to pray in the church. After about an hour David seemed to relax and was more himself. He asked Daniel if he had plans for dinner and Daniel told him that he did not. "Good, David said, we can split a pizza and a pitcher of beer." "Perfect Uncy, I'll pick you up about 5pm. David hugged and thanked him and said he'd see him later.

David went by the hospital just to be sure everything was okay. He had the head nurse's name and was able to visit with her. She assured him that Lucy was resting and had only asked for pain meds once since waking up from the anesthesia. "I'll call you if there is any change, she told him." He thanked her and went home. He had about two hours before Daniel would come after him. He decided to take a short nap and then freshen up for dinner. He laid down on the sofa in the living room and was immediately asleep. He dreamed that Amanda was holding his hand and telling him everything was going to be fine. He heard her clearly tell him that she was right there with him. When he awoke from his nap, he felt fresh and renewed. He somehow knew that Lucy was going to be fine. He went and freshened up and put on a clean shirt and waited for Daniel to arrive. They had a great visit and shared a wonderful deep-dish pizza and pitcher of dark beer. They played a game of darts and shot some pool before calling it a night. Daniel commented that he seemed more at peace tonight than he had earlier. "Oh yeah, he said, your mom paid me a visit and assured me everything was going to be fine. Goodnight, I love you. Thanks for dinner." Daniel just smiled and shook his head and waited until Uncy was safely inside the house before leaving.

After two full days David could visit Lucy for 15 minutes twice each day. She was doing remarkably well, and they had moved her to a private room but kept her sedated so she would have a chance to start healing. Her spirits were good, and she was anxious to get on with the next part of the process. The doctor told us that he was confident that the disease had not spread to the other breast. He felt like everything had gone well and that she should make a full recovery. "We will do radiation to ensure against the disease coming back, but I am not going to recommend chemo at this time. The radiation therapy is not difficult, and it doesn't hurt, it just seems to be more of an emotional rollercoaster for some patients. I think you will do fine. We won't begin any kind of reconstructive work until you're totally healed physically and emotionally. Do you have any questions?" We didn't, so he thought we were on target to be released tomorrow at noon. We visited for our 15 minutes and then he took his leave. David called the kids to let them know that he'd be bringing Lucy home tomorrow. He told them that they should wait an additional day and then they could come for a short 15-20-minute visit. Alicia and David came first. Alicia had taken a bunch of photos of the girls and put a calendar together for her mother. Lucy was thrilled and proclaimed that the girls had grown so much since she last saw them! Daniel came about an hour later. He brought a beautiful arrangement of fresh flowers and a book by one of her favorite authors. They visited and he prayed with her before he left. Debra came about two hours later and brought their dinner to them. She set up TV trays in the living room and fixed their plates for them before taking her leave. All in all, it was a wonderful day full of visits from her children.

The next couple of weeks flew by as Lucy continued to heal. She had her visit with the doctor so he could survey how the healing was going. He told her that he felt like everything was going according to schedule and that he was going to set up her radiation treatments to begin in 30 days. She would go Monday-Friday for 6 weeks. At the end of the radiation treatments, they would discuss constructive surgery. He told her to keep up her daily rests but to try and return to a normal routine which would help her to regain her strength. She and David both had questions and the doctor took the time to answer every one of them. They left feeling positive about the future.

## *More Changes*

The choir were working hard on what would be their first of four musical productions for the coming year. They had wanted to begin with Christmas and end with Easter. There were several members that had beautiful voices and they were all anxious to try out for different parts. They inquired which of the parts that he was going to have. Surprised by the questions I answered, "None. This is all about you." One of the members suggested that he might have a closing song to perform as everyone in the congregation and the entire choir loved to hear Daniel sing. He promised them he would think about it.

He had spoken again with the bishop concerning his desire for a school to be built adjacent to the church. Bishop Cornell told him that it was out of the question for this year but was being considered for the following school year. Their thoughts were to begin with a day care and progress from there. I thanked them for their consideration of my proposal but hung up feeling rather deflated. He called Debra to see if she wanted to get together for dinner. She was feeling a bit under the weather and asked if they could order soup and eat at home. "Absolutely. I'll take care of the soup and I'll see you in an hour or so." I took a quick shower to freshen up and headed to the deli downtown to get some soup and bread to take to Debra's house. I arrived and Debra let him in but headed straight back to the couch. She looked terrible. She was coughing and was looking feverish. I got her covered up and went to fix her a bowl of the chicken noodle soup and tore off a chunk of bread. She ate about half of the food and fell asleep on the couch. I started to leave and then thought better of it. I'll just stay and keep watch over her. Debra awakened about 3am and was shocked to find herself on the sofa and more shocked to find me asleep on the other end of the sofa! I woke up and saw immediately that her fever had broken, and she was on the mends to restored good health. She told me to go home so she could go to bed. I waited until she was safely tucked in and then took my leave. After all, you only have just so many baby sisters and you must be sure to take good care of them.

Debra called the girls in the office in the morning and told them she was taking a sick day. She felt a lot better but was still feeling a little shaky. Apparently, she had contacted a bit of flu or something. She lounged around all day to get to feeling like my old self. She talked with Aunty and Uncy on the phone and explained that she had a touch of something which was why she hadn't been over. Uncy wanted to know if she needed anything and she assured him that she didn't. She explained that Daniel had spent the night on the sofa watching over her. They both thought that was very sweet. She called David and Alicia and checked on them and the girls. Everyone there was in good spirits. She then called Daniel and thanked him again for watching over me. He volunteered to bring more soup if I needed it but she assured him she was fine and that we'd share a proper dinner one day next week.

# *Changes For Debra*

Morning came with bright sunshine and blue skies. I was feeling like new and readied myself to head for the office. I knew that I had a new client coming in this morning who was handling his parent's estate. My mother had handled his grandparents and aunty had taken care of his parents who were now both deceased. The owner of the boutique in Boston had sent my fall/winter wardrobe and I had chosen a beautiful navy-blue A-line dress and matching pumps. I had a multicolored sheer scarf that went perfectly with the dress. I wore my mother's jewelry and pulled my mass of chocolate curls up with two beautiful combs. I added a touch of mascara and lip gloss and decided I looked satisfactory. I got to the office and found that Melinda had everything typed and copied and ready for my meeting. I reviewed the paperwork and was ready when she phoned announcing his arrival. I went out to greet him and found myself staring into the most beautiful face I'd ever seen. I have always thought that my brothers, next to my father, were the most handsome men I'd ever seen, but I was wrong. This man was gorgeous. He had put out his hand to shake mine as I was trying my best to recover. I shook hands with him, and it seemed an eternity before he let go. I introduced myself and led the way to my office. His name was Kieran McDougall. He was about 5'10" tall, had a runner's build, beautiful dark blue eyes, black hair and a ruddy complexion. When he smiled it was to display perfect teeth that were sparkling white. He had a clef in his chin and the most exquisite mouth I'd ever seen. He had said something, and I had obviously missed it. I tried to shake myself and regain some sort of composure. I gathered the paperwork together and began my presentation of the estate. We visited and I found that conversation flowed so easily between us. I had never experienced anything to equal it. After we had gone through the estate and I had answered all his questions he asked if I might find time to have dinner with him as he was unfamiliar with Edgartown and wanted to acquaint himself with his surroundings. "My parents moved here shortly before they passed away and I never had any time to visit. I accompanied my mother's body back to Boston for burial and my father passed away less than two months later. The house is on the market but I'm unsure now whether I actually want to sell it." I asked him what his line of work was, and he had told me that he was an investment broker. "I've lived and gone to school my entire life in Boston. When I got my degree, I had already been offered a job with a prestigious agency downtown Boston and jumped at the opportunity. I'm afraid I've rather drawn a large fence around myself." We talked about our families and when he rose to leave, I felt like I'd known him all of my life. I told him that ordinarily I would decline a dinner request from a client but that I would love to have dinner with him. "Let me make a reservation for say 7pm which would give us some time to show you around the area if you'd like to." "Yes, I would he said. I would very much like that. Do you know where my parent's house is as that is where I'm staying while I'm here." I assured him I knew where it was, and we agreed on my picking him up at 5pm to sightsee before dinner. I walked him out to the lobby and then went back to my office to try and collect my thoughts. What had I just done? I just broke every rule in my book about seeing a client outside the office. I called étoile to see if they could squeeze us in. They didn't have a 7pm available but had a 7:15pm which was fine. I didn't even give a thought to the fact that I'd just made a reservation at the very restaurant where my father took my mother on their first official date! I finished up with the rest of my day's work and went home about 4pm to freshen up before picking Kieran up.

I arrived at his parent's house promptly at 5pm and he was waiting on the porch. He walked out to the car and greeted me and thanked me again for taking the time to show him the town. We chatted as we drove along the coastline to see the lighthouses and the state park. We drove by the old whaling church and the museums. I drove slowly through the lovely neighborhoods and showed off all the beautiful homes that were mostly over 100 years old and newly renovated. He was quite taken with the beauty of the area. We arrived at the restaurant shortly after 7pm and were shown to our table almost immediately. "If you enjoy lobster, I can guarantee that this would be the best you've ever eaten. He ordered a bottle of white wine for us to share and we had spinach salads. "I'm having a terrible time trying to decide about an entrée. Do you have any suggestions, he asked?" Well, are you prone toward seafood or meat? "I like both, he said." I suggested that he order the halibut that was on their special and I would order the lamb. "We can share, if you're up to it?" "Perfect, he said. That sounds wonderful." We ordered and enjoyed our wine, and he ordered a bottle of red to go with our dinner. We found that we talked non-stop and seemed to be amazingly comfortable in each other' company. He asked if I was seeing anyone special. I told him that I wasn't, and that finishing up with school, making a career choice and moving home had kept me pretty busy. "You? Do you have a wife or a special someone, I asked?" "Not really. Well, never a wife, but I did have a girlfriend through most of my college days, but she married one of my best friends and they moved away. I haven't bothered to fill that space since then. He asked why I had decided to move back to Edgartown, and I walked him through my family situation. "My aunty and uncle, who have been my parents since my own were killed when I was three, have worked their tails off for the three of us. They are the hardest working and most selfless people I've ever known. They never hesitated to make changes in their lives in order to accommodate my brothers and myself. I had thought for sure that I wanted to work in the D.A.'s office like my maternal grandmother had but I finally settled on estate planning and real estate law which followed in my mother's footsteps exactly. "Are you happy with your choices, he asked?" "I am, I told him. I find that I was very wrong in my misconceptions about estate planning. It is complicated and extremely exciting. I've been very happy with the choices I've made. My aunty found me a beautiful home here so I'm self-sufficient and in charge of my own destiny. Kieran asked if I wanted dessert and I admitted I did but was too full to eat it. He insisted on paying the bill and I drove him back to his parent's house. He asked if I would like a cup of coffee on the front porch before calling it a night. I told him that sounded like a lovely idea. He got me seated on the swing and gave me a blanket in case I was cold. He was back shortly with two steaming mugs of coffee and a plate of cookies. Perfect! When we finished our coffee, I thanked him for a wonderful dinner and a most delightful time. He walked me to my car and leaned over and kissed my cheek and thanked me again for showing him the town. "I'll be in touch, he said." I got in my car to drive home feeling something akin to loneliness. What the heck do you make of that?!

I had clients this morning, so I was up and at it early. The girls were surprised when they saw that I had arrived before them. That'll keep them on their toes! I answered emails and sorted through my mail after the two morning appointments had left. I had one more client coming into sign paperwork this afternoon and when I finished that I thought I'd swing by the parents. I also needed to give Daniel a call and take him up on his dinner invitation. Before she left the office, she phoned Daniel and asked if he was available for dinner. He was so they made plans to meet at 7pm. She finished up and headed to the parents.

Aunty was up and looking much more like her old self. She was happy for the company because she needed a break. We caught up on her visit with the doctor and how she was feeling. She asked what was new with me. "Oh, nothing much. I have had several client meetings this week and one of your client's sons came into sign the last of the paperwork and sent along his best regards for all the help you gave him and his parents. He's quite charming. Perhaps you remember him, Kieran McDougall?" "Yes, she said, I recall talking with him on the phone. He was very nice as I recall." "Well, I said, we had a lovely dinner and found that we had a lot in common." Aunty noticed that her eyes were twinkling, and she had a slight blush. "Really, she said, well isn't that nice?" "Yes, I said, he hinted that he might give me a call in the future." "Ok, Aunty said, 'fess up. Tell me everything!" I was laughing but told her how very handsome that he was and how we just talked non-stop like we'd always known one another. He's the perfect height for me. I can wear heels and he still is lots taller which is always nice. He kissed me on the cheek when I dropped him off. He's really very nice, Aunty." "Hmmm, well, my dear, she said, this reminds me of another beautiful young woman who was instantly smitten with a handsome young man and he with her. They were a match made in heaven." My eyes welled up with tears when I thought of my beautiful parents and how much they loved one another. I could only hope that someday I'd be that happy. Aunty hugged me and said, "I'm hopeful you'll hear from him soon. I think this could be an incredibly good thing, Debra." "I'll keep you posted, I said." Funny, I've always been able to tell her anything. She is such an incredibly wise woman. We talked for a while longer before I told her I needed to scoot to go meet Daniel.

I drove to the Seafood Shanty which is where we always seem to end up. Probably because it is the most delicious food ever. My cell beeped letting me know I had a message so I got it out so I could check the caller before going into the restaurant. It was Kieran! He said that he was coming back to Edgartown in a week and was spending his 2-week vacation here and was hoping if I wasn't too busy, that I could put together some sightseeing and places to eat while he was here. I texted him back and told him I would schedule some places to see and some reservations and would look forward to his return to Edgartown. I reminded him that my brother is a priest and very bossy and I would have to attend mass on Sunday. I asked him if he might want to accompany me. He texted back and said, "By all means. I'm a practicing catholic and it would be lovely to visit our local parish and that way he could meet my brother." "Oh, you'll end up meeting the whole family. They'll all be there with bells on." I believe that I was walking on air when I went into the restaurant to meet Daniel. He had already gotten us a table and the hostess escorted me there and took my drink order. Daniel stood and hugged and kissed me and as always, every eye was on the pair of us. Too funny. "You look all bubbly, Pixie, what going on, he asked?" I told him about Kieran and he just sat there listening and smiling that beautiful smile of his. "He sounds wonderful and I can't wait to me him, he said." "Well, we will attend mass and I'm thinking I might have my first dinner party at my house. I'll have to hire a private chef and serving team, but I think it would be fun. Would that make me look too much like a spoiled brat?" "Yes, he said, but we might as well let him know that now." I threw my napkins at him!

Over the weekend I planned with a local private chef to meet me at my house at 10am so we could discuss a menu. I felt like Sunday after church would be perfect for a family get together. I scoured the local sightseeing to see things that I felt like he might want to see. I had no idea how he felt about museums, but we had a couple of interesting ones to browse. There are lots of bike trails and we all had bikes at the parent's house that we could use. I booked the Martha's Vineyard Island Tour. I hadn't done that for years, but it was fun and educational at the same time. There was also a couple of wine tasting tours that looked fun. I booked two of those and made reservations for lunch at restaurants that were close to the vineyard. Charlene Dupré', the local private chef, showed up exactly on time. She was delightful! We decided to start with a puff pastry tartlet and poached shrimp for an appetizer. A citrus and avocado salad would follow at the dining table. We went back and forth trying to decide between a pasta dish or a fish dish for the next course. Finally, I said fish and she presented dover sole which sounded wonderful. A rack of lamb with potatoes, parsnips, and carrots would be the main entrée. She planned a variety of small bite sized desserts with coffee and liqueur of choice. She went through my buffet to be sure that I had adequate stock for all courses. She gave me a list of the serving dishes that I needed to obtain. She went through my wine and liquor cabinet and deemed it satisfactory for the event. Because the event was on a Sunday, we opted to have the goods delivered to my back door on Saturday afternoon. She would come by about 4:30pm Saturday evening to ensure all was there. Then on Sunday she would arrive at 10am with two servers who would also act as busser and dishwashers. Appetizers and drinks would begin at 4pm and dinner should conclude by 8pm. I signed off on the menu and gave her the deposit for the event. After she left, I phoned the store and ordered the pieces that I was missing. They had all but one serving platter which we decided would be fine if it was pure white. The items would be delivered later in the week.

After I got the serving pieces ordered I went up to my room to go through my closet and decide on outfits for the two weeks that Kieran would be here. I was sure he wouldn't want to spend every day with me, but I could hope. Anyway, I wanted to be prepared. I had three tours planned with lunch reservations attached to those. They were all casual. I had black slacks, jeans, blouses, cardigan, and jackets that would work fine for those. I might buy one new outfit if I found something I really liked. I wanted a maxi length hostess dress for my dinner so I would shop for that. I wanted a pair of capris for our bike trip so I would look for something cute to go with them. I had made three dinner reservations and I had dresses and accessories that were perfect for those. I didn't want to reserve all of his time, so I was trying to be somewhat discreet in my selections. I had my list and I had decided to go to Very Vineyard which is a wonderful local boutique. I also needed to stop at a card shop and get invitations out to the family for my dinner event. I had found a lovely piece of parchment in my stash that I would use to list the reservations for tours, lunches and dinners and send to Kieran. Oh, and the florists! Good grief, I need to have the house spruced up! I ran to shower and get dressed so I could go run my errands.

I parked right outside the boutique and saw the perfect outfit in the window. I sure hope it fits because it is perfect. The sales lady greeted me, and I gave her my list. I asked about the outfit in the window and she said that they had one in a petite size for me to try. The only difference being it was red rather than navy. Red? Not necessarily my favorite color but I was willing to try. She found me capris and a couple of cute tees and a jacket to try. While I was trying everything on, she knocked and said she had two after 5 dresses for me to try on. I opened the door to take them and gasped. They were gorgeous! She brought a maxi length halter dress in black and white floral that was stunning but there was a contender in watercolor silk which I tried on and fell instantly in love with. It would be perfect with gold or silver sandals. The capri set fit perfectly and they had it in gunmetal silver which was my favorite. I found canvas shoes that were just right for the outfit. The red outfit was quite beautiful on. I've always stayed away from red and now I'm wondering why. I paid for my purchases and headed to the card shop. I found a nice package of invitations that would work perfectly. Next, I headed to the florist. Felicity is a high school friend that owns and operates the local florist. She was busy with customers when I went inside so I waited patiently for her to assist me. She greeted me with her beautiful smile and a big hug. I told her about my event and asked if she had any suggestions for flowers to decorate the house with. She asked about my dining table and we decided on an array of small low-profile vases down the center. She chose two tall vases for both ends of the buffet in the dining room. She had a photo of a gorgeous arrangement that would be perfect for the coffee table. We selected a small vase to go in the powder room and a new fresh flower wreath for the front door. She got my address and told me she would deliver everything personally on Saturday afternoon. I paid for my order and we promised to get together soon to catch up. I found that I was starving so I headed to David and Alicia's to see if I could play with the babies and bum a sandwich from them.

David was working out in the garden and Alicia and the girls were on the patio cheering him on. The girls were all growing like weeds! You would never guess that Amy was adopted as she bore a startling resemblance to Alicia. I picked up each of the girls to hug and kiss them and then asked Alicia if I could please go fix myself a sandwich. She laughed and said, "You bet. Just bring back a glass of wine for each of us." I went in and found some deli turkey and cheese and got out two pieces of whole wheat bread. I found the mustard and mayo and got the sandwich fixed. She had pickles that looked to die for, so I grabbed a couple of those. She had her famous Wine in a Box in the fridge, so I poured both of us a glass and headed back outdoors. I scarfed down my sandwich like I hadn't eaten for weeks. Alicia asked,

"Are you okay? You just devoured that sandwich." I told her that I just realized I hadn't eaten since last night at dinner! I was starved! We've always laughed with one another about how we eat because we're both petite. Alicia is about an inch taller than I am but other than that our body sizes are very similar. She had inherited that good Asian blood from her mother. Aunty was half Japanese and had always been very tiny. David joined us and complained that he had no wine. I handed him my empty glass and told him I'd like more while he was getting his. I believe he thumped me on my head as he walked by. The twins were chattering away with one another and Amy was clinging to her mother as usual. She is by nature a very loving child, but she adores Alicia. She really doesn't want her out of her sight. Alicia and I talked about the upcoming dinner and I told her she'd be getting a formal invitation. She was excited to be able to dress up as she doesn't get to very often. "What will you do with the girls, I asked? You are welcome to bring them if you want." "I'm thinking, she said, of getting a sitter. We never go anywhere anymore, and I could use a break. What do you think?" "Well, I think you should definitely get a sitter and treat yourself to a new dress." "Tell me about this Kieran person, she said. Mom mentioned him quite favorably I might add." "Well, I said, he's gorgeous and sweet and funny and highly intelligent. He's a successful investment broker. I know that because I googled him. His parent were clients of your mom's and his grandparents were my mom's clients. He texted me that he was going to spend his two-week vacation here in town and asked me to arrange some sightseeing and dining engagements. I've got about 5 things plus dinner at my house put together so far. I didn't want to fill up the entire two weeks because I don't know that he wants to spend that much time with me. I hope he does, but I'm not sure." "Good grief, Alicia said, you like this guy! I can see it written all over your beautiful little face." I had to admit that I do. I really do like him. I told them I needed to head for home and thanked them for the lunch and the wine. I hugged and kissed the five of them and left for home.

## Father Dan And Changes In The Church

The choir and I had been practicing constantly to feel that we'd have a good program together for the holidays. He had asked the choir what they thought of the following ideas: the children could make Advent calendars and they could be sold for playground equipment, a celebration Feast of St. Stephens where they could do a potluck and feed the congregation, and end with a Posada celebration and hot cocoa in the church recreation room. Take these ideas home with you, I told them, and then let me know your thoughts at the next meeting. I felt like the meeting had gone well and we had lots of fun things to think about doing. The whole idea is to bring the congregation together and invoke some joy into the people. It is far too easy to become bogged down with family and work. We all needed to be uplifted and Jesus' birth was just the way to do that.

I had talked with Debra earlier and she was planning a nice dinner party for her new beau. I shouldn't tease her about him. She certainly deserves to find someone to spend her life with. I guess I'm just selfish where she is concerned. If she belongs to someone else than she isn't available to me and I have to admit that I don't much like that. Stupid, I know. Still, it is the way I feel. I guess I need to add this to my confession and personal prayer request.

I heard from Barbara after she got settled and she was doing great. She was so thankful for the help that she had received and the tremendous weight off her shoulders. She assured me she was attending mass regularly and prayed for me daily.

# *The Parents*

I find that my energy is pretty much nil. I cry a lot in the bathtub so David can't hear me. He would be sick with remorse if he thought he couldn't help me. He is the best man in the entire world, and I love him more today than yesterday, but believe me, not half as much as I will tomorrow. I know it is an old cliché but certainly true for me. My body doesn't seem to belong to me any longer. It isn't at all familiar and I can't say that I like it very much. However, when I consider my age and what I would go through for the reconstructive surgery I find that I'm pretty content with it just as it is. I don't have the time, the strength or the will for that matter, to go through such agony. I just want to get through the radiation therapy and be done with this. I think when I am finished with the treatments that I will get David to take me somewhere warm for a couple of weeks. We could eat, sunbathe, and be merry. Yep, that's what I'm going to do.

# Debra And Kieran

I got my invitations made out and typed up an itinerary and sent off to Kieran. I was really looking forward to seeing him. I had checked my calendar at work and found that I could pretty much stay out of office 3 days each week while he was there.

He sent me an email back thanking me for the itinerary and saying that he was really looking forward to his visit. *"The tours sound really interesting, he said. I had no idea how much history is on that little spit of land. I see that you made lunch reservations connected to the tours and 3 dinner reservations. Does this mean that I'm on my own the rest of my visit? Are you terribly busy? Did I pick a bad time to come and visit? I was really hoping to spend as much time together as possible while I'm there. Let me know, okay? Also, thank you for going to the trouble of planning the dinner party. I'm really looking forward to meeting your family and I'm dying to see your house. I'm assuming that the dinner party is somewhat semi-formal. Will slacks and a jacket be satisfactory? I'm looking forward to hearing back from you and even more to seeing you. My best to you. Kieran."* I read through the message several times and then happily responded telling him that I hadn't wanted to sound like I was hogging all of his time while he was here. I told him that I would need to go into the office once or twice during his stay, but other than that I had freed up my dance card. He answered straight away saying, "Great. We'll take advantage of this time together to see what our next step is. I am thinking that I may just want to keep you, Debra." I didn't know what to say so I just sent him back a smiley face and told him "safe travels and see you soon".

# *Decisions*

Alicia picked me up and we went to the clinic where I had my first consultation with the radiation therapy team. It was frightening beyond words but as the appointment progressed, I found myself comfortable with both the doctor and the team of therapist. They were all simply wonderful. We set up my appointments which would be daily Monday-Friday for the next six weeks. They talked to me and explained things and I felt comforted with their honest approach. This first visit was simply an introduction to what was to come. I would begin this journey for real tomorrow. Alicia and I chatted all the way home about what nice people they were. She asked if I wanted lunch or coffee or something, but I begged off saying that I was tired. In truth, I just wanted to get home, get into my bathtub and cry until all the tears were gone. I'm so scared but I don't want anyone to know. Please God, give me strength and understanding for this journey.

# David And Alicia

Alicia got home and hugged her babies and went in search of David. He had been hired by a real estate broker and was busy studying and seemed to be enjoying the tasks at hand. I told him about our visit, and he seemed encouraged that they were nice people. "Did your mom seem upset or frightened, he asked?" "No, she said she was fine, but I don't believe her. I honestly believe that she is terrified of what is to come. I don't know how to help her. We can't any of us do this for her or even with her. She has to go this journey alone." "Well, he said, your brother-in-law would tell you that you were mistaking. The Holy Spirit will be with Aunty and will comfort her through this trial as He has every journey she's ever made." "You are right. I stand corrected."

Alicia went to get the girls some lunch and play for a while. Amy was walking, well to be truthful, running everywhere. Ari and Addy were rolling over and trying their best to crawl. They looked so funny with their butts up in the air and usually traveling backwards. Amy encouraged them every step of the way. She was a fierce older sister. She adored her siblings, and they did her. The girls ate their sandwiches and cookies, and we all went outside to play in the garden area. Amy would run all over chasing butterflies and singing at the top of her lungs. I put the twins in an outdoor playpen, so they were corralled from getting in too much trouble. David joined us after a bit. He and Amy played jump rope although she was still too young to try jumping but she enjoyed watching him. She would squeal with delight at his antics. The twins would watch the entertainment and clap their little hands in appreciation of their father's athleticism. The twins were yawning so we got them all inside and Carol took them to have an afternoon rest. Mary has moved on and is officially engaged to her boyfriend. The little kids like him very much and I believe it will be a good match. She's a lovely person and deserves happiness. We miss her but I think in time she will come to visit.

# Debra And Kieran

The days seemed to rush by and before I knew it Kieran would arrive in Edgartown tomorrow afternoon. I had given him the address for my house and he already knew where my office was, so we agreed he would show up at one or the other of the places. I had made reservations at Lambert's Cove in Tisbury. It was a rather romantic setting, and the food was excellent. I laid out my dark gray suit and crème chiffon blouse to wear with it. It was business like but still very beautiful. The blouse itself was breathtaking. I was sure he would arrive in casual wear and would want to go to his house to change before dinner. At least that was what I was hoping would happen.

I didn't sleep at all well last night. I felt like I had tossed and turned most of the night away. I should have gotten up and read or work a puzzle or something rather than just rolling all over the bed. I showered, did my hair (what a joke) and make up. I got my suit skirt and blouse on and grabbed my mom's gold earrings and her ring and bracelet. I had several of her hair combs that she always used. Her hair was dark auburn and quite long and thick but just wavy unlike my mop of curls. I recall how beautiful her hair was whether it was in a ponytail or just pulled back with combs. How I wish she were still here. I love my Aunty, but I miss my mom and dad every minute of every day. Oh, well, no time to be melancholy. I need to pull this mop up and make it look respectable. There! That will work. I donned my suitcoat, grabbed my purse, briefcase, and keys and headed to the office. I got to the car and thought, you idiot. You forgot to eat again! You're going to waste away to nothing! I stopped at the bakery by the office and grabbed pastries and coffee for all of us. It was too early for the girls to arrive, so I put the stuff in the kitchen area and headed to my office. I had several emails to answer and it seemed that prospective new clients were arriving in droves. The ladies arrived, thanked me for the goodies, gave me the rest of my messages and went off to start their days. I worked right through lunch time without even realizing it. Melinda came back from her lunch break and laid a salad and cold drink down on my desk. I thanked her and had it pretty much gone by the time she got back to her desk. I must have a tapeworm or something.

I was winding down my day about 3:30 when Melinda called me and announced that Mr. McDougall was in the lobby. I told her thanks and to send him back. I stood up and headed to my door to greet him. He rounded the corner with a big smile on his beautiful face and pulled me into his arms for a big hug. He kissed me on the cheek and told me how wonderful it was to see me and to be here with me. I managed to ask what I thought were intelligent questions like how was your trip? How are you doing? I probably sounded like an imbecile. He just hugged me again and then I sort of disengaged myself from his grip. He looked kind of funny when I did that but didn't say anything. I told him I was ready to go if he was. I grabbed my briefcase, purse and keys and we left the building. When we got out on the sidewalk, I asked him if he had driven or walked from the house. "I haven't been to the house, Debra. I couldn't wait another minute to see you, so I came straight here." "Oh, I said, okay. Do you want to follow me to my house, or did you want to go and unpack at your house?" "I have a great idea, he said. Let's start over. I couldn't wait to see you. Have I misread something here? You don't seem all that glad to see me." "Kieran, I said, that isn't it at all. Let's go over to my house and have a glass of wine and I'll tell you my life story." Before I went to my car I turned and walked back and kissed him right on the mouth. Then I went and got in my car. I could see him standing there grinning, so I was pretty sure we were going to be able to drag this moment out of the toilet. He followed me to my house, and we went straight to the kitchen for ice cold white wine. We poured nice big glasses and went out and sat on the patio. "Look, I said, when I was 14 years old, I had a boyfriend. He was skinny, wore braces, and as I recall was a jerk. I hated boys. I hated school. I hated my parents for leaving me. I pretty much hated everything and everybody. I steered clear of any more male encounters, graduated with honors two years early. I was finished with college at 20 and through law school at 22. I'm somewhat of a genius. I said I hated school, which was true, but I loved learning. I'm like a sponge. Once I learn it I have it for life. Do you want more wine? "No, Debra, I'm good. Keep talking." "Oh, ok. Well, so long story short, the only boys or men that I really have any contact with are my brothers and my uncle. I don't date. I haven't had any serious or even non-serious relationships. I don't hang in bars and take guys home. Thing is, I guess, even if I took one home, I probably wouldn't know what to do once we got there. Sure you don't want more wine?" "I'm fine, Debra, he said. What time is our dinner reservation and how far are we traveling?" It's at 7pm and we're about 20 minutes away. I either have to change or you do before we go. It's fancy, romantic, and expensive." "Oh, he said, it sounds perfect. You look beautiful just as you are so we'll swing by my place and I'll change, and we will be on our way. Were you going to finish your story?" "Yes, well, the thing is I have no experience with men. I don't mean I'm stupid I simply mean that I've not had a close relationship with any man other than my brothers and uncle which is kind of different. Look, I'm a virgin, ok? I don't know a thing about life other than what I've read. I don't have girlfriends, so I don't get caught up in gossip and storytelling. My aunty has been very good to guide me whenever I've needed help, but I simply haven't asked about these things. One of my brothers is a priest and the other one has been physically and emotionally tied to his wife's side since they were born. Weird, I know, but true. So, there you have it in a nutshell. If you want to go back to Boston I certainly understand." I couldn't help that the tears were streaming down my face. Kieran got up from his chair and came over and literally picked me up and set me on his lap. He wiped away my tears and said, "Debra, I think you are a remarkable woman. I can't wait to get to know everything about you. I promise I won't rush, and I won't push. Do you believe me?" 'Yes, I said, yes

I do. I want so badly to be in your life. I knew that 20 seconds after I met you." "Ok, he said, now let's go wash your face, freshen your makeup and go get me tidied up so we can go eat expensive food in a romantic restaurant. By the way, your home is gorgeous. I can't wait to get a grand tour."

We stopped by his place so he could drop his suitcase, change clothes, and park his car. He came downstairs with dark slacks, a light gray dress shirt unbuttoned at the neck and a beautiful steel gray suede blazer. He is so darned good looking. and his coloring is very much like my brothers and my dad. We talked non-stop to the restaurant and had a fabulous dinner. We shared our appetizer and salad, and both got their fish special, which was halibut, and it was divine. They had a small band playing in the lounge so we decided to have a nightcap in there. The music was beautiful, and the band was really very good. Kieran asked me to dance and I almost said no but thought better of it. "I'm no Ginger Rogers, I said, so protect your feet." "We will be fine, he said. Just hang on tight." I felt like I was floating in air. Being held closely in his arms was what heaven must feel like. He smelled so good and I couldn't get enough of him. I figured that I was probably headed for unknown territory. We stayed and danced a couple more times before deciding to call it a night. We were doing our bike tour and lunch tomorrow and then he announced that he was cooking dinner for us. I drove to his house and thanked him for a most wonderful evening. He looked at me for quite some time before leaning over and very softly kissing my lips. "Good night, Debra, he said. Sleep well. I'll pick you up at 9am for breakfast before our outing." With that he got out of the car and was through his front door before I descended to earth. I drove home thinking that sleep might not come very easily tonight.

At exactly 9am my doorbell rang. Kieran was standing on my stoop looking as handsome as ever. He wore jeans, a Henley tee and had a sweatshirt tied around his neck in case it cooled off. I smiled and he engulfed me in one of his bear hugs and kissed me on the cheek announcing that he was starving and was I ready to go. I grabbed my tote bag and purse and locked up the house. While we were getting into his car he said, "You look beautiful as ever. Where should we have breakfast?" I gave him a couple of suggestions and he headed into town. We had a wonderful breakfast, got a coffee to go, and headed across town to where we would start our tour. Rather than using the old bikes that were stored at the parents I opted to rent new bikes for the day. There were 5 other people on the tour not counting the tour guide. Everyone introduced themselves and I discovered that I was the only local. The tour guide was well informed and remarkably interesting to listen to. We pedaled all over the area for 3 hours. By the time that the tour was over my legs felt like jelly. We decided to sit on the bench by the marina before heading off to lunch. I had booked a reservation at a restaurant that overlooked the harbor area. They have wonderful chowder and fish and chips, and I found I was getting hungry.

The weather was perfect for a brisk walk. The restaurant was only about 3 or 4 blocks away from where we were parked for the tour, so we decided to just walk over. I was hoping that my legs would begin to regain feeling other than pain. We were seated at a perfect table overlooking the marina. The sky was so blue that it didn't look real. We ordered a carafe of white wine and oysters on the half shell to start with. I ordered a small dinner salad with shrimp and a cup of chowder. Kieran wrestled with his wanting fish and chips but wanted chowder too. He finally decided on a cup of chowder, and a side of fish only. The food came and it was delicious. "I'll trade you a piece of my fish for half of your salad, he said." "Done. I was having a terrible time not stabbing it from across the table." "This has been a glorious day, he said. Did you enjoy it as much as I did?" "Yes. I believe I took this tour when I was about 9 or 10 years old. It must have been a school outing of some kind." "Do you want to help cook dinner, he asked?" "Not if you want to eat the food, I told him. I don't cook, Kieran. I don't even boil water. I'm a master at ordering delivery food. Some people can cook in microwaves, but I find that I'm somewhat afraid of anything that is a kitchen appliance. It is a phobia of sorts." He was laughing at me! "I had, he said, suspected that this was the case. Your beautiful itinerary was a dead giveaway for a catered dinner." "No, no, I said. My dinner is not catered by any means. My personal chef will arrive early and do all the cooking in my kitchen." He was still laughing. "Ok, he said, do you want to hang with me while I cook or what? It is going to be around 3pm when we get back into town and I want to have cocktails about 5pm." "Well, if you don't mind, can you drop me at my house so I can freshen up and change into something more appropriate for dinner? I would only need about 45 minutes and then I can drive myself over to your house." "That sounds perfect, Debra. I can get things started and do a quick change as well. Whenever you're ready we can head for home."

Kieran walked me to my door and gave me a hug saying he'd see me shortly. I went in and poured myself a cold glass of white wine and headed to the shower. I pulled out one of the beautiful dresses that Aunty had made me which was perfect for dinner tonight. I grabbed a cardigan sweater to keep me from getting a chill. I pulled out a white and a red wine from my cabinet and headed to Kieran's house. I knocked and he immediately opened the door and pulled me into him and kicked the door shut. He told me he was glad I was there and thanked me for the wine. "Come on, he said, let's go sit on the patio while it is still warm enough. You look beautiful, by the way." I thanked him and helped to pour us a glass of wine before heading outside. He had some iced prawns, a red sauce, cheese, and crackers for us to snack on with our wine. We walked through the gardens that were simply gorgeous. He said that there was a gentleman that kept the yard and gardens for him. "I need to decide if I'm going to sell the house or not. Right now, I want to keep it so I can come and visit you." I noticed that he had the island in the kitchen set up for eating dinner. I was secretly glad of that as it is so much friendlier than a huge table for two people. I offered to help but he told me to just enjoy my wine and he'd only be a few minutes.

Kieran hollered for me to join him in the kitchen. "Here, my lady, he said, let me help you with your bar stool." He was grinning as he helped me jump up on it. Sometimes it is a real pain to be tiny.

"I didn't ask, but judging from your healthy appetite, I'm guessing you like pasta. I fixed us a seafood medley with an alfredo sauce. I hope that sounds good?" "I think you can just put that bowl right in front of me and you'll have your answer in no time. My goodness, Kieran, that looks and smells incredible." "Well, I was going to make a salad, but I thought pasta and bread sounded so much better, he said." We both talked and ate and finished off most of his wonderful dinner. He had managed to get white fish, shrimp, calamari, oysters, and scallops all into this wonderful rich, creamy, cheesy sauce. Right up my alley! We cleaned up the dishes together. I'm quite adept at loading the dishwasher so I took over that chore. He asked if I wanted coffee which I said sounded wonderful. "Perhaps an Amoretto to go with it, he asked?" "Yes, please." He got the coffee, and I found the liqueur glasses and filled them. He took cannoli out of a small box to serve with our coffee. I was so full I didn't know how I'd manage dessert, but alas, I did. We had curled up on the couch in the living room to have our dessert and coffee. He had some soft music playing and the gas fireplace was burning in multiple colors making for a lovely ambience. However, I was full and now very sleepy. I believe he was talking when I nodded off. What seemed to be several hours later I awoke with a start and found that he was asleep on one end of the sofa and I had been on the other. This didn't seem very first-date appropriate but hopefully nobody knew what had occurred. I hated to wake him up but didn't want to leave without saying anything. I got up and went and kind of nestled in beside him and kissed him on the cheek. That wily coyote came full awake and pulled me into his arms saying, "Gotcha!" We were both laughing and then things seemed to change, and he was kissing me; really kissing me. I pulled away and told him I needed to head for home. He agreed and told me that would be my smartest move. He walked me out to the car and asked if I wanted him to follow me home? "No, I told him. I'll be just fine. I have a way of pulling the car up close and running for my door. I'm kidding. I'll be fine." "What time are we having breakfast, he asked?" I told him to just come over when he got up and around and we'd plan our day from there. I have stuff you can make for our breakfast. With that I headed to my car.

The next couple of days were simply incredible. We walked, we talked, we hugged, we kissed, and then we started all over again. We were at my house Saturday night after dinner and decided we needed an early night, so we'd be ready for morning mass and my Sunday dinner event. Everything had arrived and Charlene and her crew were ready to go. I gave her a key so she could get in the back door in case we weren't home yet from church. I walked Kieran to the door and kissed him goodnight. "Tomorrow is going to be a very busy day.

Kieran arrived to pick me up for mass and he looked even more gorgeous than usual. He had on a beautiful light gray suit with a white linen shirt that he wore open at the neck. I had chosen my steel gray A-line dress and matching shoes, so we really went together rather nicely. We were quiet on the way to the church and I asked him if he was nervous about meeting my family. "No, not at all, he said. I feel like I already know them and I'm sure they'll love me. Everyone does. I was thinking about the fact that we only have 4 more days together before I have to go back to Boston. We really need to talk, Debra. Can we plan to spend a quiet day tomorrow, perhaps a picnic or something like that, so we can make plans?" "Yes, of course. I know the perfect place. I need to go into the office for about an hour and we can plan to leave at 10am. Ok?" "Yes, that's perfect." We arrived at the church and parked relatively close to the front door. I spotted David and Alicia and the girls, and I was figuring that Aunty and Uncy were already inside waiting with bells on. Daniel was at the front door greeting everyone. I waved to David and family and we walked up to greet Daniel. His eyes were twinkling as you might well imagine, and he was in rare form. He grabbed my hand and kissed it, saying good morning baby sister while sticking out his hand to greet Kieran. Kieran was grinning watching the fun between Daniel and me. I introduced Kieran to Fr. Dan, and we stepped inside to wait on David and family. Alicia hugged me and turned to say hello to Kieran. She handed me a baby, thought for a minute, and then handed one to Kieran. Amy was clapping and giggling while being tickled by her devoted uncle Daniel. David shook hands with Kieran and in his best Irish brogue said he was looking forward to visiting with him later. I'm totally unsure what they are going to visit about but I plan to find out. While we were bouncing babies up and down the parents appeared. Uncy told Kieran how glad he was to meet him and that he looked forward to visiting with him later. Do I detect a theme here? Aunty was her usual gracious self and told him that she missed his parents as they were delightful. We gave David and Alicia back their children and went to find seats. Aunty had saved all of us a pew, so we were packed in like Donaldson/Adler sardines. The choir was singing softly as everyone found their seats. Daniel greeted the congregation and sang The Lord's Prayer. Kieran had grabbed my hand during the song and when I chanced a glance at him his eyes were filled with tears. I was so moved by his response to the song that I felt myself tear up. Daniel's voice, second only to our father's, is the most beautiful sound. He has such emotion and is so truly joyful in his calling. His sermon was light and happy, and the congregation all responded in kind. At the end of the service, he welcomed his sister's friend who was visiting the family and asked God's blessings on him as he traveled back to Boston. I kind of cocked my head on that one. Was that sincere, or rather snide on the part of my big brother?

We bid the family adieu and headed for the house. I asked Kieran if he could occupy himself at my place while I change clothes. "Absolutely. You have a bar and I have a sneaking suspicion that I'm going to need it." I laughed and then headed to my room to change. I noted that the table was set beautifully, the bar was set up and the kitchen smelled spectacular. I got out of my dress and freshened up, redid my makeup to go with the watercolor dress and pulled my mop of hair up on top of my head and fastened it with my mom's combs. I slid the dress on and actually gasped as I felt it settle itself on my body. I had found a strapless shapewear to wear under it and I felt a bit on the naked side. When I looked in the mirror, I decided that I didn't care as I looked ravishing. I put on my mom's ring and bracelet and it finished the outfit perfectly. I slipped on a beautiful pair of silver sandals that had a small heel but had a strap so I would break my neck. At this point I needed to be in control of me in order to control my family. I took one last look and then walked out to find Kieran. He was watching me as I walked out. He had the most beautiful look on his face and his eyes were twinkling. "Debra, you look gorgeous. You would outshine any bride walking down the aisle."

We checked with Charlene to see if we needed to do anything, but she was totally in charge at that point and just needed us out of the kitchen. She had made us a snack so we wouldn't be starved before dinner was served. We took our snack and some lemonade and went out to the garden to relax for a while. I asked Kieran if he had enjoyed the service and he assured me he had. "Your brother's voice is beautiful, and his song really touched my soul. My parents both loved church and that was always a favorite song of theirs. My parents were a bit older when I came along. They had been blessed with a set of twin boys, but they passed away before they were a week old. It was a terrible time for both of them and they didn't expect to have any more children, but I came along about 4 years later. They doted on me all my life and I loved them dearly. My mother was a twin, but her brother died when he was in his early 20s. My father was an only child so there are no relatives living on either side. I guess that makes me an orphan." I didn't really know what to say at that point, so I just squeezed his hand to let him know that I cared and understood. "When my parents died, I said, I was very small, but my memories of both of them are forever in place. Also, both Aunty and Uncy worked hard every day to be sure that those memories stayed intact." We had finished our lunch and cleared up our paper plate and cup and got them to the garbage. We both went to separate bathrooms to freshen up before people started arriving.

Aunty and Uncy were first to arrive followed closely by Daniel. David and Alicia arrived about 15 minutes later saying they were sorry to be late but leaving the babies was an issue. Everyone got a cocktail or glass of wine and was munching on the appetizers. David and Daniel had Kieran cornered and I was watching closely to see how they were behaving or misbehaving as the case might be. When either one of them start throwing their Irish brogue around there is usually trouble. Kieran was laughing so I'm thinking that he can take care of himself.

Uncy told me that he thought Kieran was a fine-looking lad and seemed to be a gentleman as well. "He is, I assured him. I like him a lot." "I knew that, he said. It shows all over your beautiful face. Don't worry about your brothers. They'll test the water, I'm sure, but it appears Kieran can take care of himself." Aunty and Kieran were visiting on the sofa and I'm sure it was wonderful for him to share stories of his parents with someone who knew them. Alicia and I were surveying the group. "He's very nice, Debra. I liked him the moment I met him. He is as beautiful inside as he is outside or so it would appear." "He is, I told her. He's very open and honest and so easy to be with. I'm not looking forward to his leaving in just four days."

Charlene magically appeared asking everyone to be seated for dinner. Every course was perfect, and the entire group was quietly devouring every morsel. Daniel had asked the blessing before dinner and each of us had said something that we were thankful for. When it was Kieran's turn, he said how thankful he was to have been so warmly embraced by such a lovely family. It was such a nice thing to say. It was close to 8:30pm by the time we finished the wonderful meal. We had all moved to the living room to enjoy our coffee and cordial. Charlene and the two ladies had cleared up everything and I heard them leave by the back door. A perfect evening. Aunty was tired and Alicia was anxious to get home to her girls, so people started leaving. Daniel hung back until everyone else had left. He had scooped me up into his arms and turned to tell Kieran how glad he was to meet him and that he looked forward to seeing him again soon. "You seem an honorable man and that is important when you entrust your baby sister to that person. She is very special to all of us, but particularly to me. She has been my charge since she was born." With that he kissed me on the cheek, told me he loved me, and was out the door. The tears were streaming down my face from his beautiful words. I love my Daniel so very much.

Kieran put his arms around me and said he was going to head for home. "What a wonderful day I had, he said. Thank you so much for sharing your family, also for going to such trouble to feed me. It was truly magnificent. Can I buy you breakfast in the morning when you're finished at the office or will you have already eaten?" "Let's plan to do a late breakfast," I said. "Do you want to pick me up at 10?" "Yes, that's perfect, he said. I've been studying the local maps, so I have a nice car ride for us."

I was up early the next morning and was at the office by 8am. I answered emails and phone calls and had paperwork put together for client meetings the following week. The time went quickly, and I apologized to the ladies when they arrived for being in casual attire but I was checking out about 10am and I'd see them later in the week. Kieran arrived right on time, and I was ready to walk out to meet him. He kissed me as I came through the door and walked me to the car. He had found a cute little café for us to have breakfast at. We visited over breakfast of scones, jam, crispy bacon and hot coffee. He asked if I was ready and I told him I was. "Where are we off to, I asked?" He said," I read about these two favorite Martha's Vineyard back roads that link up nicely with the above routes for a day trip out to Aquinnah. When Edgartown Road ends in a T, we will turn left onto State Road, which becomes South Road. We'll skirt along the shoreline near Lucy Vincent Beach—open to Chilmark residents only—before the road turns back inland. Then in the center of Chilmark, we'll turn left and take State Road southwest. Then we will cross Stonewall Pond and thread the isthmus between Squibnocket Pond and Menemsha Pond before eventually ending up at the Aquinnah Cliff Overlook. For a better view all the way to Aquinnah, we will take a left onto Moshup Trail, which hugs the coast." "Good grief, you sound like a tour guide!" "Well, I sort of memorized it so I wouldn't have to keep looking at the map. We can either have lunch at Chillmark or Home Port. Your choice." While we were driving along and enjoying the gorgeous scenery we were listening to some soft music and Kieran was humming along with it. "Do you sing, I asked?" "Debra, I'm Irish. I was an altar boy, I was in the choir, I've done my share of solos for my church." He found a beautiful spot to pull over and shared a mug of hot coffee that he had brought with us. He laid a blanket on the ground for us and the sun was warm. We talked about the scenery and all that he had seen while there. "It's truly a beautiful place to explore. You're lucky to have grown up here. Debra, I want to talk about the fact that I'm leaving on Thursday. I want to know that we're both on the same page going forward. I've fallen in love with you and I'm pretty sure you feel the same way." "I do, I said. I didn't want to say anything in case you didn't feel the same way." "Debra, I'm 30 years old. I've had my share of lady friends but never anything serious. I always knew that my heart would tell me when I *met the one*, and it did. I love being with you and cherish every minute that we are together." I told him that I felt the same way. "I'm in unfamiliar territory but I know that my heart knows what is right and wrong and you're right. I feel like I've met the other half of my heart." "Well, he said, then going forward from this I would like to propose the following scenario. I'm an investment broker. I can work anywhere. I am thinking I'd like to work here. If I do that, I'll keep my parent's house for now. I think if we still feel the same way in six months that we look at taking the next step. What do you think?" "I think that is a perfect plan. Should I start looking for office space for you?" "We can do that tomorrow while I'm still here, he said." Kieran suggested we head to the restaurant of choice to share lunch as he was getting hungry. They had a wonderful lunch at Chillmark Tavern and then took the back roads home. They had decided that they would have delivery pizza, a bottle of chianti and a movie tonight. They had talked about it and knew that they just wanted quiet evenings together until it was time for him to leave. The parents had made an offer for dinner, but they had opted out of it. "We'll plan to get together next time. He'll be back in a couple of weeks, I said." They didn't say anything.

The days flew by and before they knew it Wednesday night was upon them. Kieran wanted to leave early to try and get back to Boston before rush hour traffic. "We'll say goodbye tonight when I leave. No tears. No worries. I'll be back in two to four weeks for good. We've found suitable office space for me and I'll take care of putting the lease together when I get back to Boston. I need to be able to shut down my office there and be assured that my clients will still love me when I'm in Edgartown. Do you have any questions or concerns that we need to clear up before I leave tonight?" "I have a question, but I'm not sure how to ask it, so I guess I'll just blurt it out. I'm thinking that I should make a doctor's appointment and see about getting birth control. What do you think?" Kieran was staring at her, mouth slightly agape, but his eyes were laughing. "You are so precious, he said. Your poor face is beet red. "Yes, I think that is a wise notion, Miss Donaldson. A very wise notion." His kiss told her that she'd better make that appointment soon.

# David, Alicia And Girls

David's real estate business was taking off with great success. Besides being intelligent he is very charismatic. People are just naturally drawn to him and trust him without question. Alicia was busy with the girls who were growing like weeds. Amy talks your ear off, and the twins are picking up lots of words but are still prone to visiting among themselves in some kind of gibberish.

David knew that Kieran was planning on relocating to Edgartown and had been giving some thought to how their two careers might mesh. He liked Kieran and hoped that something permanent would be in the future for his sister.

David had lunch with Daniel a day or two before and had asked him if he'd noticed big changes in the parents. Daniel said that he thought Uncy had aged significantly since Aunty was diagnosed with Breast Cancer. Daniel had said that he thought that was perfectly normal given how close the two of them have always been. "It just worries me, said David. I can't imagine ever losing either one of them." "Nor can I, echoed Daniel, but it will eventually take place with them as with all of us." They decided to just keep watch over the two and to let each other know if they saw any big changes in their health.

David asked Daniel what he thought about Kieran moving to Edgartown. "I suppose it'll be fine, Daniel said. It is wrong of me to feel so protective and selfish where our sister is concerned. She has every right to finding love and happiness. I like Kieran. I think he is a man of integrity and that is the most any of us can wish for these days."

Daniel told David about the possibility of a day care at the church by early next year. "That's wonderful, Daniel. That would be great for all of us that have children. Do you suppose that eventually they will authorize a parochial school, at least through elementary grades? We need one desperately." "I know, said Daniel. It is the top of my prayer list. I would like to establish a 13-year school, but I just don't know if the funds are available or that the community will relish the idea. There are considerably more retired folks in the area than young families." "Well, David said, that is true enough, but I believe the people will rally round the idea. We could do a fundraiser to help fill the coffers." "That certainly is something to be considered. I'll mention that to the Bishop when we speak next time."

# *Debra Is In Love*

The two weeks went quickly. Kieran and I either texted, emailed or talked on the phone every day. He had been successful in leasing the office space and was in the process of shutting down his Boston business and condo. He had found a friend to sublet the condo as he wasn't ready to sell it quite yet. The clients were all amiable about his relocation. There would be some that would prefer he return to Boston to meet with them and others that would welcome the opportunity to visit Martha's Vineyard. He told me that he was on target to move the end of the month.

My business was busy, and I relished the distraction while I waited for Kieran to return. I made a lunch date with Aunty, and we talked about him and my feelings at length. "Debra, she said, I believe you've met your soulmate. We are so happy for you and encourage you to enjoy this new journey. Falling in love is such a magical time. And a long-lasting love is even better. Your uncle and I have been married for over 43 years and we still love spending every moment with each other. It isn't easy, though, as you must make lots of concessions over the years in order to keep an even keel. Couples that argue, even in jest, are not happy people. Criticism, sarcasm, and back-biting have no place in a marriage. You must counsel yourself to be open and honest, always." "Thank you, Aunty. I know that those are true words as I've witnessed them first-hand for 25 years. Kieran and I talk quite openly already. I'm sure it won't come as any surprise to you to know that an intimate relationship has not been a part of my life up to now. Kieran is very respectful and thoughtful of my feelings, and we've agreed to take things slow, really get to know each other, and be capable of making decisions as we move forward." "I believe that is a good plan, she said."

# *Daniel's Laying Plan For The School*

I needed to travel to Boston to have a face-to-face sit-down with Bishop Cornell and Fr. McMurry. I had made a business plan, outlined the possibility of a local fundraiser, and I had a spreadsheet of families in the area, number of children and their ages. It was apparent to my eye that a parochial school was very much needed. We were but a short couple of months away from the holidays, which would be a perfect time for a fundraiser as people were in the mood to *give rather than receive*. I made the appointment and left early that morning to be in Boston by noon.

It was wonderful to see Fr. McMurry. I loved him dearly and he had been a wonderful mentor to me over the years. We shared a cup of tea before Bishop Cornell arrived. After a friendly banter I proceeded to lay out my plan. Both men listened to my proposal and at the end of it had questions which I answered best I could. We made a list of the items that seemed to still be problematic. The bishop was concerned that the bulk of my congregation were retirees. I showed him where I had baptized several babies and welcomed new families into the congregation. His other concern was more obvious – money. I proposed that I could raise $500,000 by the end of the year if I were given authorization to begin the process. That would be enough to get a construction loan with the bank for the erection of a building. I explained to them that I had $500,000 left to me by my parents that had never been touched in more than 20 years. After checking with my aunt, I find that the money has earned about $300,000. I am prepared to loan the project the entire amount, interest free, to be paid back over the next 20 years. My aunt and uncle are prepared to pledge enough to pay for some of the hired help that would be needed such as school cafeteria, library and so on. I believe that this project would entice the 6-8 nuns needed for teaching the students. Rather than using church funds for the daycare as you suggested we do next year; my family wants to erect the daycare and stock it with the needed materials and it would be a gift from Timothy Donaldson and Amanda Bradley Donaldson. Fr. McMurry was profoundly moved by that thought as he had loved my dad all his life and had certainly come to love my mom as well. The bishop asked that I leave the room for about 15 minutes so they could talk. I went out to the sanctuary and prayed while they discussed my proposal. It was 22 minutes before Fr. McMurry signed for me to return to his office.

I went in and sat at the table prepared for whatever they were going to say to me. Bishop Cornell looked at me with his sharp blue eyes and said, "Fr. Dan, I believe that we agree for you to spearhead this project. We will expect a formal budget to be made available to us within the next 30 days. Also, the money that you are willing to loan the school will be repaid with the going interest rate and should be drawn up by a professional to insure you being repaid. I'm truly moved by your family and your generosity in your desire to see this dream become reality. Keep me posted." With that he took his leave. Fr. McMurry hugged me and kept patting me on the back saying, "Good job Daniel. Good job."

# *Debra And Kieran*

Kieran has settled into his new home with a bang. He had two clients before he closed his door the first day. He and I have decided that we will not wait 6-months to make the next step in our relationship. We will give it 3-months and will then start planning for a spring wedding. We love each other and there isn't any reason to wait. The family loves him, and he does them. He and David have become good friends and he has been a big help to Daniel. Afterall, investment is his strong suit. Daniel asked him if he would be the lead on the fundraiser ensuring that everything would be on the up and up. Kieran was thrilled to be asked and happily accepted the offer.

Aunty has gone through all the Bradley estate and has found several different areas that can invest or donate to the school. It will be the perfect use of the funds. She had a meeting with all of us and assured us that by making these investments and donations that it would not break the bank. We all live on the dividends and haven't touched the capital. We sold the Boston house and bought Debra's house for an almost dollar to dollar exchange. A good investment indeed. While we were all together for the meeting, she told Daniel that Debra, David and Alicia had all pledged 50% of their $500,000 inheritance to the school project. Poor Daniel burst into tears and really didn't know how to begin to thank his siblings for their generosity.

The holidays were a blur with the fundraiser, the musical events at the church, shopping for Christmas, our businesses. The events were all warmly received by the community and made quite an addition to the church coffers, so that was good. People were truly happy that young people were taking an interest in church and community. We had the big celebration at David and Alicia's as it is so much easier for the girls. The girls were so cute to watch with their gifts. They just love to shriek for joy!

Kieran and I finally found an evening to have a quiet dinner at home. We usually spend our evenings at my house as he is doing some remodeling to his place. We were getting ready to fix our dessert when Kieran stood by my chair and then got down on one knee and proposed to me. He presented me with the most exquisite ring I've ever seen. I was so surprised. We had talked about it, but now this was for real. "Debra, you've made me the happiest man in the world. If you don't feel that we need a huge wedding and would settle for family and close friends, I was thinking Valentine's Day might be perfect. What do you think?" "I think that sounds like the ideal date. I don't have close friends and really would be happy getting married in Daniel's study with my parents and siblings and nieces. Do you have special friends that you grew up with that you'd want there?" "No, I don't. I thought about asking David to be my best man and I had guessed you might ask Alicia to stand up with you." "Well, I think we just planned a wedding. Let's go tell the parents." "Now, isn't it too late?" "No, it is never too late to stop by what will always be home." We found them watching TV and so they answered the door right away. Aunty told us she had warm cherry pie and vanilla ice cream with our names on it. We went into the kitchen and I showed them my ring. They were both overjoyed. "When are you thinking for the wedding, Uncy asked." I told them just our family in Daniel's study on Valentine's Day. Uncy looked a little shocked but then thought it sounded like a wonderful idea. "Aunty, I asked, could I wear your dress to be married?" "Oh Debra, she cried, you certainly can." We ate our dessert and then hugged them and headed home. "We can tell the rest of them tomorrow, I said." "Yes, I think that will work, he said."

Kieran and Daniel spent a lot of time together with all that was going on with the fundraiser. So far, they had pledges for over one-million dollars and generous donations that matched that figure. They had spoken with contractors and had plans drawn up for the two buildings. The daycare would be a standalone building, fenced with a beautiful playground attached to it. The school would be two-story and would house 16 classrooms, a cafeteria, and a library. The Bradley donations would erect the gymnasium, a running track, and a baseball diamond with bleachers. They were planning on breaking ground for the school in the spring and hopefully concluding the project by the beginning of the next school year. The daycare would be built in the spring and be open for business for summer to help parents that work and need childcare during the day.

Kieran and I were counting the days until our wedding. It was becoming more difficult daily to wait until we were married. Our bodies cried out for each other, but we really wanted to wait.

# The Big Brother

Tomorrow my baby sister will be wed. I'll officiate at this ceremony putting my stamp of approval on her belonging to someone else. It was not right to feel this way, but I couldn't seem to shake it loose. I was feeling unusually surly toward everyone. Uncy had noticed and asked if he could help, but I had even turned away from him saying it was nothing.

That evening, I had been reading a novel late into the night sitting in front of my fire. I must have drifted off because I dreamed that my dad was sitting next to me. I dreamed that he told me how proud he was of me and how he admired my dedication to my faith, my family, and my church. He told me that I needed to let go of this feeling that I was harboring. "it's doing you no good, my boy, he said. Debra needs love and companionship the same as you have found in your faith, and your church. You need to let her go." I woke up and looked around for sure that I would see my dad sitting there. But of course, he wasn't there. I sat and thought about my dream, if that was what it was, and the words he had spoken. I found that I had an inner peace that I hadn't felt earlier. I knew that it was all going to be alright.

# The Wedding

Aunty had decorated Daniel's study with flowers and ribbon, and the small altar was draped in a beautiful shawl with baskets of flowers on both sides. Uncy was in my dressing room being sure that I was all ready for my day. He had brought me a beautiful necklace with a teardrop blue topaz for my *something blue*. I wore my mom's ring and bracelet for my *something borrowed*. Alicia had given me two gorgeous combs for my hair for my *something new*. Alicia came to tell us that they were ready. Uncy and I waited outside the study doors for our cue. Daniel had a recording of the wedding march that he played for us. David and Alicia were standing up front with Kieran and Daniel. Amy tossed flowers all over the place which was adorable. The girls were all being incredibly quiet and had promised to behave, which was something new.

Uncy and I walked up to the altar where he kissed me and gave my hand to Kieran. Daniel greeted us and said a prayer and then he sang Ava Maria as I had asked him to. It was a much shorter service than most Catholic weddings, but we felt it was just as meaningful and just as joyous. During the final prayer and before being pronounced husband and wife, Kieran surprised me by singing The Lord's Prayer. He is a tenor, different from my grandfather, father and brother who are rich baritones. His voice gave new meaning to me as I listened to him. I would venture to say that this church is going to have all sorts of surprises in the future. Daniel blessed our marriage and presented us to the family. Everyone was cheering. Aunty had arranged for a few old friends and business associates to join us for cake in the church basement. Kieran and I made our way downstairs and when we walked through the door, we were stunned to say the least. There must have been one hundred people there. Neighbors, business associates, school friends, associates of both my mother and father, and more. What a lovely surprise. We spent the next couple of hours greeting people and visiting old friends.

Kieran and I went home and this time he didn't have to leave. We would be together for the remainder of our lives, and I couldn't have hoped for more. My memories of my parents, their parents, our upbringing with trusted friends, my brothers and almost sister were causing my heart to overflow. I looked at my husband and told him that I promised to be the best wife and friend that I could be for the rest of our lives.

**Tomorrow would be our new beginning.**